FACE-TIME

FACE~TIME

Erik Tarloff

A NOVEL

CROWN PUBLISHERS, INC.
NEW YORK

Grateful acknowledgment is made to Simon & Schuster, Inc. for permission to reprint an excerpt from THE RAGMAN'S SON by Kirk Douglas. Copyright © 1988 by Kirk Douglas. Reprinted by permission of Simon & Schuster, Inc.

Published by Crown Publishers, Inc., 201 East 50th Street, New York, New York 10022. Member of the Crown Publishing Group.

Random House, Inc. New York, Toronto, London, Sydney, Auckland
www.randomhouse.com

CROWN and colophon are trademarks of Crown Publishers, Inc.

Printed in the United States of America

DESIGN BY KAREN MINSTER

Library of Congress Cataloging-in-Publication Data
Tarloff, Erik.
Face-time / Erik Tarloff.—1st ed.
I. Title.
PS3570.A626F33   1999
813'.54—dc21   98-43008
                                                CIP

ISBN 0-609-60463-5

10 9 8 7 6 5 4 3 2 1

First Edition

For my parents,
Frank and Lee
Tarloff

With special thanks to Kate Lehrer,
Wendy Lesser, David Littlejohn, and Sally Quinn
for providing encouragement and good advice
when both were sorely needed

FACE-TIME

D ON'T SHIT WHERE YOU EAT," is the way my girlfriend, Gretchen, says it. Maybe that's the midwestern version. I learned a British variant from my grandmother: "It's a foolish bird that fouls its own nest." My grandmother's rendition has the advantage of refinement, but Gretchen's is undeniably pithier.

Gretchen has a lot of those sayings, adding up to a kind of coarse folk wisdom. They come accompanied by a certain measure of irony, even self-satire, since a good part of her youth and adolescence was spent in Washington, and she graduated from Georgetown; she isn't exactly fresh off the farm. In fact, her father, Arnie Burns, was an eight-term congressman from Illinois, the southern part of the state, and she attended elementary school in the District, at Sidwell Friends. But after her parents divorced, she went back home to Illinois with her mother—it didn't feel like home to *Gretchen*, of course—and finished high school there. She continued to spend most summers in D.C., however. Part of the custody agreement, painstakingly negotiated to no one's satisfaction. "What a treat!" she says about those summers now. "My plane would land at Dulles just when everyone in his right mind was leaving. Including, sometimes, Dad." So anyway, she has a kind of Washington sophistication as part of her armature, but those Midwestern roots go pretty deep, too, maybe deeper than she realizes. When she says things like "Don't shit where you eat," I think it represents something authentic about her, no matter how much detachment she pretends to.

Which is something I like about her, incidentally. I don't necessarily like the sayings themselves—my own upbringing was too fastidiously bourgeois for that—but I'm awfully fond of the person who's comfortable expressing herself that way. I like the homespun side of her more than the sophistication, to be honest; the latter, paradoxically, seems more provincial. When she talks knowledgeably about the intricacies of the legislative process or whether an undersecretary outranks an assistant secretary, it's like a person from Detroit holding forth about automotive assembly. No doubt somebody needs to know that stuff, but it isn't awfully interesting. It's the other Gretchen I fell in love with, the girl who rode horses and did chores and developed a tomboy sexiness that works better with Levi's than evening wear. The sophisticated side seems brittle, secondhand, *learned*. And there are other people who do it more convincingly.

But since Gretchen and I live in Washington now—we have a condo near Dupont Circle—and since we're both working in government these days, this provincial expertise of hers has its uses. In the beginning, she virtually acted as my Sherpa, whispering relevant information in my ear when we socialized. "That's the house minority whip," she might murmur as the worthy in question approached to glad-hand us by the buffet table. It was indispensable, really: God knows how many gaffes she saved me from committing in the early days of the Sheffield administration, the period when we were all being assessed.

And what I liked best was, she wasn't awed by the powerhouses we'd encounter. If my first impulse was to feel small and insignificant in their presence, to feel like a high school civics student on a spring trip to Our Nation's Capital, she helped put everything in perspective. She'd known them, or people just like them, since girlhood. "Their barns don't smell like Old Spice either," she'd say later. Another Gretchenism. My British grandmother would have put it differently, but she shared the same fierce refusal to be intimidated by the high and the mighty. She'd been active in the trade union movement in Manchester; she was a lifelong Communist to whom the British class system was a constant source of outrage. Her capacity for outrage was bottomless, and provided an exuberant white-hot rage that may have been her only true joy.

Gretchen shares some of that outrage, in her own way. Even though her father was a Republican, he was the kind of small-town Republican who never felt comfortable around the East Coast Establishment types in his party. Not that he was one of those progressive Republicans in the La Follette mold; it's more he was full of an inchoate sullen resentment and distrusted any agglomeration of wealth or power or privilege. This wasn't political with him, it was a peasant's instinctive small-minded wariness. He detested Franklin Roosevelt—those class resentments of his didn't make him sympathetic to the New Deal—but at least according to Gretchen, in 1948, in the privacy of the voting booth, he actually cast his vote for Harry Truman. But maybe that's uncharacteristic wishful thinking on her part. I can easily imagine him finding Tom Dewey hard to stomach, but it's tough for me to picture him crossing over to the enemy. When Gretchen told him she had become a Democrat— this was when she was in college, naturally—he was pretty irked. He thought of Democrats as Irishmen and Jews and Negroes and AFL-CIO Socialists and disreputable college professors: not an assemblage he cared to have anything to do with.

"You mustn't go thinking Daddy's some kind of crusty old *character*," Gretchen cautioned me once, early in our relationship, when I expressed an interest in meeting him. "You know, a cute crotchety curmudgeon or something along those lines. He's a nasty, closed-minded, bigoted bastard. He finally lost his seat because, even though his district was pretty nasty and closed-minded, too, he was finally just too much for them. An embarrassment."

I guess it's pretty obvious Gretchen has a few problems with her father. That she's turned out so wonderfully is a miracle.

She and I first met during the primary season. We were working for different candidates at the time, neither of us, ironically, for

Charles Sheffield. Mine was the *bien pensant* liberal sacrificial lamb the party manages to provide every election cycle, the one who raises most of his money in L.A. and New York; and hers was the year's bloodless technocrat without a message beyond enlightened common sense. (It's interesting how the field of presidential candidates every four years is like a summer repertory company, or a *commedia dell'arte* troupe, variations on the same stock characters.) She and I bumped into each other for the first time at one of those free-for-all candidates' forums that purport to be debates. She was wryly dismissive about her own candidate's performance ("Bit the wienie," was her critique) and similarly disrespectful toward mine, but she made me laugh, and she was cute and tough and rowdy, and she had a beautiful ass, you could tell that even through her midnight blue business suit; so I worked like a son of a bitch to get her to meet me in the hotel bar for a drink after our respective melancholy pep rallies. Then, because she was bored or because I cranked up the charm or because everybody gets so lonely on the road, she came back to my room with me. A lovely night, even though both of our chosen candidates had bitten the wienie. We talked on and off till almost dawn, between bouts of lovemaking that grew in ardor as the night wore on. Very little of our conversation concerned politics.

Of course, there's a lot of pairing up among campaign workers, you're all thrown together all the time and you're traveling in this enclosed bubble, but by morning it already felt different, much more important than one of those "help me make it through the night" kinds of encounters. And we realized we were in love well before the California primary, by which time both of our candidates had dropped out and we had gone our separate ways, she to New York, I to Boston. But a couple of weeks later we were still missing each other awfully keenly—it was a relief to discover this was no short-lived campaign romance, since we'd both had our share of those—so she flew up to join me. Just for a brief visit, ostensibly. We watched the results of the California primary in my apartment, drinking jug wine and eating pretzels and jeering at Chuck Sheffield, our erstwhile common enemy and now our presumptive candidate. His one surviving opponent wouldn't acknowledge it, but it was obvious to everyone else: Sheffield had sewn up the nomination that June night. Gretchen and I knew we'd be voting for him in November; we even knew (although we weren't ready to admit it) that within a week or two we'd both be vying to get positions in his campaign. It was now the only game in town. Nevertheless, he seemed much too *assembled* for our taste, too calculated and fraudulent, even in a profession defined by calculation and fraud. We were stuck with him, and he looked like a winner, but we had some misgivings; even his slightly cool style of campaigning, which I later came to admire, originally struck me as unattractive, arrogant and aloof. The night of the California primary was going to be our last chance to jeer at him without qualms, so we indulged ourselves freely, amid much hilarity, yelling disparagement and throwing pretzels at the screen.

By that time we had already begun talking about living together. The only real question was, what city were we going to be doing it in? Events ultimately answered that question for us.

And now, more than a year later, Gretchen and I are both working in the White House, we have a nice yuppified condo near Dupont Circle and a congenial circle of friends, we go for Saturday walks along the tow path and Sunday bike rides in Rock Creek Park, we shop at Sutton Place or Neam's Market when we give dinner parties, we manage to visit friends in the country, West Virginia or Maryland or Virginia, once or twice a month. It's an ideal Washington existence, really, except for one awkward fact: Gretchen is fucking the president of the United States. And I don't know what the hell to do about it.

★

I GOT A JOB IN THE SHEFFIELD CAMPAIGN BEFORE GRETCHEN DID. A friend of mine had been chief speechwriter from quite early on, joining immediately after the senator's surprise victory in New Hampshire. As often happens in such situations, there was wholesale replacement of staff—a bloody purge—after that triumphant night, once the campaign had established itself in the front tier. Seasoned professionals were brought in, unceremoniously replacing the enthusiastic amateurs who had been responsible for the early success. The pros, who might have scoffed at Sheffield only the day before—a relatively junior senator from a small state with no particular legislative accomplishments to his credit and a disconcertingly detached campaign style—suddenly sniffed the chance to ride his train to glory. And of course, money began to pour in, so the campaign could suddenly afford first-class assistance, those hired guns who are always looking to attach themselves to the next Kennedy, Reagan, or Clinton. Candidates who seem, however absurdly to outsiders, to have some sort of magic. These professionals' claim to expertise is often based on nothing much more than previous affiliation with past disasters, but they don't seem tainted by the absence of success. Their reputation for wisdom is like virginity in a Victorian brothel, infinitely renewable, unbesmirched by yesterday's errancy. Maybe the theory is they've learned the mistakes to avoid, having already committed them.

I didn't quite qualify as first-class assistance, but I'd caught the political bug in college, I was now a veteran of three previous presidential campaigns—not to mention the bruising rough-and-tumble of Massachusetts state politics—so I wasn't an enthusiastic amateur anymore either. I had long ago made the transition from cockeyed idealist, the kind of volunteer the pols regard as useful but contemptible, to someone who'd been around the block a few times and enjoyed the game for its own sake.

Anyway, when I phoned my friend Randy, he suggested I write a few sample paragraphs and he'd show them to Sheffield. "Run them by the candidate," was how he put it. *The candidate.* People get very formal when presidential politics are involved, it gives them the feeling they're in the middle of some historic enterprise. A few days later Randy invited me to fly down to Washington—at my own expense, of course—for an interview.

"Does that mean Sheffield liked my stuff?" I asked. Perhaps I was fishing for compliments, but I told myself I just wanted to get the lay of the land.

"He hasn't read it yet. But *I* thought it was pretty good." Already Randy was acting less like a friend and more like a ranking superior. "Sheffield's a people guy. He'll want to check out the comfort level between the two of you before he bothers looking at your writing."

I wanted to say, "For Christ's sake, Randy, just *listen* to yourself. You sound like one of *them.*" But I didn't, of course. I couldn't afford to alienate him. Instead I said, "What's Sheffield like, anyway? Any hints what he's looking for? Something that might improve the *comfort level?*" A little dig at the end to assuage my self-disgust at being a toady.

"Well, the main thing you should remember is, he's really, really smart."

"Uh-huh." Campaign workers always say that about their candidate, even when he or she is a certifiable moron. And when it's coupled with "He's a people guy," it's generally a dead giveaway the candidate *is* a certifiable moron. The rough translation is, he can't even understand his own position papers until an aide explains them to him.

"And there's no bullshit about him. He's a straight shooter." Translation: He's rude to subordinates.

"Right. Is there anything I can *use,* though?"

"Well, the fact is, Ben, since I'm recommending you, you've probably got the inside track already. No promises, but I'd say it looks good." Translation: I, Randy, am part of the trusted inner circle.

"So the main thing is, just don't fuck up the comfort level?"

"You're busting my balls? I'm doing you this favor and you're busting my balls?"

Whoops. Went too far. A problem I sometimes have. So I scurried back to first base before he could throw me out. "Nah, I just want to know—"

"Yeah, I know what you want to know. The best advice I can give you is, listen close and pay attention. He'll be talking, and you'll start thinking it's a soliloquy and he doesn't even know you're there, and then suddenly he'll ask you a question, and you'd better have a relevant answer. You know what I mean?"

Oh, I knew all right. I recognized this phenomenon too. The guy was an asshole.

BUT THAT DIDN'T STOP ME FROM HOPPING THE LOGAN-REAGAN shuttle and cabbing it over to the Hill. In the anteroom to Sheffield's office in the Hart Office Building, I had to cool my heels for over an hour. Randy looked in to say a quick hello, but he didn't stick around to hold my hand. His candidate was going to be the nominee, and his plate was full. He wanted me to know it.

Finally I was admitted to the Presence. Chuck Sheffield was behind his desk, in his shirtsleeves, his back to me. And despite what Randy had said, he was reading my pages, right there in front of me while I watched. Without having had a chance to gauge the comfort level. "Sit down," he said, not looking my way. "I'll just be a minute."

He meant it literally. After a minute, he swiveled around to face me. "So...," he began.

He seemed larger than he did on television, broad shouldered and imposing, with very big hands. In general, I'd have to say he was more attractive in person, too. He had a balding head and heavy features—unusual for a candidate in this day and age, a fact much commented upon—but it was a kind of rugged, craggy look that worked well face-to-face. Many news reports described him as "handsome," but I didn't really see that. I could, however, recognize that he might be considered a good-looking man, virile and commanding. Men have more latitude than women in the ways they can be attractive. He also looked older to me than his forty-nine years, but it's possible this was a response to his male-pattern baldness, another much-commented-upon fact. The first cue ball to run for president since Stevenson and Eisenhower faced off. The face itself was youthful, I suppose. And he had a very good smile, manly and friendly and apparently genuine. But you expect that sort of thing from a politician's smile. Nevertheless, the fact that *People* had, in its profile, proclaimed him a "sex symbol" didn't seem outrageously off the mark.

"Randy told me you can write," he went on, gesturing toward my pages. "And you can, you can. But if you're going to write for *me*, there are a couple of things you need to know. I don't split infinitives. The word 'media' is plural. 'Impact' is a noun, not a verb. I try to keep the patriotic bullshit to a minimum. I don't like numbering my points. I prefer concrete examples to orotund pronouncements."

I was meant to be impressed, and I was. "All right."

"You can manage all that?"

"I think so."

"And my jokes have been lame. This may sound trivial, but it makes a difference to the press. They like to be entertained. If they think you're funny, they're much more forgiving. You write jokes?"

"Not really."

"You think that might present an insurmountable obstacle?"

I smiled. "Not insurmountable, no."

He suddenly rose—he was taller than I expected—and I did too, and he leaned across the desk to shake hands. He gave me one of those politician's handshakes, firm grip, deep, sincere gaze. My own hand seemed to disappear into his mammoth fist. "So...welcome aboard," he said.

I was startled, I admit it. "That's it?"

"You want me to bring in the marine band, have them play a fanfare?"

"Well…might be premature."

He actually laughed, which surprised me. "Maybe," he said. "But only slightly. I *am* going to be the next president of the United States, you know."

"Yes," I said, and realized as I said it that I meant it. "I believe that."

"Yeah. Me too. It's just starting to sink in." He shook his head at the sheer improbability of it and then added, "So don't fuck up, okay? You don't want to be the fella who buggers up my rendezvous with destiny."

This may not have been much, but it was more irony than I'd encountered in any other politician for whom I'd worked. I left his office liking him. One final surprise.

GRETCHEN GOT HER JOB A COUPLE OF WEEKS LATER, A RELIEF TO both of us. I put in a good word, of course, but she had a number of other friends in the organization better connected than I, so I can't claim any credit. The position she ultimately got involved travel and logistics, a fairly unexciting assignment. Stuck in Washington, living out of a borrowed apartment near Capitol Hill, she was totally involved with nuts and bolts and had virtually no face-time with the candidate, which is how cachet is gauged in a presidential campaign. And since, as things transpired, I had to travel with him, it also meant our time together, Gretchen's and mine, was pretty catch-as-catch-can. When the campaign returned to home base for a few days, we were passionate and inseparable, but those days were rare.

Which had its own paradoxical advantages. An impediment or

two at the beginning of a relationship concentrates the heart wonderfully. Our reunions were always joyous and lubricious.

But I also suspect she was a little jealous of me. Not only was I
traveling with Sheffield, not only was I part of the road show—
quite exciting in itself—but I was developing a relationship with
him. When an entire enterprise is built around one person, your
sense of importance is determined by your access to him. By face-
time. The campaign becomes a traveling court, with the candidate
as sovereign, the rest of us courtiers vying for his attention and favor.
It's almost independent of his personal qualities. I mean, to get that
far, he's probably got *something,* but whatever he might personally
lack, his position supplies. So Gretchen was always full of questions,
both when we talked on the phone and when I saw her in D.C., and
always pressed me for more detailed answers. But for all her enthusiasm, I think my evolving closeness to the fellow must have rankled
a little, must have made her feel all the more peripheral.

It started with chess. Sheffield was an enthusiastic chess player.
And though I had barely played in years, I had been pretty good
once upon a time, with a strong expert's rating in high school and
an all-city scholastic championship to my credit (due to luck; in the
final round, my opponent, a player far superior to me, had nervously
blundered away an easy draw in a queen and pawn ending); and
when word went out on the campaign plane that Sheffield was
looking for an opponent, I volunteered. Why not? I was bored too,
and besides, win or lose, this was something I could brag about for
the rest of my life.

Sheffield wasn't terrible, but he was many points shy of an
expert's rating; and rusty though I was, it was no great achievement
to beat him. I don't think he had expected much of me, just a spar-
ring partner, really, so he came out punching. Typical Sheffield, on
or off the chessboard. I quickly tied him up and slaughtered him,
and he was surprised and peeved enough by the result to demand a

second game immediately. He must have thought the first outcome had been some sort of fluke, and he wanted to put me in my place as soon as possible, reestablish the natural order. But even though he played more conservatively the second time, it was over even more quickly than the first.

"You know how to play," he said, staring down at the wreckage of his position on his little magnetic traveling set.

I agreed with him. Minimizing my own skills would have been insulting. Then he glanced up and gave me a look—it wasn't a friendly look exactly, more an appraising look. As if he had underestimated me but wouldn't in the future. And I didn't get the impression this reappraisal was restricted to chess.

"We must play again," he said.

"I'd enjoy that, Senator."

"I'm sure."

When I told Gretchen about the experience on the phone that night, she was appalled. "You didn't throw the game?" she demanded.

"Good God, no."

"Not even the second one?"

"Chess players don't do that," I said huffily, inventing a code of conduct right there on the spot. She'd put me on the defensive. I was wondering if she might not be right, if it wasn't insensitive of me, not to mention impolitic, to make him lose twice in a row.

"You don't want to jinx him," she said.

"Chess is one thing, politics another," I replied. Defensiveness sometimes renders me pompous.

"In the middle of a campaign, everything is politics." Then, perhaps to mitigate the harshness of the implicit rebuke, she laughed and added, "My hero."

The very next day I was summoned to the front of the plane again. Sheffield already had his magnetic kit set up and ready. "Okay, Ben, I'm braced for another lesson," he told me. Which I took to be permission to beat him again. Not that I necessarily *required* permission, despite my conversation with Gretchen the previous night: the opportunity to crush someone on his inexorable way to the top of the world was close to irresistible. And when, in the middle of this game, an aide approached to show him a position paper he'd need for his next stop, he waved her away. "Later," he said brusquely. He was already trying to extricate himself from a mating net. I had his undivided attention.

The next night, at a hotel in Denver, I was summoned to his suite. We had some business to discuss—revisions on a speech he was giving next day—but he also had his little chess set out. And Randy wasn't there, a first as far as speech preparation went. When Claire Sheffield admitted me to the living room of the suite, she said, "Now see here, Ben, you mustn't keep him up too late."

"No, Mrs. Sheffield, I'll try not to. I mean, I have to write a speech after he's done with me, so I've got my own selfish reasons."

She smiled at that. Her smile was an appealing combination of the maternal and the quasi-flirtatious. She had really perfected the politician's wife role. It was clear already that she'd make a first-rate First Lady. "Chuck thinks very highly of you," she told me. "Not just the chess. He likes the way you write. He likes the way you *think*."

Which was a lovely thing to hear, of course. But I suspect that without the chess, my other sterling qualities might well have gone unnoticed and unmentioned. When I related this exchange to Gretchen, I could hear the rue in her voice, along with the shared excitement. "God, Ben, you're going to the White House," she said.

"Well, there's many a slip, you know." But I'd be dishonest if I denied enjoying her envy just a little.

"You're brushing shoulders with greatness."

"No, I'm brushing shoulders with Chuck Sheffield."

"Jaded already, are we?"

I wasn't, in fact. Charles Sheffield was proving to be quite an interesting person, at least as candidates go, and proximity didn't cause immediate disillusionment. He was clearly smarter than most—Randy had been right about that—and occasionally indulged a surprisingly sly, refreshingly subversive wit. He campaigned with a certain cool detachment, a visible reluctance to feign emotion, which contrasted attractively with the stump styles of most of his colleagues. At first I'd disliked this reserve of his, considered it a manifestation of arrogance. Over time, though, I saw it differently, as a determined refusal to pander, a fastidiousness both moral and aesthetic. His staff seemed to like him, and he was perfectly collegial with them, often organizing an ad hoc end-of-the-day cocktail party for senior staff, either on the campaign plane or in his suite, in which the conversation was fast, rude, and unstructured. While I doubt that any of us would have been moved to say, as John Hay once did about *his* boss, Abraham Lincoln, "He is the greatest character since Christ" (talk about managing to be a hero to your valet!), it was my impression that they all believed Sheffield worthy of the job he was seeking. Which God knows isn't always the case.

And he did seem to have taken a shine to me. Over the course of the campaign, when we discussed the speeches I'd written for him, our conversations eventually became wider ranging. My efforts to enunciate policy sometimes turned into discussions *about* policy, and the words of greeting to local dignitaries I wrote for him became the occasion for uncensored ruminations about their strengths and weaknesses. As far as I could tell, he valued my honest opinion, and he trusted me with his own. And while, unlike some of the inner circle, I never addressed him as "Chuck"—I guess I had joined the team too late for such familiarity, when he was already too close to the presidency—I felt we had some sort of genuine personal relationship, given the inevitable limitations inherent in our situation and the disparity in our ages.

And I think he liked the fact that I wasn't a sycophant. When your wagon is hitched to a probable winner, it's easy for respect to start bleeding into fawning obsequiousness. But maybe because of my Bolshie British grandmother, I just couldn't do that. I could hear her saying, in that odd Yiddish-British accent of hers, "So he walks on water, maybe?" While I certainly addressed him with proper deference, and gradually came to regard him with a respect that verged on the filial, I didn't suck up. Sometimes, when somebody else *did* suck up, Sheffield would catch my eye, sharing his sardonic amusement with me.

In early October I was able to do him a small favor that further cemented our relationship. It came about because, at the end of a long day of campaigning, I was having dinner with Chris Partridge in the coffee shop of our hotel. In Akron, Ohio, if I remember correctly. Chris was a Brit, the *Guardian*'s man in Washington, and he and I had become casually friendly over the previous few weeks. I had some misgivings about him—his cynicism edged toward the nihilistic, and as a consequence he sometimes struck me as potentially dangerous, a very loose cannon indeed—but he was also far and away the most enjoyable company in the Sheffield press entourage. He cultivated this totally inauthentic Fleet Street seediness (a not uncommon affectation among well-born, Oxbridge-educated English journalists who've read their Waugh) that could be very entertaining in small doses. It wasn't uncommon for us to meet for a drink in some bar, or in his hotel room or mine, when the day's dust had finally settled, and we occasionally shared a meal; over time, to my surprise, I came to trust him about as much as I trusted any reporter. For all his raffishness, he was punctilious about observing the code, and he was always happy to offer some tidbits of gossip (usually scurrilous) of his own in exchange for anything useful I might have. In a social setting his cynicism was amusing without being coercive or tendentious; he didn't, in other words, make us political operatives feel like horse's asses for believing in the system or being loyal to our candidate, even though he himself disliked Sheffield intensely and thought the whole political process a corrupt sham.

After a couple of derogatory comments about his BLT and American cuisine in general, he took a sip of his beer and said, "By the bye, your fellow may have a little problem." He said it with a studied casualness that told me it was probably something serious.

"Little problems we can live with."

"This may not be so little, in point of fact."

My first thought was, Oh God, there's a woman. There had been stray rumors. But before I had a chance to give that possibility too much thought, Chris went on, "The *L.A. Times* has a story....It seems your Mr. Sheffield has a police record. A DWI conviction. He pleaded *nolo contendere*. It's going to be in Sunday's edition."

"Jesus." Was this worse than a sex scandal? I honestly didn't know. It was hard to see any serious relevance: Sheffield might like to have a drink before dinner—sometimes even two—but I'd never seen him intoxicated. A lot would clearly depend on the details.

"It's the sort of business that can take on a life of its own," Chris continued. "You know, with all those Pecksniffian pressure groups casting gloom everywhere. Have fun and go to jail sort of thing. The peculiar propensity you Americans have for taking the fun out of life, in the thoroughly dubious interest of protecting children. If this were a story unmasking your Mr. Sheffield as a lying manipulative shit, I'd be overjoyed, I'd be cheering them on from the sidelines. But as things stand…" He shrugged. "Well, in any event, you might want to look into it."

"Yes," I said, already repenting of my "Jesus" and trying hard to sound offhand, "I will. Thanks for the heads-up."

Of course, I knew he wasn't relaying the information solely out of benevolence. If he could sabotage a colleague's big story, it was in his interest, too. Nevertheless, the more lead time we had on this, the better, so the thank-you wasn't out of place. He certainly had no obligation to warn me.

Because appearances matter, I forced myself to finish my meal as if nothing momentous had occurred. But you never know in advance what sort of story is going to do you serious harm and which will turn out to be a trivial one-day wonder. So as soon as I left Chris, I dashed up to the candidate's suite and shared the news. After some discussion back and forth, it was deemed sufficiently alarming so that some brave soul went into Sheffield's room and roused him from a much needed slumber. He emerged a couple of minutes later, wearing only a pair of Dockers and a Harvard Law School sweatshirt—no shoes or socks—looking tousled and cross. "This better be really bad," he said. He wasn't joking.

When the reason for the untimely wake-up was explained to him, he responded incredulously. "Aw, Christ," he growled, "I was eighteen years old when that happened! This is utter crap!" I'd never seen him really angry before, but he was clearly furious. And since no representative of the *Los Angeles Times* was present, we, his loyal staffers, were going to catch the full brunt.

Randy, tone-deaf to the candidate's raw and querulous mood, said, "Still, it's the sort of thing that could hurt us. Drunk drivers aren't the most popular people in the country right now. We ought to prepare a statement. Get ahead of the curve."

Sheffield groaned with annoyance and said, "It's certainly reassuring to know everyone's focused on the welfare of the country." Then he turned to me with a sigh. "All right, you'd better write me something, Ben. Youthful indiscretion, suspended sentence, no repetition in over thirty years, long-held belief in responsible drinking, support tougher penalties for drunk drivers, contributor to MADD…"

"Are you?" I asked. "They may try to verify it."

"I think so. I did it once, I'm certain of that, or maybe it was Claire. I remember claiming the damned deduction on my tax return. Anyway, let's go for full disclosure. Right away. We should issue it first thing in the morning."

"Yes, sir."

No one in the room looked happy. It was one of those bombshells that might be catastrophically destructive or a total dud, it was almost impossible to predict till the thing was detonated.

"Well, what are you waiting for?" Sheffield demanded testily, looking straight at me. I hadn't moved from my seat. "Get started."

But I had had an idea, which was why I was hesitating. "I will, Senator. Right away. But...something occurs to me. Something that might help us even more."

Sheffield eyed me curiously. "Go on," he said.

"This may be a total shot in the dark, but...I was thinking...The current president of MADD. Does anyone here know what her politics are?"

Randy, probably annoyed that I was speaking out of turn, violating the chain of command—my direct access to Sheffield was already an established and throbbing sore point with him—muttered audibly enough, "What the hell does that have to do with anything?"

But then Alice Hahn, Sheffield's Senate AA and a major player in his campaign, spoke up. "She's a supporter. We got a contribution from her. It was personal, not institutional." Alice never forgot things like that.

"Well," I said, "a public endorsement from her might be awfully timely right now. Even if it is personal rather than institutional. That's the kind of distinction that might easily get blurred in the heat of the moment."

Sheffield suddenly broke into an exultant grin. A number of other people in the room started to nod. "Great!" the candidate announced. "Alice, get her number and call her. Right away. Wake her up if you have to. Say it's an emergency." Then he turned to me. "Good thinking, Krause. Now, get busy and write the damned statement. Hurry. We'll hit 'em with a one-two punch tomorrow."

So, glorying in the man's approval, I scurried to my room and hacked out something on my laptop. I didn't aim for eloquence, just a simple, straightforward statement. The alchemy of these things is mysterious. I suppose the whole business could have blown up in our faces, but instead the alacrity and apparent candor of our response—coupled with the unexpected endorsement from the MADD woman (of Chicago, not Chaillot)—did the trick. By the time the actual story appeared in the *Los Angeles Times* several days later, its substance had already been analyzed and dismissed, and the piece itself seemed overblown and carping. I got a call from Sheffield in my hotel room that Sunday morning, while I was shaving. "Great work, pal. Thanks for the early warning *and* the statement. Not to mention the absolutely inspired notion of the endorsement. That's why they say we're the Rolls-Royce of campaigns, because of the way we handle these problems. We're in the clear now. The Sunday shows barely mentioned it, except to say we're MADD's choice for president. It's a fucking net plus, of all things. Who would've thought it?"

"I'm pleased it worked out, Senator."

"What would I do without you?" He said it humorously, but I felt the warmth behind the humor. And was thrilled at finding myself deeper in his good graces.

During the prep for his first debate with Vice President Norris, Sheffield asked me to feed lines to Senator Jared MacMillan, his closest Washington friend, who was standing in for the vice president. When I asked Randy why I'd been chosen, he said, "The candidate doesn't want the rehearsal to turn into a game of patty-cake, and he knows you're willing to hit him with both barrels." Which sounded like carte blanche. So I let my quasi-Oedipal imagination run wild. And I must have done a pretty good job, because afterward, when I congratulated Sheffield on his performance, he said, "Fuck you, Krause," and turned his back on me. He seemed genuinely irritated. A far cry from his earlier attitude. I honestly didn't know whether to feel abashed or amused. But after the debate itself, the general consensus being that he'd won handily, he invited me to his suite, where both he and his wife thanked me extravagantly for the work I'd done. "After the crap you had MacMillan throw at me, I was ready for anything," he said with a smile while pouring me a glass of champagne. The "fuck you" was apparently forgotten or perhaps was now meant to be interpreted as a rugged gesture of respect, macho campaign freemasonry.

But I didn't really deserve any credit. Typically, Sheffield had been so aggressive from the start that Norris had no opportunity to throw any punches, let alone land any. He was reeling from the opening statements on.

THERE WAS A REASON WHY MY FIRST THOUGHT, WHEN CHRIS had told me we might have a problem, was of sex. Most of us had heard vague rumors of Sheffield's womanizing during the primaries. But I have to say I saw no sign of it during the general election campaign, the period I was present, a personal witness. Which isn't to deny categorically that it was taking place, merely to suggest that if it was, he was awfully discreet about it. Mrs. Sheffield had her own separate travel schedule, they were apart during most of the fall, so I can't say for sure what went on in his various hotel suites late at night. But with all the comings and goings, it's hard for me to imagine he was up to much. His staff would have known. And there would have been talk. We gossiped incessantly. Besides, by the end of the day he was usually so exhausted that he could barely mumble last-minute instructions to us before dragging himself off to his room. It's hard to imagine him rallying for some amorous activity.

I can't quite claim the same. I had a lapse. There was so much coupling in the Sheffield camp that it became something of a group ethos, as if we were a touring rock show. Besides, toward the end we were all in a sustained state of euphoria and shared the close-knit camaraderie common to a successful campaign (a similar phenomenon occurs in unsuccessful campaigns, now that I think about it). So one night after we'd collaborated on the script for a voice-over, I succumbed to temptation and slept with Amy Blaustein, one of the team in charge of crafting television commercials. We had been fighting over the wording of the penultimate sentence in a thirty-second spot, it had grown heated, and then we suddenly ran out of steam, ran out of arguments, stared at each other in silent hostility, and then fell into each other's arms. Amy had a husband back in New Jersey, and I, of course, had Gretchen, so we both felt guilty and compromised the next day. We had probably been the only two chaste ones left, until we weren't anymore.

"This may not have been such a terrific idea," I said as I pulled my clothes on at five A.M. "I mean, it was great and everything, but—"

"Yeah," she said, "I know. Look, you don't have to confess to Gretchen or anything. I won't tell Ron. It was just...you know, one of those things."

"Right," I agreed, "a trip to the moon on gossamer wings," giving her a quick gentlemanly kiss before tiptoeing out of her hotel room and back to my own. We acted like strangers for the remaining weeks of the campaign.

It isn't something I like to think about. And I haven't, until recently.

October felt like an extended victory lap. The polls were so good, the crowds were so enthusiastic, the press was so laudatory, it was impossible not to believe that the election was in the bag. It had looked to be a Democratic year all along: the country still hadn't fully recovered from its two-year recession, and Vice President Norris was a dull and drearily familiar presence on the scene. But some of the credit had to go to Sheffield. His campaign was generating the kind of electricity that's rare even at the most rarified political reaches. So while we all were very careful not to say anything too optimistic—I once did to Gretchen, over the phone, and she damned near took my head off—and while we all lived in fear of the evil eye or some nasty last-minute scandal, the unsuperstitious realists among us were already speculating on the composition of our candidate's cabinet.

I had been invited to spend election night in Albuquerque with the Sheffield party, but, perhaps foolishly, I chose to spend it instead with Gretchen in Washington. "You're an idiot," Randy said. "It's a big honor. And this is the night you want the candidate to remember your existence."

"I'd rather sleep with my girlfriend," I told him. Call me a cockeyed romantic. Or maybe a stubborn grandson. I needed to prove to myself, perhaps, that I still had my priorities straight.

"Are you out of your fucking mind?" Gretchen herself demanded when I told her my intentions. But I think she was flattered. At least I hope so. My ardor felt like a tribute to her; I could only hope she regarded it in the same light.

It worked out okay. Randy was officially designated head of speechwriting the following morning, and three or four days after that he phoned me at Gretchen's to offer a position under him. "The president-elect asked for you personally," he said. The tone in his voice suggested I might not have gotten the job had it been up to him. It was clear enough he'd come to resent my relationship with Sheffield. In the previous month or so I'd had as much face-time as Randy had, and he hadn't bothered to disguise his resentment. But he couldn't very well ignore a direct request from the president-elect.

"Well, that's exciting," I allowed. "When do I start?"

"You'd better get down here tomorrow. There's lots to do. Several statements a day. And it isn't too early to start thinking about the inaugural address. Sheffield wants it to be memorable. Think you can manage that?"

"Ask not."

GRETCHEN GOT HER WHITE HOUSE JOB IN THE WEEK BEFORE the inauguration. In the nick of time, you might say. The social office. Not a stellar assignment, but we both were relieved nevertheless. Neither of us wanted her to have to go back to New York, and the thought of returning to her old job—she was an editor at a small artsy publishing house specializing in twee short-story collections and incomprehensible poetry—was abhorrent to her. It's not that she didn't like the work, it's more that she'd given her heart and soul to the campaign, and it would have eaten her up to watch from the sidelines as so many people she knew joined the new administration while she slunk home. And of course there was our relationship to consider. We'd already been apart too much. A weekend romance wasn't going to cut it now that real life had resumed.

Newly flush—my White House salary was the most I'd ever made in my life, and Gretchen's was more or less comparable to her New York take—we jointly put some money down on the condo near Dupont Circle. It was a heady time. I bought a tux. No more rentals for me. I was a presidential speechwriter. I even sprang for an Armani.

My inaugural address (the history books consider it Sheffield's inaugural address, but not me, and not my mother) was interrupted by applause twenty-three times. Gretchen and I weren't up with the really big shots in the bleachers on the west front of the Capitol, but we had good seats, in among the first rank of nonpolitical celebrities. She kept nudging me proudly each time my words garnered an ovation, and after it was over she even confided to Leonardo DiCaprio, seated nearby, that I was the fellow who had written it. He didn't seem terribly impressed. I guess he had the traditional Hollywood disdain for writers.

It was okay, though. During the parade, the new president waved me up to the front of the reviewing stand. I brought Gretchen with me. He was drinking hot chocolate out of a mug emblazoned with the presidential seal. It was warmer where he was sitting. The heating system favored the front of the booth. "Nice work, Krause," he said.

"Thank you, Mr. President." It was the first time I had called him that, and it felt good. He seemed to like it too. "I heard your voice inside my head while I was writing it," I went on. "That helped. And you hit it right out of the park." I was tempted to say something about Joachim and Brahms but wisely forbore. This wasn't the right time to show off, and it certainly wasn't the right time to suggest I was a creative artist and he was merely a sympathetic interpreter. "You were great," I said instead.

He smiled and then gave Gretchen the kind of once-over that would have seemed brazen coming from anyone other than the president of the United States. I remember thinking I was glad she was wearing her overcoat; it made his gesture a little less vulgar. I was relieved for him, not her. "So, Krause, who's your friend?"

"She works for you too, sir," I said, and then made the introductions. After Mrs. Sheffield murmured a few complimentary words to me, the interview was over. Still, for all its brevity, I was glowing. I even liked the fact that he seemed to find Gretchen attractive. My girlfriend now had a presidential imprimatur, no less. And the next day the papers were full of praise for the speech. Randy glowered at me when I reported for my first full day of work at the Old Executive Office Building. "It ain't gonna be Gettysburg graveyard dedications most of the time," he warned. "There's plenty of boilerplate."

I knew there and then I'd be getting shit assignments for a while.

Which was fine with me. The sheer excitement of working at such an exalted level carried me through the first few months, even when forced to write banal greetings to trade groups and Girl Scout troops. You have to work for losing candidates a few times to understand how thrilling it is to be with a winner.

And living with Gretchen was an absolute joy those first few months. We did everything together, furnishing the condo, shopping and cooking—in my bachelor days I'd paid no attention to that side of things—and exploring Washington with her as the guide. I found, somewhat to my surprise, that I liked the city. It was smaller than I'd imagined, at least the northwest quadrant in which we usually found ourselves; the scale was surprisingly human, almost like a small town.

Gretchen had household skills and a household orientation that were new to me and which I came to delight in. It's not just that she could cook, although that accomplishment certainly wasn't negligible; previously my meals at home had consisted of take-out and frozen dinners. But in addition, she knew something about wine (a residual benefit from an earlier relationship) and taught me to notice and appreciate the difference between drinkable stuff and swill. She had an eye for furnishings and tchotchkes. We haunted the antique shops and flea markets in Virginia and Maryland on weekends, usually over my grumbling resistance when we set out, although I now count those days as being among the happiest of my life. And she usually managed to find something that looked ridiculous to me when she first pointed it out and insisted we buy it but fantastic once we got it back to the apartment.

She had a relationship to our condo—to the whole concept of home—that was totally alien to me, at least at first. During my adult years I had lived in a succession of bachelor digs in the Boston area that were little more than mail drops and places to crash. But Gretchen had a nesting instinct; she wanted our home to be a refuge and to express something personal about us. And as the weeks went by, it became increasingly quirky and attractive and welcoming.

The relationship itself was exceeding my wildest expectations. It sounds so corny to say this, but I truly didn't know such intense feelings existed. I was falling more deeply in love with Gretchen with every passing day. It was a genuine consuming passion. Simply looking at her made me happy. I went to sleep holding her, I woke up invigorated by the thought that when I opened my eyes she would be the first thing I'd see. And in between, I missed her as keenly as if we were separated by decades and continents. I was so besotted with her that I sometimes found it hard to concentrate on anything else, even work; my thoughts kept drifting in her direction, replaying a conversation we had had the previous night, or remembering something that had made her laugh, or looking forward to getting her into bed the moment I got through the door, gourmet dinner be damned. Even though I phoned her several times a day, I frequently found myself doing a sort of countdown of the hours remaining till I could go home, and the process made my heart beat faster in anticipation. Literally.

And my feelings were returned. She was so warm to me, so unreservedly affectionate, so unconditionally loving, it felt like a miracle. As if it validated, or redeemed, my very existence.

Admittedly, part of this heady excitement may simply have derived from our exhilaration at being together at the beginning of a grand historic enterprise; to be young at such a time was very heaven. But there was so much more to it than that. This wasn't a generic emotion. I felt as if, at long last, I'd found a soul mate. She embodied so many of the qualities I valued but had, over more than a decade of serious searching, come to despair of finding in a single person. She excited respect, interest, limitless tenderness, and uncontrollable lust.

She was smart and funny and tough-minded, of course. That much had been clear from the first night. And would have been more than enough. But there were other things about her that were far rarer and more precious, and which became apparent only over time. Things I hadn't begun to suspect initially. She was, for example, in closer touch with her emotions than anyone I'd ever met. For all her worldly cynicism in some areas, and her ability to look at the world with detached objectivity when necessary, there was something almost childlike about the way her feelings came to her without mediation, the way her vulnerabilities were on display without protection or disguise. She cried easily, she laughed easily, she expressed anger without guilt or hesitation, joy without irony, she took uncomplicated, unself-conscious delight in everything from Shakespeare at the Landsberg Theater to strolls along the Potomac. She certainly knew how to be polite and pleasant with people she didn't care for, but when she really liked somebody, there was no mistaking the warmth. I don't know how it happened, but she succeeded in reaching adulthood free of any conscious need for self-presentation. Aside from everything else, this proved to be an extremely effective self-presentation strategy, but that was just a happy accident.

She taught me how to look directly into another person's eyes and hide nothing. She taught me how to fight fair, expressing pain or anger clearly, without any clever verbal window dressing. She taught me how to be emotionally generous. I'd had my share of girlfriends—I'd even been engaged to someone once upon a time—but here at last was a woman with whom I wanted to spend the rest of my life.

Nevertheless, even though her extraordinary qualities weren't calculated, it would be a mistake to think they had come naturally to her, without effort or struggle. She made it seem that way sometimes, so easily did she manage it, but then she would say something that let me know she'd had to fight her way through to this state of apparent ingenuousness. For example, she taught preschool for a couple of years immediately after college, and when she assessed what she had learned from her observation of little children during that period, she said, "After a while, you begin to realize that innocence is an acquired characteristic."

Which may have been the key. Some remarkable strength of character had permitted her to acquire innocence. She found a way to feel comfortable inhabiting her own skin. If she ever feared that emotional honesty entailed the risk of embarrassment or loss of face, it was never apparent. But then, she never had to: she combined frank self-exposure with the kind of personal grace that allowed her to bring it off successfully.

She was equally able to ask for solace and to offer it. If she stubbed her toe or cut her finger, she would come to me, like a child, to be held. If I had a difficult day at work, she would force me to permit her to give me a backrub or even a foot massage. This didn't come at all easily to me, but she overrode my objections as if I were being stubborn and perverse. Also like a child, a stubborn and perverse child.

And then there were the nights. I'm not referring only to sex, although our sex life was a revelation to me. She took a delight in her own body so pure and so candid it was almost infantile. There was nothing of *performance* about it. She was without sham and without shame. I'm tempted to say she was without modesty, but that would suggest she was consciously shucking off years of ingrained conditioning, and it didn't seem like that at all. Rather, there was something almost prelapsarian about it. As if pleasure and sensation came to her without any cultural overlay or mental construct, without guilt, without social context, without the whole nexus of attitudes and expectations that had always seemed so integral a part of sex to me that I'd never even noticed it was there. Not until I encountered Gretchen, who seemed to be entirely innocent of it. Not *freed* of it, but genuinely innocent of it.

"Have you always been this way?" I asked her once, after a particularly torrid episode. I suppose I was angling for a compliment of some sort.

"Pretty much," she answered. Honesty was another of her qualities, undeniably admirable, but one that sometimes took a little getting used to.

But as I say, it isn't only, or even primarily, sex that I'm talking about. It was our nighttime conversations that were so extraordinary. It was then that I felt closest to her, felt that no two people had ever been so intimately joined. Lying beside me in the dark, she would talk about her life so frankly and so feelingly that I felt privileged to have gained such astonishing trust. She could weep at slights suffered when she was seven, she could howl with laughter at memories of faux pas and gaffes dating back to junior high school, she could discuss former lovers—of whom there were quite a few—with tender regret, she could talk about her parents with wry, affectionate wrath. And more incredible than all this, she somehow managed to elicit something similar from me. I'd never felt that sort of security before, so little need for emotional camouflage or cover. It was a revelation, being able to reveal myself totally to another person without worrying about repelling her.

"Most people," she once said to me, early on, when she was encouraging me to open up to her, to give her more of myself than the canned autobiography I had fed to countless dates over countless dinners over the years, "most people just don't think, deep down, that they're lovable. It takes guts to believe you can show yourself to somebody without losing their respect. But it's worth the risk, Ben."

I frankly couldn't believe my luck in having found her and having somehow gained her love. Before I'd met her, even my most extravagant romantic dreams had involved settling for so much less. I'd been in love before—at least I'd thought I was—but now those past relationships seemed like nothing more than the enacting of some conventional, socially sanctioned mating ritual. This was different. This was the real thing. I know it sounds dopey and sappy, but during those first months with her, I felt as if she completed me and I completed her.

But if I'm giving the impression that we nestled in our own private little cocoon, formed what Kurt Vonnegut calls "a nation of two," then I'm misrepresenting it. We led a very active social life, we developed a network of lively relationships with our administration colleagues. The Sheffield administration, everyone seemed to agree, was an especially tight-knit and collegial group of people. The ordinary hierarchical pecking order wasn't much in evidence, at least socially, at least after business hours. So in addition to our peers, we had cabinet secretaries and White House muckety-mucks over for dinner, in addition to, one memorable night, the vice president and her husband. (It was a kick to look out the window during our final preparations that evening and notice a couple of glowering Secret Service agents standing outside our door.) Plus, we suddenly found ourselves on the invitation lists of *le tout* Washington. Gretchen and I could have gone out every night of the week in those days if we'd chosen to, could have made ourselves at home at embassies and Georgetown dining rooms for drinks at one location and dinner at another, and still have been forced to send regrets to the majority of people who sought the pleasure of our company. It was heady and hilarious. People who a month before would have had us forcibly ejected now vied with one another to entice us into their homes.

Gretchen did occasionally feel self-conscious about the lowliness of her job. Those invitations all came to me rather than to us, and she was always aware of it. Perhaps this was a function of her having lived in Washington in the past, because as far as I could see, no one else seemed to bother about it at all. The people who liked us liked both of us. And as far as the others were concerned, what difference could it possibly make? Embassy parties were as boring for me as they were for her, regardless of our respective status.

Those were exhilarating days for all of us in the administration. Sheffield, unlike so many of his predecessors, seemed to lead a charmed political life for the first year or so of his tenure. It went beyond the traditional honeymoon. He didn't make a single misstep.

This wasn't all skill on his part. Some of it was plain dumb luck, a confluence of inchoate political forces and a chastened opposition and a set of issues susceptible to a clear-cut resolution. He concluded a difficult trade pact with China, but most of the scut work (although none of the credit) adhered to the previous administration. A revolution in Iran, for which he couldn't in fairness take any credit, rendered the region far less dangerous. The economy, which had begun to pick up only in the final quarter of the previous year, continued to improve dramatically. And he had the luxury, as a result of the size of his victory, to make sound appointments. He could even afford to default on some of his political debts without serious risk of alienating his base. As a consequence, all of us who served him acquired a kind of glow, a glamour that came from being part of a successful, exciting enterprise. The press regularly referred to all of us as "the dream team." Books and magazine articles (they all echoed each other, of course) asserted we were the most impressive group to form a government since the Kennedy administration.

And this included Gretchen as well as me. I remember one day when we were shopping at Dean & DeLuca, when she was wearing her Sheffield administration sweatshirt, which bore the presidential seal and the words "Sheffield Administration" and her initials, and I was dressed in jeans and a sweater. An elderly couple approached us. They identified themselves as tourists from Iowa and started praising her, the work she was doing, her association with Sheffield. They barely acknowledged my existence as they showered compliments on her, expressed their admiration and gratitude. The experience wasn't so terribly unusual; everyone who worked for Sheffield basked in the glow.

FROM THE START, I WONDERED WHETHER THE RELATIONSHIP Sheffield and I had established during the campaign would survive the election and inauguration. At first, unsurprisingly, the answer was no. He was busy, he had people he had to cultivate, he was canny about the political advantages of mixing with permanent Washington society, and as a result, my initial contacts with him were businesslike and impersonal. He was pleasant enough, but when he dealt with me our conversation was restricted to the work at hand, the speech I was to write or had already written. There were no games of chess. And some subtle, ineffable change in his manner clearly told me that things were different now, that he was no longer in any way to be regarded as a fellow human being, even the fellow human being who happened to be my boss. He took his new position very seriously. He even, rather more surprisingly, took *himself* very seriously. During the campaign, his ability to distance himself from his position—or at least to seem to—was one of his more appealing qualities.

In fact, this was made very clear the first time Gretchen and I were invited to a social event at the White House. It was an informal affair for staff and some old Sheffield friends from New Mexico, a relatively unpretentious buffet dinner in the East Room. We were beside ourselves with excitement simply at being there, occasionally catching each other's eye and giggling surreptitiously at the sheer unlikelihood of it. But at the end of the evening, as we were preparing to leave, one of those old friends, a woman who was there with her husband, hugged Sheffield and said, "Oh, Chuck, I just can't believe you're president now!" It was sweet and affectionate and didn't strike me as remotely disrespectful, but Sheffield stiffened, mumbled something unintelligible, pulled away from her embrace, and unceremoniously directed his attention to someone else. A rather chilling moment. She had been trying to break down the barriers, and he had restored them immediately, adding a couple of new layers in the process.

When Gretchen mentioned the incident on the drive home, I said, "Well, she probably shouldn't have called him 'Chuck,' all things considered. It was a little presumptuous." I was troubled by the incident too, but was inclined to give Sheffield the benefit of the doubt. In that sort of environment, the sovereign makes the rules, and the rest of us have to try to internalize them.

"But she's known him for decades," Gretchen protested.

"Doesn't matter. He's the president of the United States."

"Does that mean Claire Sheffield's supposed to call him 'Mr. President' too?"

"That's different. She's *married* to him, for Christ's sake."

"What about his mother?"

"Family's different. But other people should observe the proper forms."

"You surprise me, Ben. A guy in Sheffield's position, he *needs* people who can call him Chuck. More than ever."

We didn't discuss it further, but about an hour later, when we were in bed and drifting off to sleep, a peculiar bit of trivia from an old college history course floated unbidden into my mind: When Louis XIV was a small child, he was required to put his mark on an official document granting his nanny permission to spank him if he misbehaved. Had he not done so—because the king's person and the state itself were deemed indivisible—she would have been guilty of treason.

MOST OF SHEFFIELD'S CONCERNS THAT FIRST YEAR WERE DOMESTIC, and with a compliant Congress, he got most of his program through. A series of bills that, among the liberal community at least, were considered quite uncontroversial. These ideas had been percolating up, in one form or another, from think tanks and universities and state legislatures for almost a decade. They were timely, they were fashionable, they didn't rattle any china. Of course the Republicans squawked a bit, but their squawking was pretty perfunctory.

In foreign affairs, except for the Iranian situation, things were reasonably quiescent, with one other serious exception: The war in East Africa was appalling, civilian casualties were astronomical, and it was my impression that Sheffield was genuinely concerned.

"I want to do a speech about Africa," he announced to me one day in the Oval Office. It was a lovely May afternoon, and he had summoned me unexpectedly.

"Okay. What do you want to say?"

He shook his head. "What the hell *can* I say? Killing is a bad thing? War is hell? I've talked to State about this, they're adamant I stay out of it. But there has to be something. At least we should indicate our human horror at it all." He looked out the French doors into the Rose Garden. "Europe is hopeless, that's one problem. The alliance is a joke. They wring their hands and go tut-tut, but they won't *do* anything. They won't even follow our lead if we do the heavy lifting."

"So you just want to deplore the situation?"

"Well, it's a start. At least it demonstrates someone has noticed." He shook his head. "'The most powerful man in the world,' they say. Frankly, Ben, I don't feel any more powerful than I did last year. More coddled, but not more powerful."

"But you want me to write a draft anyway?"

He stared at me. His look could almost be described as hostile. Maybe he regarded my question as impertinent. "Don't bother," he finally said. "I guess I'm just venting." The hostility probably wasn't personal; perhaps it resulted from that coddling he had referred to, from being accustomed to having his wishes acted upon instantly, even in circumstances like this, even when he wasn't sure precisely what they were. And it's possible he wanted someone to show him the way out of the corner in which he now found himself. It annoyed him that I couldn't help him, even though I was only a lowly speechwriter.

That evening, at home, Gretchen was watching something on PBS that didn't appeal to me, and the novel I was reading wasn't holding my interest. So I sat down at my computer and started surfing the Net for information on East Africa. I knew so little about it, I was honestly just curious. What I learned was fascinating and appalling: the baffling complexities of the various tribal relationships, the miserable colonial background, the catastrophic slaughter. It was almost two A.M. and I was bleary-eyed and headachy when I finally felt I had acquired some very rudimentary grasp of the subject. And then, even though I was exhausted and bed was beckoning almost irresistibly, I forced myself to try writing a few words about the situation, just to see what came out. I made myself some coffee, returned to my computer, and struggled to express how I felt about what I had just learned. And inspiration struck. As I sat there at my desk contemplating it, the sheer horror of the thing hit me in a new, vivid way, and the words started to flow. I didn't include any policy recommendations, of course—the president hadn't given me any guidance along those lines—but there was still plenty to say. An overview of the troubled history of the area and some prose pictures of the carnage that was occurring there now. My sentiments may have been conventional and generic—might even be dismissed as sentimental—but I had learned something about the bloodletting, I had internalized Sheffield's mood of frustration and indignation, and I had somehow found a way to translate those feelings into passionate rhetoric. Perhaps because I felt haunted by the carnage, and even more by the fact that it was taking place while the world averted its eyes. And also because I admired Sheffield for evincing a reaction more human than political.

I was up writing all night. When I finally checked my watch, it was already after six, dawn was breaking, and I could hear the beginnings of rush-hour traffic on the street outside. There was no point in going to bed. I showered, shaved, read the *Post*, and drank a whole lot more coffee, waiting for Gretchen to get up so we could drive to work together.

My purpose hadn't been careerist. Nor had I written the thing in order to repair what I perceived as slightly damaged relations between me and the president. But what I did next wasn't quite so innocent.

I didn't show my pages to Randy. I presumed on my friendly relations with Sandra, Sheffield's personal secretary during his Senate
years, now guardian to the entrance to the Oval Office, and handed
her the manila envelope containing my work and a cover letter. "Can
you see that the president gets this?" I asked.

I told myself that this was the appropriate course of action. After
all, the speech hadn't been written for a specific occasion, and the
president had mused about it to me personally. Nevertheless, at this
stage my motives were no longer pure. Among them was simple
vanity: Randy had gotten into the habit of disparaging my efforts
when he read them the first time, and I didn't want to have to deal
with his jealous, sardonic dismissal. But in addition, I suspected that
the president would be pleased with what I had wrought, or at least
with the fact that I *had* wrought it, and I really didn't want to share
credit. Also, I didn't want to have to rewrite it for Randy, to enable
him to say to Sheffield, as he often did, "Ben's ideas were pretty
good, but we had to work with him to get it right." I always hated
that. And the way the hierarchy functioned in the Sheffield White
House—with Randy the principal and me a mere staffer—I would
just have had to sit there silently, as if I accepted his version of
events.

Later that afternoon, while I was struggling to stay awake, the
phone in my office rang. A rare enough occurrence. I assumed it was
probably Gretchen, to say hello, or share some gossip about the
social office, or suggest we go out to dinner that night rather than
eat in. But the female voice at the other end of the line said, "Please
hold for the president." That had never happened before, and it gave
me a sharp jolt of adrenaline, woke me right up.

"Ben? Great work. I love it. It's exactly what I was looking for."

"Yes? I'm pleased, Mr. President. Thank you."

"No, thank *you*. I can't wait to deliver it. State and the NSC will
be furious, but so what? Let 'em bitch. It's the speech I've been
dying to give. I just have to find the right occasion."

My heart was racing. Nevertheless, I found the temerity to say, "Well, you *are* scheduled to deliver the commencement address at American University next month."

"Am I?"

"Yes, sir. Randy mentioned it to me just the other day. Told me to start thinking about it."

There was a long pause. "Jesus, that would be perfect. It's where JFK delivered that fantastic thing about war and peace, isn't it?"

"I believe so."

"Yeah. Great. Extra resonance. Listen, Krause...you've out-Sorensened old Ted this time. People will remember this one. I mean that."

I stammered out a few more expressions of gratitude, and the conversation was over. But despite my fatigue, I was in the stratosphere, in a state of elation for the rest of the day. And Sheffield was right: it's proved to be the most quoted speech of his presidency, at least so far. Bill Safire even included it in the most recent edition of *Lend Me Your Ears*.

"Randy will be furious," Gretchen observed gleefully that evening. I had taken her out to dinner, to Kinkead's, to celebrate.

"I didn't do anything wrong."

"Like that'll make a difference."

"Well, the president requested the speech. Randy won't be able to do anything about it."

"Except make your life a living hell."

"Yeah, he's still got that arrow in his quiver, I guess." We were both grinning. The triumph was too fresh for Randy's prospective vindictiveness to bother us any.

"Still, if you're the fair-haired boy now, he'll probably have to proceed kind of carefully."

"The dark-haired fair-haired boy."

"The fair- but dark- and kinky-haired boy." After sipping her wine, she said, "Poor Randy. You don't really play any of those

bureaucratic games, do you? You don't even know how. But somehow you always end up besting him. He must rue the day he
brought you on board."

"I don't imagine the thought gives him much pleasure, no." I let
the reference to the purity of my MO pass. I hadn't, after all, done
anything wrong. I'd ridden into the president's good graces on sin-
cerity and talent.

WHEN I WAS IN HIGH SCHOOL, MY OLDER BROTHER, DAVE, WHO
was in his sophomore year in college at the time, suddenly dropped
out of school and joined a cult. He had always been so sensible, it
took all of us by surprise and made my parents frantic. Without letting us know anything beforehand, he abandoned his small apartment and moved to the primitive rural compound that served as the
cult's headquarters.

The first time we went up to visit him, on a Saturday—the cult's
Sabbath, hence the only day visitors were permitted—proved to be
extremely painful. His personality was unrecognizable, he seemed
like a zombie, and he shrugged off my parents' questions and
protests with a serene, smug smile. No special little big-brother
wink for me, either, which was something he'd always vouchsafed
me in times of stress. At the end of our private time with him, he
took us to meet the leader of the group. I gather this was standard
operating procedure for the initial visit of new members' family and
friends. Whether it was designed to reassure them or to rub their
noses in their new irrelevance, I'm not certain.

At any rate, seeing my brother in the company of the leader—
named Marcus and always addressed by his first name—and his
inner circle was especially distressing. The man had a certain presence, unquestionably, but the extraordinary deference shown him by
everyone in the room other than us was profoundly disconcerting.

If you had met him in a living room, you wouldn't have necessarily been overwhelmed, but in that context, in that setting, you began to wonder whether you were possibly missing something essential. Everyone else in the room seemed to see it. And Dave kept shooting us little covert glances, as if to say, *"Now* do you understand?" As if every word and gesture of the man bespoke something manifestly majestic and holy.

Dave left the cult on his own after about ten months, without much fanfare—no kidnapping, no expensive force-fed deprogramming required—went back to college, resumed what was, to all appearances at least, a normal life. He's a chef at a good San Francisco restaurant now, married with two children, and doing very well thank you very much. It's an aspect of his personal history no one ever mentions. I don't think his wife is even aware of it.

But it's something I sometimes recall when I'm in Charles Sheffield's company. The president is an interesting and able man, undoubtedly, but does he really merit the deferential kowtowing that is shown him as a matter of course? If he didn't have the mantle of the presidency about him, would any of us think of him as anything terribly special?

I doubt it, frankly, but the fact that I can't be sure—that the man and the office are inextricable even to me, even now—is almost as distressing as was the adulation everyone showed Marcus during that first family visit to the cult's compound. I sometimes get the feeling Dave isn't the only Krause brother who joined a cult.

AFTER THE AFRICA SPEECH, THINGS CHANGED FOR GRETCHEN and me. The Sheffields had a small coterie of personal friends, but their social life also included the people with whom the president worked, and the favorites of any given moment tended to be those who were engaged in whatever was occupying his attention at the time. Perhaps that was merely a function of the superficiality of his affections; his warmth was directed toward whoever showed up on his radar screen.

And now I started to register.

Even before the AU commencement, Gretchen and I were invited to a state dinner, for the newly installed president of Nigeria. It wasn't unprecedented in the Sheffield White House for someone at my pay grade to be invited to such a grand event, but it wasn't exactly common either. I suppose the African connection was the determinant.

"Payoff for the speech," I said to Gretchen the day the invitation arrived. She had got home after me, and I greeted her at the door with the thing in my hand.

After glancing at it, she said, "Unless it's for my groundbreaking work in the social office." And then she smiled, to show me, quite unnecessarily, that the joke was benign, that she didn't feel competitive.

"Our first state dinner. Not bad, you have to admit."

"Not bad at all," she agreed. "Keep up the good work."

And it was a grand event indeed, great glittering fun, not to mention an opportunity to trot out my Armani tux. But totally impersonal. Except for our few seconds in the receiving line, we didn't have any contact with either president. "Glad you could come," Sheffield said to me as I shook his hand. That's all I got. When Gretchen glided up beside me, he said, "It's Gretchen, isn't it? Good to have you," and then smoothly moved us on toward Mrs. Sheffield and her Nigerian counterpart. His remembering Gretchen's name made the evening for her. His graceful delivery of the toast I had written for him went a long way toward doing the same for me.

That might have been that—favor performed and favor repaid—except for what happened two days later. Randy and I were in the Oval Office with him at the end of a long day—it was well after six—discussing a speech he was scheduled to deliver before some trade group or other. The worst sort of assignment imaginable, for him, for us, and no doubt in many ways for his audience too, although for the audience the novelty of seeing the president of the United States in the flesh might compensate for the tedium somewhat. Anyway, Sheffield was having a Scotch-rocks—Randy and I declined when offered, although the drink looked mighty attractive every time Sheffield brought it to his lips—and was trying to unwind while simultaneously focusing on the speech. It wasn't hard to see that his heart wasn't in it.

Wasn't hard for me, that is. Randy, on the other hand, was otherwise engaged, droning on, reading the speech out loud, experimenting with alternate word choices, defending certain paragraphs as representing requests from the Commerce and Labor Departments and USTR, all the while blankly oblivious to the fact that the president's eyes seemed to be glazing over. Randy had a job to do, damn it, and he was going to do it whether or not the person for whom he did the job showed the slightest interest.

And somewhere along the line, Sheffield looked up wearily and our eyes met. And then something untoward happened. More than untoward: Incredible. Incomprehensible.

What happened was, he raised his eyebrows quizzically, and we suddenly started to giggle. Sheffield and I just totally lost it. It was an amazing thing. We were like kids trying to be solemn in school, our efforts at stifling our hilarity ultimately making it even more uncontrollable, and Randy's effort to understand what we were laughing at, and his visible effort not to take offense—he couldn't very well get huffy with the president of the United States, especially right there in the Oval Office—making it *completely* uncontrollable. Finally we abandoned any attempt at decorum and just threw back our heads and screamed with laughter, clutching our sides and doubling over. It was a couple of minutes before we were able to pull ourselves together, and when our laughter finally subsided, we both had tears in our eyes. Randy, on the other hand, was flushing a bright red. He still didn't know what had happened, but he could tell he was, in some obscure way, the butt of the joke.

"Sorry, Randy," the president was finally gracious enough to say, "it's been a very long day."

"Of course, sir," said Randy. "I understand." But he didn't. And the look he shot me was the unfriendliest in our troubled history.

"I suppose we ought to try this again another time," the president said with a sigh.

As he was showing the two of us out of the Oval Office, he suddenly put one of his big hands on my shoulder. "Stay behind a minute, Ben. There's something I want to talk to you about."

Randy was too exposed at that point to give me another glare, but I could feel the impulse to glare coming off him like a noxious odor. After he left, Sheffield said, "Claire and I are having a few people over tonight to see a movie. Very informal. Would you and, uh, and Gretchen like to come?"

It was a spur-of-the-moment invitation coming directly out of our shared laughter. I knew that within an hour he would wonder what had possessed him, so I didn't wait to consult with Gretchen before accepting. "That would be terrific," I said. "Thank you, Mr. President."

Gretchen's initial reaction, when I called her from my office with the news, was mild irritation. "Not exactly a lot of notice, is it?"

"No, it was one of those sudden inspirations."

"What time?"

"Eight."

"Damn. I won't have a chance to wash my hair. I'll barely have time to change."

"Don't you want to do it?"

"Well...I suppose it's kind of exciting. I just wish I'd known in advance."

"Yeah, that was darned inconsiderate of him. Wanna call to complain?"

"Sure. *Somebody* should teach him some manners. You happen to know his personal number?"

I had to work late that evening—Randy made sure of that—so I was in an even worse position than Gretchen, unable to get home at all. By the time she came to fetch me in my office in the OEOB, I felt as if I'd spent a month in the suit I was wearing. But when I saw her, I let out a small involuntary, "My goodness."

"Well...he said informal, didn't he?"

"It's not that, it's—" What was it, in fact? I suppose it's that she looked so utterly *sexy*. Without overtly violating any norms, she looked almost indecent. Or was that just my own reaction? Simply to describe her outfit wouldn't begin to convey the impression it made. She wore a pair of pleated herringbone tweed slacks and a black turtleneck. But both were tight and made of thin material, and they showed off her body. Boy did they show off her body. Still, you couldn't say they were inappropriate—no flesh was revealed, the colors were tastefully muted—but they certainly grabbed your attention. By the throat. "You look fantastic!" I said. "Gretchen my dear, you are one hot babe."

"Why...thank you." She was pleased.

I was thoroughly familiar with her body by then, but I felt as if I were seeing it for the first time. The bounteous curves, the flat belly, the trim hips. I couldn't keep my hands off her, is the simple truth of the matter. I would have ravished her right there in my office, except she called a halt. "We're going to be late, Ben."

"So what? Afraid we'll miss the credits?"

"That's what I was thinking, uh-huh."

Despite the exigent promptings of lust, I could see she was right, of course. You don't keep a president waiting. It took me a minute or two to get myself into a presentable state, and then we proceeded out the side entrance of the OEOB, across West Executive Avenue, and through the basement entrance into the west wing of the White House. Our arrival at the area near the movie theater was perfectly timed. Most of the guests were already present—there were fewer than twenty of us, all told—but the president and Mrs. Sheffield hadn't arrived yet. Then, as we gave our drink orders to a white-coated steward, our hosts slipped in. No *Ruffles and Flourishes,* no applause; it wasn't that kind of night.

The two of them separated to greet their guests. Gretchen and I got the president just as the steward brought our drinks, which made shaking hands comically difficult. After that awkwardness, he put one of his big paws on my shoulder and said, "Good to have you, Ben. That was quite a meeting today, wasn't it?" His eyes were sparkling with amusement; evidently the experience hadn't lost its risibility in the intervening hours.

Then he turned to Gretchen. I saw his eyes widen as he took her in. They didn't travel back up to meet her gaze right away either. They lingered for a moment. Only then did he say, "Gretchen. I'm glad we finally convinced this fella to bring you to visit. He's been doing great work for us. I'm proud of him."

"Me too, Mr. President," said Gretchen. There was something about her tone of voice and something about her smile—something in her eye—that let him know she was quite aware of the once-over he had given her, that she was amused by it, and that he didn't intimidate her in the slightest. Her demeanor wasn't exactly flirta-tious, it was something else for which no word exists; to me, at least, it seemed to convey a message that said, "If you want to look at me the way a man looks at a woman, then you'd better expect me to talk to you as a man rather than a president."

Something registered with him—the moment was very quick, but you could see it in his face—and then he said, as if nothing in particular had happened, "You know, I just learned your dad is Arnie Burns. I was a page back when he was in Congress. Crusty sort of fella, wasn't he?"

"If that's a polite way of saying a pain in the ass, he still is," answered Gretchen. "More than ever."

Sheffield grinned. He was enjoying himself. "That's what I meant all right. Glad to hear he hasn't mellowed."

"Nope," she said, her accent easing into the country drawl she sometimes affected. "He's ripened some, but he hasn't mellowed any."

"Where is he these days? Gone back to Illinois, or stayed in the area?"

"Neither. He's got a place in Rehoboth Beach. Cohabiting with a woman not his wife."

This was a bit of data for which Sheffield was unprepared. He took a moment, trying, I think, to gauge how much bitterness Gretchen was introducing into the conversation. He finally decided the ground was reasonably safe. "Well, good for him," he declared jocularly.

"Yeah," said Gretchen, "he's living life in the fast lane all right, shacked up with a sixty-eight-year-old bimbo."

"Those are the ones you gotta keep your eyes on," Sheffield said.

I was entertained by this conversation—admired the gutsy way Gretchen was handling herself, relished the way Sheffield obviously liked her—when someone sidled up to me and said, "Ben! Good to see you!"

I turned to find Senator Jared MacMillan at my left shoulder. I hadn't seen him since the campaign, when I'd prepped him for the first practice debate, during which he had stood in for Sheffield's opponent. It was flattering and rather surprising that he remembered me, even more so that he would bother to seek me out at a White House function where virtually all the other guests were more important than I. As a result, and despite my reluctance to leave Gretchen and the president, I really had no polite choice but to pivot around and engage him.

"I've been wanting to tell you," he went on, "how much fun it was, being able to say all those awful things to Chuck. Downright cathartic. I've wanted to rag on him for years, and I knew this would be my last opportunity. Man, you really went after him with the full nuclear arsenal, didn't you?"

"That was the assignment," I said. "Or at least, that's what they *told* me was the assignment."

"Caught some hell for it, did you?"

"A couple days in Coventry."

MacMillan laughed. "Me too. He could see how much I enjoyed it, I think *that* was the problem. But"—and here he gestured with his glass, taking in the entire White House—"we seem to be back in his good graces."

"Yeah, well, being the most powerful person in the world must encourage benevolence."

"You're obviously too young to remember Richard Nixon."

This would have been a good moment to extricate myself from the conversation and rejoin Gretchen—in addition, my wineglass was empty, so I even had a plausible excuse—but at that moment the First Lady joined MacMillan and me. Trapped! I looked across the room. To my surprise, Gretchen and the president were still talking animatedly. Then Mrs. Sheffield said some words of praise to MacMillan about my work on the Africa speech—she had just read the latest draft, she said—so I gave her my full attention. Partly because it was socially unavoidable, and partly because I've always been greedy for praise.

The First Lady moved on after a few minutes, but then, as I was wending my way over to Gretchen, the guests started to be herded into the theater. And that's when something really unexpected happened: Because Gretchen was still talking to the president, when I approached her—at the same time the First Lady approached from a different direction—Gretchen and I found ourselves entering the theater with the First Couple and then sitting beside them in the front row. The order was, Claire Sheffield, the president, Gretchen, and me. I was a little concerned that this arrangement was a bit presumptuous on our part, since there were so many other people with whom Sheffield might have wanted to schmooze and since we hadn't been expressly invited to this place of honor. But neither Sheffield nor his wife looked put out in the slightest, and once we were seated, it was impossible to do anything about it anyway.

The movie was a romantic comedy, neither particularly good nor especially bad. I laughed out loud a few times, smiled a few times more. Occasionally the president whispered something to Gretchen, and every time he did it made her laugh, but I was unable to hear any of the things he said. And once, I glanced over, and he was looking at her and she was looking at him, but when my eyes met his he immediately turned away and faced the screen. I remember thinking, Gee, Gretchen has really made quite a hit with this guy.

On the drive home I asked, "What was the president saying to you? He seemed awfully chatty."

"Yeah, he did, didn't he?"

"What was he saying?"

"Oh, nothing really. Just comments about the movie. He didn't seem to like it much."

"Were you...*flirting* with him?"

She laughed first, and then she said, "I guess I was, wasn't I? Or at least, *he* was flirting with *me.*" And she laughed again. At how surreal the whole situation was, most likely.

When we got home I wasted no time completing the ravishing I had initiated in my office several hours before. That she had just been flirting with the president of the United States added to the kick.

THE NEXT DAY, WHEN I GOT HOME FROM WORK, GRETCHEN WAS sprawled on the living room sofa, on the phone. When she saw me she gave a little wave and then said, "Listen, Ben just came in, I really should go.... Yes, good, that would be great.... Bye."

She may have looked a little flushed, but not enough for me to be consciously aware of it. It's a detail I'm supplying after the fact, in all probability. "Who was that?" I asked.

"Nobody. My mom."

"Which is it?"

She smiled. "My mom. She said hello." Very cool, she was.

I didn't suspect a thing. I didn't suspect a thing for a long time.

I didn't suspect a thing when Sheffield offered me the use of Camp David for the weekend when I had to make the final revisions on the speech. Should I have? It seemed like a high honor, a magnificent sign of presidential favor. I had no misgivings, no qualms, I was on top of the world. "It'll be empty," he told me, "except for the staff. You'll have the run of the place. It's a fabulous setting for getting work done."

"That's awfully kind of you, sir. Do you think…that is, I hope this isn't too presumptuous, but would it be okay to bring Gretchen?"

There was the briefest of pauses—just long enough to make me think I might have overstepped—before he said, "Of course, feel free. Just so long as you don't let her distract you."

Ha ha ha. Masculine chuckles on both sides.

But when I told her the exciting news, she didn't respond the way I expected. "Oh, Ben, I can't. I just can't. We're gearing up for the First Lady's Women in the Arts luncheon. I'm going to be working all day Saturday."

"Can't you get dispensation? This is a pretty big deal."

"I don't even want to ask. The whole East Wing is in a tizzy over this thing. You wouldn't believe it."

And I didn't suspect a thing when I phoned home from Camp David a few times and there was no answer. I was reveling in the beauty of the setting and wanted to let Gretchen know what she was missing, wanted the two of us to share our regrets about not being able to enjoy the experience together; but hell, she had said she was going to be busy, so it wasn't a huge surprise that she wasn't there. I had no reason to think the president had dangled this plum in front of me simply to get me out of the way.

And I didn't suspect a thing at the American University commencement, to which Gretchen and I were invited. It was a beautiful spring day, and the Africa speech went like gangbusters. When I glanced over at Gretchen while it was in progress, I saw an odd half smile on her lips, noticed that her eyes were glistening, and I thought these were signs of pride in my handiwork. When we rode back to the White House in Sheffield's limousine—I'd been part of his motorcade before but had never ridden in the limousine with him—and she told him how well it had gone, I thought she was cleverly boosting my stock in the guise of paying him a compliment. When our invitations to White House social events increased—and they increased astonishingly in the weeks that followed—and when he took a little extra time with us in the receiving line, I thought it was an indication of professional favor and appreciation, even of friendship.

In other words, I was a complete idiot.

Although perhaps I'm being a little hard on myself. Because, you see, he didn't become nice and attentive to Gretchen alone, he became far more solicitous toward me as well. And it wasn't merely the invitations, although evenings at the White House soon became, on average, an almost weekly occurrence for us. He also sought my advice more frequently, he laughed harder at my jokes, he seemed to share more of himself. It strikes me as a little creepy, now that I'm finally aware of what was going on. Maybe it would be less creepy if it had been entirely an act, if it had been intended as misdirection, but I don't think that's the case. For Sheffield, taking on Gretchen seemed to mean taking on both of us. As if in some peculiar way we both became his clients. A sort of noblesse oblige kind of deal. So with all this personal presidential attention, whatever suspicions I might have otherwise entertained were allayed before they reached the level of consciousness, were headed off at the pass.

I remember, for example, a few days after he had given the American University commencement, he called me into his office simply to tell me how annoyed the administration's foreign policy apparatchiks were. "Their noses are so out of joint they're gonna need rhinoplasty," he said. "Guess we showed *them* who's boss, right?" He had a playful glint in his eye, he was obviously enjoying the ruckus, and he was seductively including me as an ally in his mischief making. No, it went beyond that: an ally in his presidency. *We* had shown them, he told me. And it worked. I believed him. Chuck and Ben were in this together, two decent people fighting for humane values while the establishmentarian fuddy-duddies clucked their hidebound disapproval.

When I was leaving the Oval Office that day, he said, "And Ben, listen. I don't give a good goddamn about lines of authority. If anybody tries to hassle you about the speech, I don't care if it's the secretary of state himself, just refer them to me. This is a good thing we're doing. And you deserve a lot of the credit. You really did your homework, and you wrote me a great speech." Of course, I was glowing all over again. And even now, even today, I don't believe he was dissembling, I don't believe this was some calculated stratagem to mislead me; Sheffield was able to compartmentalize the different facets of his life in such a way that he could cuckold me one day and feel genuine good fellowship toward me the next.

So I keep struggling with the question. From a practical point of view, can I really blame myself for not figuring things out sooner? I still don't know the answer. The idea that you're being cuckolded by the president of the United States isn't the sort of thing that just pops into your head, even when your life is taking a few strange turns.

And—this is more evidence against my idiocy, incidentally—it's not as if I didn't notice something dubious going on with Gretchen. In fact, it was pretty early on that I began to suspect, however dimly, that she might be seeing someone else. There were those phone calls that concluded abruptly when I entered the room. Sometimes she said she was talking to her mother—they had never talked that often before—and sometimes she said it was one old friend or another. There were occasional Saturday afternoons when she said she had to go to the White House and put in a few extra hours of work—unusual but not unprecedented in the social office—and there were evenings when she didn't get home till eight or nine, a couple of hours later than her usual. It became almost commonplace for me, alone at the kitchen table, to eat the dinner I had made for the two of us, with a magazine or book for company, and then leave a plate for Gretchen to microwave when she got home. Sometimes she explained her lateness by invoking the crush of work, and once or twice the excuse was that she had gone out for a drink with a co-worker. And occasionally the phone would ring, I would pick it up, and there would be silence on the line. Now, when I think about who was holding the phone at the other end, those calls strike me as being almost as funny as they are painful: the leader of the free world covering the mouthpiece with his palm and cursing his bad luck. But at the time, I rarely gave them a second thought. In fact, none of these things, taken by themselves, would have aroused any suspicion; it was only over time, taking them all together, that they began to put me on alert.

In addition, our sex life was suffering. It wasn't in complete abeyance, but we were definitely making love less frequently, and Gretchen was far less aggressive, and far less adventuresome, than she had once been. Less receptive too.

Still—as I seem to need to keep insisting—it wasn't clear-cut. She continued to be affectionate and caring, continued to tell me she loved me, continued to devote herself to our conjoined life. We still entertained as much as before, still shopped together and played together, still shared gossip and impressions. She continued to offer much more than she withheld.

And then, one night, I went into the bathroom and found her sobbing. I took her in my arms and asked her what was the matter.

"Nothing, nothing. Just hormones or something. You know what women are like."

"Jeez, Gretchen, if *I* ever said something like that, you'd take my head off."

She smiled through her tears and kissed me. "You're the best thing that ever happened to me, Ben."

"You sure?"

"More every day," she answered.

"Then tell me...Gretchen, are you having an affair? Something along those lines?" I just blurted it out; my suspicions had been gathering steam for a while.

If she started guiltily, I missed it. And trust me, I was looking. She merely said, "No, sweetie, of course not. Where did you get a crazy idea like that?"

So I dropped it, of course.

Meanwhile, providing some distraction, our social life was taking an exciting turn. As I said, we found ourselves invited to the White House almost once a week. Sometimes it was for big events—dinners for campaign contributors, musical evenings, celebrations of one kind or another—but sometimes it was for remarkably small and almost intimate gatherings. To watch a baseball game in the family theater, to join a small party for dinner in the family quarters, to entertain a visiting celebrity from L.A. or New York. And sometimes we even went out, to a restaurant, to the theater, to a ballet at the Kennedy Center (Claire Sheffield was a great balletomane, and although I don't believe her husband shared her enthusiasm, he occasionally indulged it). It was never just the Sheffields and us, but still, this was heady stuff. When a president wants to show you you're in his good graces, he's got plenty of resources to draw on.

And this president was letting us know in lots of ways that we were in his good graces. I chalked it all up to the Africa speech, along with our youthful charm, Gretchen's and mine. Sometimes embarrassment vies with rage these days when I look back at the late spring and early summer of that year.

In retrospect, I sometimes ask myself if I were missing hints and clues all over the place, if there weren't all sorts of behavior on display that I should have noticed. After all, I saw Gretchen and the president together quite a lot. Of course there must have been something, little glances, stray touches. But I don't believe it could have been anything terribly obvious. My antennae never quivered. Besides, Sheffield was such a gregarious fellow in social situations, any particular attentions he was paying Gretchen probably blended in with, got lost against, the general background noise of his affability. He often called women "honey" and "sweetheart," he sometimes called men "pal" and "fella," his hands were frequently on one's shoulder or arm. It was very effective natural camouflage, whether intended as such or not.

But then, there were several turning points. It's humiliating to admit that there were several, that things became clear to me only in stages, but that's how it happened. Once again, my only defense against the charge of blank stupidity is that the reality is so damned implausible.

One Friday, Gretchen and I were scheduled to have dinner with a couple of friends at Germaine's. She had a hair appointment after work that day, so we arranged to arrive separately at seven-thirty. I got there on time, our friends appeared about ten minutes later. We ordered drinks and waited for Gretchen to show up.

She didn't.

By eight-fifteen I started to worry. I called home, but she wasn't there. I called her office at the White House, but there was no answer. I phoned the hair salon, George at the Four Seasons, but it had already closed. I was so desperate, I then called the concierge at the hotel itself and, exploiting my White House affiliation for the first time ever, demanded that they check the hair salon appointment book for me. I told them it was an emergency. They didn't want to help but finally agreed—I had to hold at the pay phone at Germaine's for over five minutes—and they then assured me that yes, Gretchen had kept her hair appointment.

Visions of muggings and rapes danced in my head. My friends ordered a bottle of wine and tried to get me to calm down. But they weren't mindless about it, they were sympathetic and concerned and even offered to drive around Georgetown with me to search for her. That didn't seem like a very practical plan, but it was difficult to come up with an alternative. I was about to call the DCPD—not a bureaucracy you want to deal with on a Friday night, but I couldn't think of anything better—to ask if they had any record of a street crime in the Georgetown area. That's the moment, as I was heading back toward the pay phone, that Gretchen appeared at the top of the stairs.

She looked flushed and upset and out of breath. "Oh God," she said, "I'm so sorry, Ben. What a mess! I hope you ordered without me."

Since we were in the entrance foyer, right at the top of the stairs, far enough from our table so our friends couldn't hear, I hissed at her, "Where the fucking hell have you been?"

"Don't be angry. I had to go back to the White House. They paged me. It was the last thing I wanted, but...You know what it's like, it's impossible to say no in that situation."

"An emergency in the social office?"

"You're always making me feel like my job is trivial. There *are* emergencies in the social office. Not matters of war and peace, but...other things."

"I called your office. No one answered."

"I was in and out. Why are you interrogating me like this?"

"But you did keep your hair appointment?" This was a trick question, of course. Sherlock Krause.

"Yeah, that's where they paged me. Can't you tell?" This last was a small joke. It had been raining, one of those miserable hot wet nights you get in Washington at that time of year, and her hair, though perceptibly shorter, was a mess.

"You could've called."

"I did. I left a message at home. But things were a little crazy once I got back to the White House, I didn't feel as if I could make a lot of personal calls."

I left a brief interval before saying, "We'd better sit down."

"Aren't you relieved I'm okay?"

"I'm not sure." At which point I turned and headed back to the table. I didn't trust myself to have any further conversation with her in a public place.

I don't remember much about our dinner that night, except that I had no appetite, that my taciturnity was all too evident, and that I called for the check before everybody had finished eating. No one protested.

When I got home, Gretchen was already there. Miraculously, she must have found a parking space nearer to Germaine's than I, even though she had arrived so late. I didn't know whether I'd encounter bravado or remorse. As far as that goes, I wasn't sure what tack I was going to take either.

"It isn't what you think," was how she greeted me as soon as I got through the door. So no tack was necessary. She was in the foyer, still in her raincoat, waiting for me.

"No? And what is it I think?"

"That I'm having some sort of affair."

"Yes, you're right, I do think that."

"Listen…not only don't I want to, but I don't even have time for it, Ben."

"Well, sure you do, as long as you're willing to keep me waiting and worrying at Germaine's while you tear off a quickie."

"This is really demeaning, this conversation. I'm sorry you're upset, and I'm willing to accept most of the responsibility, but this shit you're saying is totally unworthy of you. Why don't you check the White House logs on Monday? You'll see. I went back there at about seven-fifteen."

Well, what was I to do? I didn't quite believe her, but I wanted to, and I certainly didn't have any conclusive proof to the contrary. Nevertheless, I did check our answering machine, and sure enough, there was a message from her saying she had been called back to the office. And I did check the White House logs the following Monday. And was relieved to discover she hadn't lied.

WE WENT AWAY FOR THE FOURTH OF JULY WEEKEND, VISITING Wilt and Liz, some friends who owned a vacation house in Bethany Beach. They had no connection to the political world, which made them relatively rare among our Washington circle. I had met Wilt, an attorney, at my gym. And the holiday was going pleasantly enough, I suppose, although I wasn't easy in my own mind and thought I sensed a certain abstraction in Gretchen's manner, as if her mind were off wandering elsewhere. But it was all so vague; I found my mood swinging back and forth like a pendulum, deeply suspicious one moment, angry at myself for being paranoid the next. Either way I felt ridiculous, a comic figure out of some Italian farce.

Sunday morning, sitting in the Bethany Beach sand beside Gretchen, soaking up carcinogens and doing the *New York Times* crossword puzzle, I turned to her. We had made love that morning, to the oddly exciting accompaniment of our oblivious hosts rattling around in the kitchen, and on the surface everything was fine, actually better than it had been in some weeks. But I heard myself saying, "Tell me, is this working out, as far as you're concerned?"

"'This'? Meaning…what? You and me?"

"Meaning that, yeah."

Which got her attention. She had been lying on her stomach, reading the "Arts and Leisure" section, and now she hoisted herself up on one elbow, adjusted her halter as she did so, and said, "As far as I'm concerned it is. Absolutely."

"There's something different about you, Gretchen. Something's going on."

"What do you mean? Different since when?"

"You want me to provide a specific date? I can't do that. Since lately."

The look on her face acknowledged the edge in my voice. Then she said, "I love you, Ben. Until I met you, I didn't know I could care about someone this much. Isn't that enough?"

"Isn't that enough as in, 'What the hell else do you want?'"

"No, I think I was expressing a more generous sentiment than that." Now there was an edge in her voice too.

"Well," I said, rolling into a prone position—I didn't know how else to terminate such an uncomfortable discussion, other than by body language—"I'm glad you think things are working out."

"Well…I *did.*" Getting the last word, and the upper hand, rather neatly. But not quite providing the reassurance I was seeking.

That afternoon, as the four of us were sitting around the living room table playing a game Liz taught us—which involved supplying plausible first sentences for novels that none of the participants have read, hoping to trick your opponents into voting for the one you've written—the phone rang. Although we were pretending to be casual and frolicsome about the game, we were all deep into overachievers' competitive mode, especially Liz. She was ahead, but I wasn't far behind, and she wasn't too skillful at disguising how much the outcome of the game meant to her. (She was much more skillful at writing convincing first sentences for the paperbacks lying around her vacation house.) So when the phone rang, she said, "Oh, just let Alex get it." Alex was their thirteen-year-old son, off in his room playing video games. She didn't want to stop the competition, even for a minute.

A couple of moments later Alex came into the living room, looking very impressed. A rare thing for a thirteen-year-old boy. "Mr. Krause, it's for you. *It's the president!*"

I was startled. Sheffield had called me at home maybe twice—at most—in the months I'd been working for him, and I couldn't think of any reason he'd need to speak to me now. As I got up to answer the phone, Liz said, "I bet you arranged this with some friend before you left town, right? Just to impress us?" But the flippancy was camouflage; she seemed, beneath the facetiousness, pretty damned impressed. I occasionally got the impression that our White House connection added to our luster as friends in her estimation, made us just that little bit more attractive than we might otherwise have been. Hardly a unique phenomenon in Washington. It wasn't specifically political with her, I don't think—in fact, the relative absence of any political discussion among us led me to suspect that she and Wilt were Republicans—it was more that our jobs lent Gretchen and me a bit of reflected glamour.

"I probably should have some privacy for this," I said.

"Awww…can't we eavesdrop?" Whining humorously. But then she told her son, "Show Mr. Krause the phone in our bedroom, Alex." Suddenly becoming very grown-up and serious.

I followed him in. The phone was already off the hook. It was the one he had picked up. I nodded my thanks to him—his back was already to me, he was on his way back to his video game—and then said into the receiver, "This is Ben Krause."

"Please hold for the president."

I had to hold long enough to wonder again what the call could possibly be about. Then Sheffield came on the line. "Ben?"

"Yes, Mr. President."

"How's your vacation going?"

"It's very pleasant down here. How about you?"

"Claire and I are up in Camp David, we have the kids visiting. It's lovely. You know, you've been. One of the better perks that come with this job. I had to do a couple of events earlier, just quick 'show the colors'–type things in the Baltimore area, then I choppered up. Very convenient, having Marine One at the ready. Another nifty perk. But for all that, I kind of envy you, just loading yourselves into the car and rolling off somewhere. Bethany Beach, is it?"

"Yes, Mr. President. And I can't tell you how much it means, hearing that the leader of the free world envies me."

He laughed, briefly. Then he said, "So…gonna be traditional? Got any fireworks planned?"

Which is the point I entertained the notion he might have gone nuts. We had reached a point in the conversation where the transition to business would have been easy and natural, but instead he pressed on with vacation chat. Hadn't we vamped enough, even for a phone call on a holiday weekend? What was his agenda, and what the hell could he possibly be waiting for?

Nevertheless I answered, "No fireworks here. There might be some in town." You can't very well demand of the president of the United States, "Do you honestly care?" You follow his lead and hope he's going somewhere.

"It's a nice holiday, the Fourth of July. I've always loved it. Especially in nonelection years, when you don't have to spend the whole damn day doing drop-bys at all those picnics and wienie roasts and things."

"Yeah, I hate that."

But he didn't even hear me this time. "And so redolent of summer, you know? Of the things that summer meant to you as a kid. Softball games and lazy hot days and no school as far as the eye can see."

It now struck me that this call had come during Sheffield's traditional cocktail hour, about six o'clock. Perhaps that explained the serpentining conversational path he was taking to his goal. I don't mean to suggest he sounded drunk, or even slightly tipsy, merely that he was unwinding at the end of the day and therefore taking his own sweet time about getting to the point, sipping his Scotch and relaxing a little along the way.

"It sounds as if you'd like to go back to those days, sir." Shit, I still had to keep my end up, I had to say *something*.

"Like a shot, Ben. Without a backward glance." He cleared his throat. Okay, I thought, here it comes, whatever *it* is. "Uh, Ben, have you given any thought to, to, uh, to that roast for Jared MacMillan?"

"The MacMillan roast isn't till September, sir."

"Yeah, I know, but I was just starting to worry about it. The Gridiron and the Alfalfa and those other speeches last spring didn't go so great, I'd like this one to be really first-rate. Up to the Ben Krause standard."

We had had some problems with those humorous speeches the president, by tradition, delivers annually. They don't get much coverage outside the Beltway, but within Washington they're considered important, a gauge of his ability to be funny and self-deprecating, to show his human side, to share something with insiders withheld from the rest of the country. And the prevailing opinion afterward was, we had blown it. We had misjudged the tone, we had tried to score points off our opponents rather than make fun of ourselves, and our jokes hadn't been nearly funny enough. The experience had clearly unnerved him at the time. Charles Sheffield breaks out in flop sweat! Film at eleven!

Still, it was damned peculiar that he would be calling me about such a topic now, two months before he was due to deliver the speech, especially a speech that, regardless of his personal feelings, was really quite a trivial matter in his presidency. But what could I do? He was my boss, and he seemed to want to talk about it. So I assured him that Randy and I were painfully aware we had let him down before, that we planned to do whatever it took to improve on our handiwork in the future, that we knew his relationship with MacMillan made him want to do as good a job as possible.

We went back and forth this way for a few minutes, and then he said, "Well, good, I feel better about this. Just wanted to be sure we're singing from the same hymn book."

"Not the best metaphor to use in my case, Mr. President, but yes, we're certainly in accord."

"Excellent." Then, after a very brief interval, he went on, "Say, is Gretchen there? Let me say hello."

"Why, sure, I'll get her, sir. That's very kind of you." Which was the last entirely stupid thing I was ever to say on the subject, but also one of the very stupidest.

I went out into the living room and told Gretchen the president wanted to say hello. She looked pleased, and—maybe this is hindsight—a little less startled than I expected. Wilt laughed in amazement, and Liz twittered.

After Gretchen had left the room, Liz said, "Now see here, Ben, just how friendly *are* you guys with the Sheffields?" It was the sort of question she had never asked us before but might have posed to Wilt, and to herself, more than once.

"Oh," I said, "hardly at all. This was business. It wasn't a social call." But I was thinking, It *wasn't* really business. As a business call, it didn't make any sense. It didn't make much sense as *any* kind of call.

Then Wilt told Liz, "They say you can determine who has real influence in Washington by keeping your eye on the people who *deny* they're close to the president. The ones who don't feel the need to brag about it. So maybe we have us some mighty influential people in our humble household this weekend."

"I hate to disillusion you, Wilt, but we're just a couple of lowly drones."

"Keep on saying it, it just tells me how important you are."

"And what if I say we're their best friends?"

"I'd believe you."

"So I can't win."

"No, you can't lose."

"Let's get back to the game," said Liz. I think she'd been itching to get back to it as soon as it had become clear I wasn't going to be spilling any hot presidential gossip.

"When Gretchen comes back," said Wilt.

"Aw, we can give her a bye this round. She wouldn't care, would she, Ben?...Ben?...Hel-*lo?*"

She had noticed my mind was wandering, and she was right. To be specific, it was wandering in the general direction of the burning question, How the hell long does it take a president to offer a quick hello to a speechwriter's girlfriend?

But I forced myself to focus. "Oh," I said, "sorry. By all means, let's play. I'm sure Gretchen won't object."

"She wasn't doing so hot anyway," Liz observed.

I headed back to the table, but my mind felt as if it were exploding. I kept saying to myself, Nah, it isn't possible, just let it go, don't make yourself crazy. But I wasn't finding myself terribly convincing. And then, just as I sat down, Gretchen entered the living room. I didn't try to meet her eye, so I can't say whether she was avoiding mine.

"Well," exclaimed Liz, "big doings! What was *that* about?"

Gretchen was taken aback by Liz's ebullience. She hadn't been privy to the conversation that had preceded it. "Oh, I just—"

"Was he explaining his entire domestic agenda or something?"

"That's it," said Gretchen, and then, "No, actually it was just chat. Our holiday and his, the attractions of Camp David in July, just shooting the breeze. It was odd, to be honest. He must be bored up there or something."

"Maybe he's lonely," I said.

Gretchen glanced over at me—our eyes finally met—and there was one of those moments of recognition when you can literally *see* the thought passing through the other person's mind. But she recovered very quickly, and her expression was abruptly neutral again. "No, they've got their kids with them, apparently. The Sheffields' first family visit to Camp David."

"How lovely for them," said Liz. "Now...can we get back to the game?"

We resumed play, but I was no longer any sort of threat to Liz's commanding position. My concentration was totally blown.

SINCE WE WERE SCHEDULED TO LEAVE THE FOLLOWING DAY, there was only one impossibly horrible night to get through, where I had to pretend that nothing was wrong and play the part of a good-natured and enthusiastic guest. I just barely managed. Gretchen played her role better, but then, she'd been playing it for a while now, and besides, I don't think she was altogether convinced she'd have to abandon it yet, even with me. One quick glance between us...it could've meant anything. And I held my tongue that night. I had a bad feeling that if I started talking, I'd end up screaming. I held my tongue through the remainder of the parlor game, through dinner (where Liz, with that breathtaking sensitivity of hers, drew attention to my brooding silence several times; maybe she just thought I was a sore loser), and right past bedtime, when I didn't say a word to Gretchen after we got into bed. And I know she knew what I was thinking, because she didn't ask me what was wrong. She didn't have to. She knew. And she didn't want to hear the answer.

We were polite to each other the next morning, saying only those things that needed saying. About who would shower first, about packing, about the timing of our departure. We were quieter than usual during breakfast with Wilt and Liz, but I don't believe the constraint was especially obvious to them. People are funny in the morning under the best of circumstances; our hosts couldn't know we were being a lot quieter than our norm. We were probably both dreading—I know *I* was dreading—the moment when we'd suddenly find ourselves alone together in the car.

When the moment arrived, and I pulled onto the freeway and began the drive, we remained silent for maybe a quarter of an hour. Not a word passed between us. Then Gretchen said, "What?"

I looked at her for a moment, then looked back at the road.

"What is it?" she said after a few moments went by without my responding. "Something's obviously bothering you, and I've been waiting patiently for you to tell me what it is."

I think I shook my head a little, but I still didn't say anything.

"Ben, will you please say something?"

I felt that static inside my head, that gathering electric noise—it's probably just blood flow resulting from an elevated pulse—that for me signals the onset of rage. I tried to keep my voice steady when I finally choked out, "Just don't treat me like a complete idiot, okay?" I actually gasped for a breath and then continued, "I mean, I know I've been awfully stupid for quite a long time, and I'm sure that's encouraged you to feel you can take some risks, but please…" Another deep painful breath. "Don't act as if that's carte blanche to treat me like a *complete* idiot." I wasn't yelling, but my voice wasn't even slightly under my control.

A longish silence ensued. I suppose Gretchen must have been considering her options. Finally she exhaled slowly, her body slumped a little, and she said, "What do you want me to say?"

"You might start with the truth. If that isn't too big a stretch."

There was another long silence. So I helped her out. "Why don't you start with when it began?"

"Yes. Okay." She actually sounded grateful for the assist. "Remember the night we went to the movie?"

"At the White House? Of course." I was seething. Even when you think you know something like this, you hold out a little hope to yourself, however unconsciously. Having it confirmed changes everything.

"He called the next evening. You walked in while I was talking to him, I told you it was my mom. Remember? Well, it started the day after."

"But you knew it was going to? I mean, that's what the phone call was about?"

"More or less. It wasn't so direct as that, but his intentions weren't what you'd call ambiguous."

"You want to tell me what that means?"

"Not really."

"Do it anyway."

"He…he talked about my body. About the effect it had on him."

I felt my heart pounding in my chest. But I still struggled to keep my voice steady. "In delicate poetic terms?"

"No." She ventured a half smile, hoping I had intended my question at least semihumorously.

I hadn't. "In…would you say, in crude, vulgar terms?"

"You might."

"But you weren't offended?"

"No."

"Would you have been offended if it had been someone else saying those things?"

She hesitated. To her credit, she seemed to give the question serious consideration. Then she said, "I don't know." And then she said, "I suppose I might have been. Probably."

"Do you find that fact interesting in any way?"

"I don't know. I haven't had time to think about it yet."

"You'll get back to me on it?"

"If you like."

"Just trying to get the lay of the land here. So anyway, after he talked about your body in crude vulgar terms, you said—?"

She sighed. "Is there really any purpose being served by all this, Ben? We had a very flirty conversation. I think you get the drift."

"And you said—?"

She sighed again. "I told him I was flattered."

"Is that all you told him?"

"No."

"You told him other things?"

"Yes."

"In a similar vein?"

"I was flirtatious back."

I let that hang there for a second, but I didn't have the heart—or is it the courage?—to pursue that line of questioning. So instead I asked, "Did *my* name come up?"

"In passing."

Another area I didn't have the guts to explore. "And then he invited you to drop by?"

"Well…eventually, yes."

"And you accepted?"

"Not that night, no. I said I couldn't. So I went in the next day. He cleared some time for me." A small smile. "I hope the Joint Chiefs didn't mind."

"But that night, he expected you to drop everything—which included *me,* of course—and come over right then and there?"

"He isn't a patient man, Ben. You probably know that about him. He's used to getting his way."

I suddenly didn't trust myself to drive. I pulled over onto the highway shoulder, stopped the car, and turned to face her. And couldn't control myself anymore. I heard myself screaming, *"How could you do this? What the fuck were you thinking of?"*

She quailed under the barrage, and suddenly she too lost her cool, which she'd managed to maintain rather impressively (and rather chillingly) until this moment. But now the color suddenly drained from her cheeks, and she started to sob, burying her face in her hands. "Oh, Ben, I'm so sorry. I'm so very, very sorry."

AT THE TIME, WHILE DRIVING THE REST OF THE WAY HOME IN silence and brooding fiercely, I was assailed by the most miserable thoughts you can imagine. Pornographic mental images of Gretchen and the president. Notions of profound personal betrayal. Feelings of impotence and inadequacy: How could I ever compete with someone who occupied such a position, regardless of who and what he was as a man? And feelings of the most abject clueless stupidity when I rehearsed Sheffield's kindly solicitude toward me and Gretchen's empty reassurances. How could I have been so gullible, so credulous? They must even have discussed the deception between themselves: Will the fool stay duped? No matter how nicely they phrased it, that would have been the nature of their discussion. Gretchen and the president of the United States, conspiring together about my cuckolding.

It was broad daylight, a very hot, very bright summer day, but to me it felt like Walpurgisnacht, replete with horrid visions and black despair. I assumed at the time, even as I was living through it, that those few hours, when I finally reviewed my life from the vantage point of my deathbed, would qualify as the worst I'd ever experienced, the absolute nadir, ground zero.

But it wasn't, ultimately, even the worst part of the day.

Once we got back home, I poured myself a beer and went into the living room, where Gretchen was seated on the sofa, staring out the window at nothing. The air-conditioning hadn't kicked in yet; the condo was stifling. I still felt sweaty and rank from the drive, my shirt was sticking to my back; it wasn't a state conducive to the confidence you want when initiating the sort of conversation we were about to have. But events weren't going to wait for me to feel fresh as a daisy. Events aren't so considerate.

"So," I announced as I entered the room, beer in hand, "let's consider our situation, shall we?" Miraculously, my voice was no longer out of control. I had invited my reliable old friend irony to share my corner, and he was proving a steadying influence.

She regarded me mistrustfully. She knew even better than I that nothing pleasant was in the offing.

"Okay," I said, "I suppose the first burning question facing us is, should we just end the relationship right now? Shrug our shoulders and say, Well, it was a shorter run than we expected, but hey, it was fun while it lasted. Good-bye and amen."

"No," she said quietly. "Or at least, that isn't what *I* want."

"And that's because—?"

"That's because I love you."

"Ah, I see. You love me. Thank you for clarifying that." Considering the situation, I think I showed admirable restraint as far as sarcasm was concerned. "And the president?"

"Well, no, he likes you well enough, Ben, but I don't think he loves you."

I can't say this quite broke the tension, but she did get a grudging smile out of me.

On the other hand, her being cute and funny made the whole thing hurt worse, of course. "Gretch—"

"I don't want us to break up, okay?" she said.

"Well, that's kind of interesting, I suppose."

"I think we have a future."

"Ah ha."

"Do *you* want to break up?"

"I haven't had as much time as you to consider the question. But I don't think so. No. I don't know. Not when I can get my mind off this. Which may be *never.*"

"I *don't* love him, Ben. If that helps any. I like him okay, he's been very nice to me, and, you know, he has his own air force and everything…but…but even the way I like him isn't…you know, it isn't *romantic*. I mean, that's not what this is about."

"Just a hot sex thing, was it?"

She looked up at me sharply, probably to gauge the sarcasm level. And then answered as if I had posed a simple uncathected factual question: "I wouldn't even say that. It's not really about the sex. At least not for me."

"But is it—"

She didn't give me a chance to finish the question. "It's more… Jesus, Ben, think about it. He's the *president of the United States!* It's just an amazing phenomenon, more than anything else. An amazing thing to have happen."

"Something you can tell your grandchildren."

"That's one way to think of it." Another half smile. "Maybe after they're fully grown." Not getting an answering smile, she frowned slightly and went on, "And it's, it's *flattering*. You know, given his position and all, he can have almost anyone he wants. This may be the worst sort of vanity, but the fact he picked *me* makes me feel special."

"Yeah. You know, it's too bad Golda Meir is dead. Without her around, I don't have much chance for revenge, do I?"

Gretchen shook her head. The pretending-to-be-amused part of the conversation was clearly over. "I was kind of hoping you wouldn't see it in those terms. In terms of revenge. Even in terms of…you know, of cheating. That you'd understand what a unique, bizarre situation this is. I was kind of hoping you'd agree that ordinary rules don't apply."

"You were kind of hoping for a lot, weren't you?"

"I suppose I was." She looked thoughtful. "I don't know whether you can understand this, but…See, it's just, so much of life involves balancing your obligations to other people against your obligations to yourself. It's a constant struggle. And I don't think I'm a terribly selfish person that way, I *don't* automatically resolve most of those questions in my own favor. But this…it just seemed to occupy a special sort of niche. It seemed too extraordinary an opportunity to let go by."

"And the lying to me? You've always seemed like such an honest person, I honestly didn't know you were even *capable* of lying that way. Were you comfortable with all of that?"

"No, I hated it. *Hated* it. But…I mean, you can't separate the lying from the affair. You can't treat them as two separate offenses. The one pretty much implies the other, you know? Once the first happened, the second was unavoidable."

I didn't expect such a cogent defense. Sophistry or not, it had enough internal logic that it would have taken energy to argue. More energy than I had at my disposal. So I moved on to something more immediately relevant. "All right, so what are you proposing, Gretchen? That I just make my peace with it? That I let bygones be bygones, and we proceed as if it never happened? I don't know if I can do that."

I saw a flicker of something in her eye, and I knew it didn't augur well. But she remained silent. "Am I even warm?" I asked.

"Ben—"

The way she said my name was ominous, and the way she didn't say anything else was *really* ominous. "Look," I said, filling the breach a little desperately, "if we're *not* breaking up, but I'm not supposed to let bygones be bygones and pretend it never happened, then…I mean, what other choices *are* there? Which part of that doesn't work for you?"

She took a moment to steel herself before she said, "The bygones part."

"I'm afraid I'm still not following."

She got up and left the room. I hesitated—maybe she just had to go to the bathroom—then went in search of her. And found her in the bedroom, where she had already begun undressing. Through the bathroom door I could hear the shower running. I have to say, this was a very disconcerting sort of conversation to have while the other person was taking off her clothes.

"Gretchen? Please. What are you telling me, exactly? Are you saying that you don't intend to stop?"

Her jeans were off, and now her T-shirt was coming off, and God help me, all I could think of was, President Sheffield has seen this too. Did she make a bigger production of it when she undressed for him? Did he still express his admiration in crude vulgar terms? Did she like hearing it? Did she say similar things to him? And what had he done with her? And even worse, what had she done with him? Which of the intimacies I thought were ours alone were also theirs? It was all suddenly too much. A wave of nausea washed over me, my head was reeling, I tasted bile. I sat—no, I *collapsed* on the bed, almost doubled over, and covered my eyes with my hand. I felt as if I had absorbed several brutal blows straight to my solar plexus. It must have looked pretty dramatic, this sudden collapse, because she sounded alarmed rather than solicitous when she said, "Ben? Are you okay?"

"Never better," I gasped. And then scurried into the bathroom to vomit.

THERE WAS ANOTHER OUTRAGE THAT INTERFERED WITH MY pure, primary sense of outrage. It didn't make things better—far from it—but it made them more complicated.

I understood.

I understood what Gretchen had been trying to tell me. How could I not? We were both breathing the atmosphere of the same feudal court. There had, for example, been quite a few nights when we'd made plans to see friends, and then the White House had called with a last-minute invitation. We had very few qualms about canceling our friends in order to accept the invitation from the president and First Lady. Very few qualms and virtually no debate about whether it was wrong to do so. The invitation was a seigneurial summons, not a request. But even putting it that way misstates the case, because it portrays us as passive, reluctant pawns being moved around without volition, whereas the truth was nothing like that: we didn't feel compelled to go to the White House, we were thrilled at the prospect. And we stiffed our friends without compunction.

And they always understood, they always gave us their blessing (not that we required it). They were, after all, breathing the same atmosphere we were. Regardless of whether they worked in government or not. One way or another, however indirectly, they too conceded the president's preeminence, they acquiesced just as Gretchen had.

And why, when all was said and done, had I written that damned Africa speech in the first place, the speech that had initiated the complicated chain of events that had brought us to this awful pass? *Not* out of simple careerism, despite what I told myself: I accused myself of careerism in order to camouflage an even more unattractive truth. I knew that writing the speech was going to have, at best, only a marginal impact on my job situation. There was no conceivable promotion in my immediate future in any case, and my continuing employment wasn't in any jeopardy, so what help could I really do myself? No, it wasn't careerism, it was something no worthier than careerism and a lot less dignified. I did it for the simple pathetic reason that I wanted the president's approval. It's a grotesque thing to admit, perhaps, but there it is. And I wanted his approval not because the opinion of Charles Sheffield, esq. meant that much to me, but because the approval of the president of the United States was so damned seductive. If Sheffield had lost the election and had then asked me, as a personal favor, to write him a speech he could deliver from the Senate floor, I doubt I would have bothered. And if one of his opponents in the primaries—one of those fellows whom Gretchen and I had derided for habitually bit-

ing the wienie during the entire primary season—had somehow
bested Sheffield and made it to the White House instead, I would
have been just as eager for *his* approval.

So here was Gretchen, the unexpected object of the president's
lust. I honestly still believe that had any other man approached her,
crudely, suavely, forcefully, seductively, none of that would have
mattered; she would have rejected him out of hand. And had Mr.
Charles Sheffield, or even Senator Charles Sheffield, propositioned
her, she would have found his attentions importunate and unwelcome and intrusive, would have dismissed him as a Humbert Humbert–style letch, would have had some choice observations about his
style and character and sexual inappropriateness. Along with, I'd
very much like to think, his phosphorescent pate.

But that wasn't how the situation presented itself to her. Nevertheless, understanding how she felt in an abstract sort of way doesn't
make the situation any easier to accept. Something in me absolutely
recoils at the notion that some man, any man, by virtue of his position, has the right to just move in and casually wreck my life because
it happens to be his whim. And aside from everything else, it's
awfully hard for me to forgive Gretchen for confirming that pre-
sumption of his, for validating his sense of entitlement. Especially
at my expense.

Of course, someone is going to be willing to do it. Lots of someones. But why would anyone with a modicum of self-respect want
to be one of those someones? Why would she choose to let herself
be turned into a mirror reflecting Sheffield's vanity back at him?

My understanding had limits.

And yet, and yet... I wasn't so principled, I wasn't so firm, I
wasn't anything I'm proud of, when we finally confronted the issue
head on. It's a good thing I didn't think about my British grandmother till later, or I would have been vomiting all night. In tears,
Gretchen helped clean me up, urged me into bed, and suggested we
continue the discussion in the morning. But it was still midafter-

noon, and the wisdom of her suggestion was lost on me. It was a wisdom divorced from psychological reality. After making this immense awful discovery, I wasn't capable of postponing further discussion for almost eight more hours of waking consciousness, which was the most optimistic projection, since it didn't contemplate the insomnia that was certain to keep me up for eight further hours while the rest of the world slept.

Even there in that afternoon sunlight, with the phone occasionally ringing and the radio on and all sorts of other distractions, I kept picturing Gretchen with the president, kept imagining their Oval Office antics, kept hearing swatches of obscene dialogue between them. Kept hearing her amorous murmur, a murmur I knew so well, directed his way. I could only dread the visions that darkness and silence and lying supine were sure to bring.

There was no way I could face sixteen tortured hours of limbo. So once cleaned up and changed, and lying in bed with my head propped up by three pillows—Gretchen had taken care of me with maternal solicitude, and I had responded with a grateful, infantile docility—I resumed the conversation as if it had never been interrupted. "Now listen, I must have misunderstood you before. You weren't actually telling me you plan to keep on seeing him, right? It's just not possible you would suggest something like that. Even if you wanted to, you wouldn't have the chutzpah."

"We're both upset now, Ben. We really should hold off on this."

"Like I'll be able to examine this tranquilly in the foreseeable future? Trust me, tomorrow I'll be at least as upset as I am now. And even less well rested."

"Okay. I can see that."

"Our first breakthrough. A Eureka moment."

She sighed. "Listen, I hate the way this makes you feel. I really do. I love you, and I know how much I'm hurting you. It's possible that someday I'll look back at all this and positively *writhe* with remorse and embarrassment. It's possible. But this...this *thing* is kind of extraordinary. It's not on a continuum with anything else. And I know down deep you understand that. It's like...it's like, if I was an astronaut, and I was picked to go on the first manned flight to some distant planet. I mean, I'd be gone for years, and I'm sure it would do terrible damage to our relationship, but still, you'd understand why I might decide to go ahead with the mission anyway."

"You want me to tell you all the different ways that analogy fails?"

"No, Ben, I really don't. I'd rather you focused on the way it applies."

The way it applied, alas, provided no comfort. Sometimes people want something for themselves with such intensity, such passion, that nothing else matters, no one else matters. I'm sure Chuck Sheffield, for example, ranked winning the presidency above any human connection he had, including his connection to his wife and children. He might not have admitted it, to them or himself, but it was obviously the case (just as it was obviously the case with most of the men he had defeated). And Claire Sheffield had had to accommodate herself to that fact, had had to factor it into her notions of how her marriage functioned. Perhaps she had understood it from the first, though it's never pleasant to fully grasp your secondary or tertiary importance to the person you love. It isn't pleasant when your centrality has been displaced by, say, a job, or a hobby, or an addiction; but when you find you're taking a backseat to another lover—to someone who occupies the same general category you do—when you're asked to understand why it's obvious your rival's appeal supersedes whatever consideration and loyalty and compassion you might reasonably expect, it's immeasurably worse. Worse than words can convey.

And that was what Gretchen was asking me to understand. It was the part I *did* understand.

"You know he's just using you, don't you?" God, it was like being back in high school, with Sheffield the captain of the football team.

"Of course. That's what he does. That's what presidents do. They use people. I accept that. But…well, it isn't quite so simple. I also think I'm getting to know him better than other people. Men relax their guard a little in some situations. So I'm in kind of a privileged position."

I'm sure she didn't intend this to be hurtful, but it was like a slap in the face nevertheless. "Just because I'm a liberal Democrat, I guess you don't consider me capable of domestic abuse," I finally said.

She didn't look even slightly alarmed, which was disappointing. Maybe even insulting. "That isn't the reason, but I know you're not."

"And what if I decide I want to see someone else, too?"

"Do you?"

"Let's say the answer is yes, for the sake of argument." I hadn't even considered the possibility until that very second, but I sure as hell wasn't going to tell her that.

"I guess I'm in no position to object."

I lay there glaring at her. I hated her right then, although, at the same time, I had never loved her more desperately. Her capacity to hurt me—which I'd never had to confront so directly before and so had never really gauged—was a direct measure of my feelings for her and was now revealed as vast. The whole thing was demeaning beyond description. My anger and my need were equally overwhelming and equally undignified. I felt like a buffoon.

"What do you tell yourself to make this acceptable?" I demanded.

"I'm not claiming it *is* acceptable. I'm just hoping you can accept it. That isn't the same thing."

"And if I can't?" Damn she was facile. Suddenly I was the one on the defensive. Not that she seemed cool and contained; she was fighting tears. But that didn't stop her from maneuvering for the upper hand. I waited for her answer in fear and trembling, but also with a strangely detached curiosity. I had no idea how she'd answer. After a long pause, she said:

"I don't know."

My heart sank. The situation just kept getting worse and worse. "You'd pick him over me?" I sounded incredulous, I suppose, but at the same time I was reflecting that it probably wasn't an occasion for incredulity. Most women would have made the same decision without a second thought. Who's a more interesting choice for a sexual partner, this guy named Ben Krause or the president of the United States? Uh...gee, give me a few seconds to think it over. More humiliation. And the heart of the matter: Once you're put in the position of having to defend your worthiness in terms of status, something's been lost that can never be salvaged. Even if—as was obviously not the case here—you're ultimately able to establish a superior claim. Just having to play that game at all certifies you as a loser. "I can't believe you'd pick him over me," I said, but of course it wasn't true.

"No," she answered, "that isn't how it would work. I might pick the *situation* over you. I might. I don't know what I'd do. I obviously hope it won't come to that."

I lay back on the pillows and stared at the ceiling. And contemplated what breaking up would mean. It's funny how your mind works in this kind of situation: the immense loss of this person I loved was part of what I was thinking about, of course, but also the misery of having to unload the condo, divide the furnishings, and find another place to live, of starting to date again, of reorganizing my life so soon after this recent big move to Washington, of no longer being part of a popular couple, of having to find a way to explain the breakup. I suddenly felt weary beyond belief.

"How long do you think this insanity with the president is going to last?" I finally heard myself asking, to a renewed wave of nausea.

"Not forever. How could it? And you know, the fact is I'll be relieved when it's over."

★

FROM *THE HUMAN ZOO,* BY DESMOND MORRIS:

> "... *The existence of powerful, dominant individuals, lording it over the rest of the group, is a widespread phenomenon amongst higher primates. The weaker members of the group accept their subordinate roles....*
>
> "... *Status sex infiltrates and pervades our lives in many hidden and unrecognized ways.... [It] is concerned with dominance, not with reproduction, and to understand how this link is forged we must consider the differing roles of the sexual female and the sexual male....*
>
> "... *We do know that certain male South American monkeys use penis erection as a direct threat to a subordinate. In the case of the little squirrel monkey, it has become the most important dominance signal in the animal's repertoire.... When in a threatening mood, a superior male of this species approaches close to an inferior and obtrusively erects his penis in the inferior's face...."*

Do tell.

DESPITE ALL THE STURM UND DRANG OF THAT JULY FOURTH weekend, what ensued was actually a period of quiescence. Or at least latency. Summer in Washington is so awful, most people who can afford to go somewhere else do so. The president and First Lady were no exception. They spent several weeks at the "Summer White House" in Albuquerque and several more weeks with their children at a rented house on Cape Cod. They were in Washington for less than a week in between those two trips. If Sheffield and Gretchen saw each other during that brief interval, I never found out about it.

They spoke by phone occasionally. That I did find out. He never called her at home—she must have warned him about that, in what manner I'd be awfully eager to discover—but when I asked, she admitted he called her office for a chat every couple of days or so. I guess he wanted to be sure she would remain on the reservation during his absence.

A week or so later I asked if she had "heard from her friend lately," and she bristled. "Do you expect me to keep you informed about every contact, Ben?"

"I don't know *what* I expect. My expectations have already been so confounded, I'm just kind of thrashing about in the dark." There. Having neatly regained the initiative, I went on to say, "So we don't have to regard this question as any kind of precedent. Just tell me if you've heard from him."

And that's when she told me he phoned her at work.

"Still praising your body, is he?"

"I think this segment of the conversation is officially over. In fact, I think we probably should establish a few ground rules."

Her manner was maddeningly elusive. She was so matter-of-fact about these issues, neither angry nor apologetic. As if she had made her peace with all the complications, and I had damned well better do the same. And yet, if forced to describe what was going on with her, I don't believe she was being intolerant, let alone punitive; rather, I think she really believed she was acting out of concern for me. I think she was worried that if I started obsessing about the minutiae of her affair with the president, started wondering about the when and the what and the how, I'd end up torturing myself into near insanity.

Her mistake was believing I had some choice in the matter.

Still, during that summer *Sitzkrieg,* that phony war, I managed to cope fairly well. After all, President Sheffield wasn't around, the affair was an abstraction, I had her to myself. If he phoned occasionally—more than occasionally—it was while she was at work, out of my hearing and seeing, and didn't directly impinge on our relations. She wasn't pining for him in any obvious way, and all the things that had been worrying me in the period immediately preceding our Independence Day confrontation, her odd absences and her inexplicable remoteness, actually disappeared. When she was with me, she seemed to be entirely with me.

Which isn't to say I was enjoying the situation or kidding myself that I could handle whatever fate had in store for me. I was perfectly aware that this was summer vacation and summer would end and the shit would be hitting the fan soon enough. But she was caring and affectionate, I didn't doubt that she wanted us to stay together, and I occasionally let myself believe that this whole ugly business was a stage she would pass through relatively quickly. Those occasions being the odd few minutes during the day when I didn't feel like screaming and yelling and sobbing.

And wondering. It still feels like a shameful fact, but I persist in believing my reaction wasn't unique in this respect, even after months of reflection. It was simply impossible not to wonder what Gretchen and the president were like together, and to be tortured by the question. It would have been difficult in any case, a subject for endless excruciating speculation, but when I factored in his position, it was even more irresistible. Irresistible the way probing a toothache is irresistible. Everything about his position made everything about their relations unique and mysterious. Everything from the logistics to the blunt physical facts.

"Do you call him Chuck?" I asked her one night after dinner, more or less out of the blue, while we were washing and drying dishes together.

"When I call him anything at all," she answered in a voice that didn't encourage further inquiry. Nor did she look up from the sink. "He invited me to, but I don't find it too comfortable."

"Unlike everything else," I said. Thoughtlessly indulging my bitterness, thereby destroying any chance of getting more information that night.

And there was a Saturday morning, driving home from a little shopping jaunt at Neam's Market, when I asked her, "Tell me something. Does Sheffield talk to you? I mean, really talk. About politics, say, or policy, or his family, or the people he deals with? I mean, does he, like, *confide?*"

"Occasionally. A little. He lets his guard down with me some- times."

"That must be pretty amazing."

She smiled a very private smile, bespeaking some very private sort of satisfaction, and it felt like a knife plunged into my heart. "Yeah, it is," she said. I was dying inside, but I tried not to show it. I didn't want to discourage her. I waited for more, but she didn't offer anything. And I couldn't figure out an acceptable way to phrase my next question, so it remained unasked.

Another night, I was lying in bed beside her in the dark, and I could tell from her breathing that she was still awake (I was sleep- ing so badly during those weeks that it felt as if I were *always* awake). "Is it different with him?" I let myself ask. Again, as always when I asked about this business, I asked it out of the blue. There was no way to build up to this sort of thing. Nevertheless, regard- less of the absence of conversational preparation, the pronoun's antecedent was unnecessary. She was never in doubt about whom I was referring to.

There was a long silence. Perhaps she was debating whether or not to feign sleep. Then, with a patience she managed to make man- ifest, she said, "It's different with everyone, Ben."

"Yeah, granted. But I mean…" How to find words that conveyed what I meant? "Is it distinctively…*presidential?*"

"Jesus, Ben. If the shoe was on the other foot—"

"How could it be?" I interrupted.

But she plunged on. "—I wouldn't want to know *anything*. I sure as hell wouldn't ask, and if for some crazy reason of your own you started to volunteer some tidbit or other, I'd run from the room with my hands over my ears."

"Maybe," I said. "It's the sort of thing you can't know until it happens."

"Believe me, I know."

"And therefore we can conclude it's the correct response?"

"I didn't say that. But it's certainly simpler all around."

"Oh yes. And not loving you would simplify things even further."

She sighed deeply. "You want me to apologize again? I really am sorry about this. Profoundly sorry. In many ways, I wish it had never happened. But in other ways…" She stopped and then started again. "Listen. You can assume I'm apologizing to you daily. Hourly. All the time. And meaning it. This business is really shitty, I'm not pretending otherwise. And I appreciate how you're struggling to put up with it. Don't think I don't recognize that. But we just can't have this conversation. I don't blame you for wanting to, whether or not I understand what's behind it, but it isn't a place I intend to go. Period."

The really maddening thing was, having said all this, she was asleep in less than a minute. Some people can do that.

Although my workload was light during the summer months—almost nonexistent—I still reported to work every day, and Gretchen and I still drove together to the White House most mornings. We had been commuting together from the start, except when something unusual on either of our schedules (which until recently almost invariably meant mine) required one of us to arrive early or leave late. But this part of the day, our joint arrival at the portals of political Valhalla, an occasion I once treasured, I had now come to dread. Just passing through the northwest gate was a horror. This was *his* house, *his* realm, *his* baronial estate. It was where the affair took place. It symbolized everything against which I was powerless to compete.

Even in the summer, during his absence, he haunted every corner of the complex. Figuratively, but also literally: large full-color photographs of him were hanging on walls all over the West Wing and in many of the offices on the first floor of the OEOB. The president regal, receiving visiting dignitaries; the president charismatic, delivering a speech before a huge cheering throng; the president exuberant, shaking thousands of outstretched hands at an airport rope line; the president contemplative and affectionate, in a quiet chiaroscuro moment with his wife; the president vigorous and youthful, debarking from Air Force One; the president magisterial, reviewing the troops. There it all was: a ubiquitous pictorial representation of exactly what I was up against.

What could I do all day? Mostly doodle on a legal pad, play solitaire on my computer, and brood. I also started writing this account of what I was going through, on the simple theory that since I wasn't able to stop thinking about it anyway, I might as well embrace the obsession wholeheartedly. (The idea of doing so on government time also exerted a certain appeal.) Occasionally Randy would call me into his office for a desultory discussion of a speech that was scheduled for delivery in the early fall (he was at loose ends too, of course) or to order up a statement about some pressing current event, a few apt words that had to be released during that news cycle over the president's name. But in general this was downtime; with the president on vacation, our operation had ground to a virtual halt. Which left plenty of time for doodling and brooding and obsession embracing. I was making myself crazy. And I wasn't a pleasant colleague. Those times I joined co-workers for lunch in the cafeteria in the OEOB basement or in the White House mess, I was taciturn, distracted, and downright grumpy. Especially when the subject turned, as it inevitably did, to presidential doings. The gossip and political speculation and character analysis everybody offered were nearly intolerable to me.

There was something else I was doing during work hours in those weeks, although it may be a violation of federal law even to admit it: I was indulging in assassination fantasies. Not that I was seriously considering the option, mind you; no Hinckley I. Nor would actually doing it have given me any real satisfaction. My primary problem wasn't with Sheffield, after all—much as I'd come to detest the sight of his smug, self-satisfied mug and the sound of his resonant voice—my problem was with Gretchen's having accepted his advances. Had his eye alighted on another woman, I wouldn't have had any particular qualms about it. My objections weren't moral, not in any categorical-imperative sort of way. So wiping him off the face of the earth wouldn't do anything for me, wouldn't alter the choice she had already made. It might even make things worse, providing her with a reason to romanticize him, mourn for him, cherish his memory. So these were fantasies for the sake of fantasy, nothing more. Nevertheless, I got some small measure of amusement out of my imaginings. It was just a way to pass the time, which was weighing heavily upon me.

Additionally, along with the doodling and brooding and memoir writing and spinning out homicidal scenarios for my own grim entertainment, I was, without being fully aware of it, doing something else. I was counting the days till Sheffield's return to Washington. I knew life would take a definite downward turn as soon as that happened, and I was trying to prepare myself for it.

I CHOSE NOT TO JOIN EVERYBODY ON THE SOUTH LAWN TO welcome the president and First Lady back to the White House from their summer vacation. A memo was circulated among the staff, informing us of the arrival time and obliquely encouraging us to go down there to greet him, in order to create the proper welcoming atmosphere. But it wasn't required, and I wasn't especially worried that, among the press of bodies, my absence would be noted. I sort of hoped it would be, really, but I knew the likelihood was remote.

I did get to see the event on the network news that night, though. Doing so plunged me into a state of deep despondency, but I can't claim total innocence in the matter, I can't say I was blindsided; there was obviously a reasonable chance I'd catch a glimpse of Gretchen in the news footage.

And sure enough. First, Marine One hovered and landed, and a few moments later Sheffield and the little woman emerged and descended the stairs, waving gaily. After saluting his military escort, he ambled over to the staff assembled behind a rope line. The first person he encountered was Gretchen. This was too striking to have been coincidence; one of the people charged with running the Office of the President must have arranged it deliberately. Which meant there was at least one other person beside myself who knew their secret. The thought made me sick to my stomach, but I couldn't tear my eyes away. The president gave Gretchen a chaste little kiss on the cheek—not perceptibly different from the sort of kiss he planted on most female cheeks, I have to say—and then whispered something in her ear. She laughed and gave him a humorously disapproving look. Then he laughed himself and moved on to the next person in the line.

It was all very quick and quite innocuous. Except it wasn't.

I was watching the news with Gretchen. I stole a look her way, but she didn't look back at me, she sat perfectly still, her expression didn't change. Her body was tensed, though; she was waiting for me to say something. I didn't. It took an effort—any number of harsh comments were clamoring for expression—but I resisted.

I got up and went into the kitchen, where water was already on the boil for pasta. I turned it off. I had no appetite for pasta or anything else. Then I slammed out of the apartment. It was still light out, although dusk was gathering. I set off along P Street, heading west. I had no destination, no plan. None of the diversions and escapes traditional to scorned lovers appealed to me. I didn't want to pull a Sinatra and go to a bar to get drunk, I didn't want to see a movie, I didn't want to talk to a living soul. I didn't even care to spend time in my own company, but there was nothing to be done about that one.

So I simply walked. I wasn't thinking coherently, just wallowing in rage and self-pity. So I was surprised to discover that, just before

I reached Wisconsin Avenue, I had come to some sort of conclusion. It wasn't anything that brought me peace of mind, but it allowed me to turn around and return home.

The affair was a fact. Its existence was established. And I had already resolved to try to live with it, at least on an experimental basis. So I now realized that I simply couldn't afford the psychic energy required to feel outrage at every manifestation, every piece of evidence, every occurrence that confirmed what I already knew. If I accepted the fact of the affair, I also had to accept the fact that I would frequently be confronted with reminders of it. I didn't necessarily have to accept this with equanimity, but I had to recognize it as a natural concomitant of the first, fundamental accommodation. Gretchen was sleeping with the most visible man in America. I'd better get used to the idea, and I'd better anticipate that my nose would often be rubbed in it. I'd better get used to the sight of him. There just wasn't going to be any place to hide.

When I got home, Gretchen was on the phone. She started guiltily when I walked in. They must have devised some way for her to signal him when I was out. But this was a chance for me to put my new resolve into action. I gave her a quick casual wave and proceeded to the bedroom. Where I beat the hell out of my pillow for a minute or so, until the waves of rage began to recede, leaving a dull throbbing despair in their wake.

GRETCHEN EXACTED A PROMISE FROM ME. YOU MIGHT THINK she wasn't in any position to bargain, and God knows in most ways she was deferential to me during those days, she seemed to understand she had no chits to call in, no reservoir of goodwill to draw upon. But she obviously regarded this issue as being of such paramount importance that she was prepared to violate the strictures of good taste and insist on my acquiescence.

"Listen, Ben, whatever happens, you mustn't let him know you know." This time it was her turn to use the pronoun without supplying the antecedent.

Of all the issues that had been bedeviling me, this was one to which I hadn't given any thought. A simple oversight. Once she brought it up, I was amazed that I had, in my comprehensive brooding, neglected it.

"Why not?" I asked. I wasn't being contrary. As I say, I hadn't considered the question, so I had no notion of my own preferences in the matter. Rather, I was honestly curious. She made it sound so urgent.

"Because...because...Jesus, things are so complicated and awful already. If he has to cope with your feelings, too...and wonder what you know about him...and worry about how you feel about him... It's just unthinkable."

"In other words, you want to protect him."

"Well, in a way."

"And what about *me?* What about protecting *me?* Shouldn't *that* have been on your damned agenda?"

She nodded. She wasn't about to argue. "I wanted to. I tried to. But you were too clever for me. You figured it out on your own."

"I don't mean by *deceiving* me, for God's sake. I mean by taking care of me."

"We've been around and around on this, Ben. You deserved to be taken care of. But I couldn't do it. I've apologized, I've thrown myself on your mercy, I've begged you to try to understand how it feels from my point of view. I can't do anything more. I certainly don't intend to defend myself."

"But you still want me to cooperate in protecting him?"

"I think it's a way of protecting all of us, really. Not just him. You and me too. Our jobs. Our position. His trust in us. This very delicate balance we're trying to maintain. You've got to promise me."

The only reason I gave her the promise she wanted was, I couldn't in all honesty see myself confronting him. How do you confront the president of the United States? You can't slug him, you can't ask him to step outside, you can't even yell at him and tell him you don't want to have anything to do with him ever again. And since I didn't have any nuclear weapons handy, I was in no position to go toe to toe with him. So giving her my promise was easy, even if I made a show of doing it grudgingly. She was absurdly grateful, even though it wasn't really an occasion for gratitude. It didn't derive, after all, from any largeness of spirit on my part; it was just further confirmation of my powerlessness. It didn't change a damned thing, it didn't forestall a face slap with a glove that otherwise would have taken place. If Gretchen thought I had some sort of intention in that regard, I can only say her understanding of how testosterone works and her grasp of social hierarchical behavior among the higher primates were both surprisingly deficient.

"Maybe I should just quit," I said. "Resign and be done with it. This situation would be bad enough under any circumstances, but with me working for the man…"

"You can't do that," she said, sounding alarmed.

"Why not? Are you afraid he'll figure out the reason?"

"No, no. You may find this hard to believe—I wouldn't blame you if you do—but my concern isn't about him this time. It's about you. This is a position you've been preparing yourself for over your whole life. It's a great thing. God, Ben, you're the envy of every thirtysomething in Washington. You can't just give it up. I'd never forgive myself if you did."

"Oh, I'm sure you'd manage. Forgiving yourself is something you're good at."

She let that one go. "Besides, your commitment to the job isn't personal. It isn't about loyalty to Chuck. To President Sheffield, I mean. No matter what your personal feelings are, you approve of the things he's doing. And you're part of it all. This may be the greatest thing that'll ever happen to you."

"Jesus, I hope not."

"You've got to try to stick it out. You're making a huge contribution. You know, he talks about you sometimes. To me, I mean. He really likes you. He says you're one of the smartest people on his staff. And he thinks you're the best presidential speechwriter since Ted Sorenson."

"He does?" May heaven forgive me, I felt a flush of pleasure when she told me this. My sense of the sheer creepy inappropriateness of his praising me to her took a distant second place to my delight in his good opinion. I knew it would be a long time before I could live comfortably with this datum. But I also now knew that I wasn't going to offer my resignation.

I guess Gretchen wasn't the only one who needed to feel special.

But even if I could in time come to accept my corrupt emotions—come to accept *all* the uncomfortable facts with which I was contending—acceptance would be no help when one of the moments I'd been dreading all summer finally arrived: my first encounter with Sheffield since learning about him and Gretchen. And within a week of his return to Washington, it happened. God knows it was an event I'd rehearsed in my mind about a million times, but I'd never been able to find a way to make it seem all right, even in fantasy. My musings always seemed to spin off into violence or crazy misbehavior. So despite all my attempts at internal preparation, it was with deep pervasive misery that I accompanied Randy to the Oval Office for a meeting with the president about his upcoming speech to the AFL-CIO.

He looked tanned and fit, relaxed and genial, as Randy and I entered the room. He gave Randy a quick hello and a quick handshake, then turned his baby blues on me. "Ben, my boy!" he said.

Randy winced. So did I. We winced for different reasons, but neither of us was happy.

Sheffield put his arm around my shoulder. "Come on in and sit down." Then, in obedience to good manners, he added, "Both of you. It's great to see you both. Hope your summers have been as relaxing as mine."

Jesus, I hated this. The worst part was, even while seething inwardly, I found myself smiling at him, lowering my head slightly, not meeting his eyes, docilely permitting myself to be steered toward one of the two matching sofas. My reactions were out of my control somehow.

Jane Goodall, in her book *In the Shadow of Man*, describes a chimpanzee named William: "If another adult male showed signs of aggression toward him, William was quick to approach with gestures of appeasement and submission, reaching out to lay his hand on the other, crouching with soft panting grunts in front of the higher-ranking individuals. During such an encounter, he would often pull back the corners of his lips and expose his teeth in a nervous grin."

The most I can say for myself is that I somehow managed to omit the panting grunts. That one trivial bit of primate behavior to the side, I felt quite a kinship with William as I took my seat. During *his* encounters with dominant males, I wonder if his heart raced as fast as mine was doing now.

Still, the worst part of this first meeting was its beginning. It was bad enough so that, at one point, just as we were getting started, Sheffield gave me a concerned glance and said, "Are you okay, Ben? You look a little peaked." Pronouncing the last word in two syllables.

"I'm fine, Mr. President," I lied.

But as we got down to work, I became a bit calmer. My heart never stopped racing, and I never felt I was breathing entirely normally, but fortunately I managed to stop repeating to myself, This bastard is fucking my girlfriend. The nuts and bolts of a dreary speech began to assume some measure of precedence over my chaotic emotions. It obviously helped to have something specific to focus on, and for once it helped to have dogged, humorless Randy there to *keep* us all focused. Schmoozing was never his forte. Human intercourse was never his forte.

Why couldn't the president be fucking *his* girlfriend? He probably wouldn't even have noticed. Neither, probably, would she, if she could put up with Randy.

When the meeting was over, and Sheffield was escorting us to the door, he gave my face another close inspection. "Are you sure you're feeling all right? You don't look good. And there's supposed to be some bug going around."

Oh, there was a bug going around, no question about it. "Fit as a fiddle, sir," I said, leaving out the next line of the song, "And ready for love."

"Tell Gretchen she should take good care of you, Ben. I need you functioning at capacity."

I almost literally had to bite my tongue. The familiar rustling static filled my ears, the rage was rising. I closed my eyes for a moment and then concentrated all my anger into a slightly insolent shrug. It was obvious from the look in Sheffield's eye that this impolite gesture registered, although he didn't mention it. But as Randy started out of the room, he did say to me, sotto voce, "Stick around for a moment, will you? I need to tell you something."

My stomach dropped. Was I going to have to deal with a reprimand along with everything else? That might be over my threshold. I stood waiting anxiously while Sheffield bade Randy good-bye, said a few words to Sandra about needing an extra minute or two, and turned back to me. Then he said, "Maybe this'll cheer you up." He was smiling.

Now I was totally flummoxed. "Maybe what will, Mr. President?"

He granted himself a short dramatic pause before speaking. "Something's up. Something big, at least potentially. Huge. The sort of thing that makes you feel all the shit is worthwhile."

He waited. I was supposed to provide some sort of verbal punctuation here, express some sort of eagerness to hear more. But every impulse I possessed urged me to resist being manipulated by him, even when the manipulation was perfectly innocuous. So I just stared at him, saying nothing.

"Aren't you curious?"

"Yes, sir. I'm waiting for you to explain."

This was enough for him. He smiled and went on, "All three major parties in the civil war have contacted us, Ben. Independently. Through third parties."

"You mean the civil war in Africa?" I caught the excitement in his voice and heard something similar in my own.

"Indicating their willingness to try to find a formula to end the killing." He stopped, waiting again for a reaction.

This time I didn't balk. "That's fantastic, sir."

"It may be. It's a start, anyway. We're at the beginning of a very long, very difficult road. Nobody's offering to give up anything yet, God knows. But it's a glimmer of light where there wasn't any light before. And…" He put a hand on my shoulder, brought his face uncomfortably, intrusively close to mine. "Ben, a lot of the credit belongs to you. You should be proud of yourself. You got their attention. I guess the lesson is, sometimes, when you least expect it, someone's listening. Without your speech, none of this would have happened."

"Well…I think it was *your* speech, Mr. President."

He smiled winningly. "Hell, if this works out, there'll be plenty enough credit to go around. And if it should fail…it was *your* speech."

There was no way I could refuse him the smile he was after now, even though I disliked myself for giving in.

"Look," he continued warmly, "the thing is, you didn't have to write it. I was just venting that day, just letting off steam, musing out loud. You really did it on your own initiative. And you could have done it half-assed, I would have been pleased enough you gave it any effort at all. But instead you researched it deeply and thought it through. That's why they were listening, it's why we're where we are today. It wasn't just a set of fatuous bromides, it was serious and well informed, it conveyed our sense of *urgency*. And that's leaving aside its eloquence, which assuredly didn't hurt. And all of that was *your* doing, not mine. I have no trouble admitting it."

Damn it, I was suddenly proud to be associated with him. The thought was sickening, but there was no denying it; everything I had ever admired about him was on display that afternoon. It was the most peculiar thing: I stood there in the Oval Office hating the sight of him, finding the weight of his hand on my shoulder almost unendurable, while at the same time feeling privileged at having the opportunity to work for him. "I—I'm pleased it may have done some good," was all I could stammer out.

"Yes, well, I just wanted you to know." His expression changed, and his voice became earnest. "Sometimes, Ben, we get so caught up in the game that we let ourselves forget that things we do might actually have results, can have an effect on people. And in this case, if we're very lucky and very persistent and we play our cards just right, the effect will be to save thousands of lives. Not a trivial matter, is it? It's the sort of thing that makes me glad I'm president, reminds me that the job is about more than flying on Air Force One and living in this building and seeing myself on the cover of *Time*. And for what it's worth, it's also the sort of thing that makes me very glad I have you on my team."

After I left him, it must have been at least three whole minutes before I thought about him and Gretchen. A personal best.

A COUPLE OF DAYS LATER WE WERE INVITED TO SEE A MOVIE AT the family theater. "Why don't you go alone?" I suggested to Gretchen.

"Don't be silly. I'm not his *date*. We're both invited."

"Are you aware how hard this is for me? Do you have any idea what I'm going through?"

She took my hand. "I am. I do. It isn't easy for me either. Everything about this setup is difficult. Not that I'm putting our discomfort, yours and mine, in the same category." She gave my hand a squeeze. "When this is all over, I'll do anything I can to make it up to you. Anything you want. For the rest of our lives. It's a debt that won't ever be repaid."

Anyway, I ended up going, of course. It wasn't the promise of eternal repayment that tipped the scales; it was the awkwardness inherent in not going. And let's say I begged off this night, pleading illness. What good would pleading illness do over the long haul? Sooner or later I'd have to say yes. I couldn't plead illness every time an invitation arrived, and if the autumn in prospect bore any resemblance to the preceding spring, plenty of invitations would be coming our way. Besides—this sort of datum always comes last and always feels like a confession—despite everything, socializing with the president and First Lady remained something of a thrill. It was a complex, corrupt, and etiolated thrill for me, and I despised myself for continuing to feel it, but it hadn't disappeared altogether.

This would be the first social evening we'd spent—I'd spent—with the president since learning the big secret he and Gretchen shared. I dreaded it at least as much as I'd dreaded my first work-related meeting with him. "Just don't embarrass me, please," I said to Gretchen as we walked across West Executive Avenue, going from my office in the OEOB to the White House basement entrance. "Don't force me to see things I'm trying to avert my eyes from."

"It won't be an issue, honey. There are going to be people around. He's very discreet."

And he was, by and large. He gave Gretchen a deep soulful look when he greeted us, but the accompanying kiss, and the words he

spoke, were well within bounds. Of course, Claire Sheffield was by
his side, which by itself would have discouraged any attempted intimacies with Gretchen. And we weren't seated next to them in the
movie theater this time, so there were no opportunities for impro-
priety there.

For an hour or so before we went into the movie, as had also happened that ill-fated other occasion we'd attended one of these
events, there was a kind of cocktail party in the area next to the theater. What I found myself doing during that part of the evening, no
doubt as a defense against my own misery, as a distancing strategy,
was to observe how the various guests dealt with the fact that the
president of the United States was in their midst. Margaret Mead
would have been proud of me, Desmond Morris and Jane Goodall
even more so. A very elaborate quadrille was taking place. I'd performed in it myself many times, of course, but I'd never really
observed it until tonight, had participated in it without being fully
conscious of its existence.

Because there were forty or so guests, and the president could be
only one place at any given time, there were many separate conversational groupings in the room. And these had every appearance of
being real conversations, about real subjects, animated and lively.
Nevertheless, every participant had the corner of his eye cocked in
the president's direction. As soon as Sheffield glided up to any particular group—he made it his business to circulate—the group
would part for him, all eyes would turn to him, everyone would
lapse into respectful silence, and he would start to talk about whatever came into his mind. Sometimes he talked about a book he was
reading, sometimes about something he had seen on television or
read in the newspaper, sometimes about some sporting event or
other, sometimes a reminiscence about some old political intrigue
dating back to his New Mexico political apprenticeship. His contributions were unrelated to anything anyone else had been saying and
were often of surpassing banality, but the people in his immediate

vicinity would smile and laugh and nod their agreement and hang on his every word. When he eventually moved on to the next group, there would be a few moments of silence, and somehow the conversation wouldn't resume, but instead the people in the group would disperse to other groups or go off to refill their drinks. As if the real purpose of the group had now been fulfilled—to be visited by the president, not to have the conversation that ostensibly was engaging everybody—and there was no longer any compelling reason to remain together.

Now, I was obviously watching all this with a very jaundiced eye. And as I say, it was a phenomenon I had dimly recognized before, when I had no personal investment in its operation and hence no particular attitude toward it. But even in my present state of mind, I remained susceptible to the governing ethos. I too was aware of the president's location in the room at all times (of course, it was partly in order to observe how he was behaving with Gretchen, but that wasn't the whole story), and I felt a little surge of energy whenever he approached the group of people with whom I was talking. No doubt I judged his pointless little contributions more harshly than I would have previously done, but I still found myself smiling and laughing and nodding along with everybody else. And when he put his fat hand on my shoulder once, my revulsion wasn't unmixed with something other, a shameful something that resembled pleasure.

In other words, I still resembled William, my monkey brother.

You might think that the movie itself, when we finally got to it, would have provided some respite, something else on which I could focus. But no, nothing of the sort. Even though it was avowedly escapist entertainment, it provided no escape. A spy thriller set in New Delhi, it failed utterly to hold my attention. Spies generally work for governments, governments are often headed by presidents, and a president happened to be sleeping with my girlfriend. In those days, all roads led to Rome, all my thoughts sooner or later turned in on themselves. I had started to brood even before the lights dimmed, and the movie provided no relief. The utter ignominy, the utter humiliation, of my position poured over me, and for ninety minutes I sat in the darkness wishing I was dead.

On the drive home Gretchen was bold enough to say, "There, that wasn't so bad, was it?"

"I've had better nights." I contented myself with that, having no desire to explain how I was feeling. It wasn't only that I found the evening close to unbearable. My own conflicted reactions to it struck me as grotesque.

Ben: Dave? Hi. It's Ben.

Dave: My God! It's been a long time, bro. How are you doing?

Ben: I'm doing all right. Coping. How about you? How's the family?

Dave: We're okay. Everybody's thriving. Say, you calling from the White House?

Ben: Yeah. Well, not exactly. The Old Executive Office Building. It's right next door. Part of the White House complex.

Dave: Cool.

Ben: It's not the West Wing or anything.

Dave: We all brag about you, Ben. And everyone we know thinks Sheffield's doing a great job. Michael did a whole report thing about presidential speechwriters for a school project.

Ben: Great. What'd he get on it?

Dave: He didn't get a mark, Ben. He's in the second grade. But he loved being able to tell everyone his uncle writes speeches for President Sheffield. The kids were all very impressed. His teacher even asked me if it was true. I said, "Hey, a seven-year-old kid couldn't make up something like that."

Ben: Well, that's terrific.

Dave: I hope you'll come out and visit us here sometime. You and, and…

Ben: Gretchen.

Dave: Right. Gretchen. You can be my guests at the restaurant. And it would give you a chance to get to know the kids a little. They're dying to meet you. Especially Michael, of course. *[laughs]* He feels he has a special relationship with you already.

Ben: Yeah, it's way overdue, isn't it?

Dave: I'd say.

Ben: Or you should all come out here. We could arrange a White House tour and everything, if that would interest you.

Dave: Yeah, that would be terrific. We really ought to keep in closer touch.

Ben: Absolutely.

Dave: *[after a long pause]* Uh…is there…?

Ben: A point to this call? Well, yeah. In a way.

Dave: Not that you need one. Just saying hello is point enough. It's great to hear from you.

Ben: Yeah. *[pause]* I'd like to ask you something.

Dave: Okay.

Ben: It's…it may be a little sensitive. I don't want to offend you or anything.

Dave: Now I'm intrigued.

Ben: Just please understand I'm not asking casually.

Dave: *[humorously exasperated]* Will you just come out and ask it already?

Ben: Well, it's not so easy.

Dave: Ben—

Ben: It's just…Remember, back when you were in college—?

Dave: *[laughing]* Barely. My brain cells have taken quite a beating since then.

Ben: Yeah. But remember...there was a time...a short period of time...when you...when you joined that...What was it called?...The Church of the Elect?

Dave: Oh, Christ.

Ben: Should I cut my losses and stop right here?

Dave: No, no. Jesus, I haven't thought about that in ages. Christ. I thought everyone had forgotten that by now. I have.

Ben: Well, it isn't something I ordinarily think about very much either. [*laughs*] Until recently.

Dave: How come? Don't tell me you went and got religion.

Ben: No, no, it's more complicated than that.

Dave: This sounds interesting.

Ben: Well, let's leave that question for another time, Dave. Okay? It's...well, let's just say it doesn't really have anything to do with religion and leave it at that. But...I was wondering about...Was his name "Marcus"?

Dave: [*long pause*] Yes, that's right. Marcus. Jesus.

Ben: I have this memory....Remember when Mom and Dad and I came to visit? At the compound?

Dave: Not really.

Ben: No?

Dave: The whole thing's kind of a blur to me now. Fortunately.

Ben: It's just...I sort of remember how everybody deferred to Marcus, everybody hung on his every word, everybody treated him like a god. You know?

Dave: Yeah, that sounds about right.

Ben: And I was wondering...looking back, do you think he *was* impressive?

Dave: Are you joking?

Ben: No...I mean, I realize the whole thing was sort of delusional...

Dave: Sort of?

Ben: But still, I mean, history is full of charismatic people who are delusional too. Do you think he was one of them?

Dave: You're serious, aren't you? [*pause*] It's really hard for me to remember, Ben. And I probably would have had a hard time answering your question even when the memory was fresh. [*pause*] See, the thing is...if you bought into the system, then you bought into Marcus's place in the system. You know what I mean? You couldn't disentangle the elements, they were all woven together. [*long pause*] He was kind of clever, I guess. I mean, that must be how he attracted followers in the first place. He carried himself with a lot of confidence, as I recall.

Ben: I remember meeting him and thinking, What's the fuss? Am I missing something?

Dave: Well, I don't think he was a nebbish or anything. He had a certain flair. And when he gave us these long rambling talks in the evening, I don't remember their coming across as stupid or, or, like totally fatuous. I don't think I was so far gone that I'd have failed to notice if he'd been a complete idiot. And sometimes, if someone had the temerity to ask him a question, his answer usually seemed more or less cogent. I mean, considering how nuts the whole business was at its core. But...I mean, what can I say? The community was built around him. If you were there, you looked up to him. That's how it worked.

Ben: Yeah, I see. But...like, when you left, did you think, What the fuck was *that* about?

Dave: Of course. But I wasn't concerned with Marcus at that point. I was worried about *myself*. I didn't differentiate between Marcus and the rest of it. [*pause*] Look, he obviously liked the adulation, he liked the attention, he liked telling people what to think and how to behave. I'm sure he must have been screwing a lot of the women. I imagine he must have had some kind of personal presence. He was glib. He certainly made you feel he was more spiritual than you were, that he possessed some kind of *secret*.

And he had an instinct for when to give you approval and when to make you feel like you had let him down. He certainly had a knack for finding people who needed someone to look up to. Like a lion crouched in the bushes, observing the wildebeests in order to identify the slowest and weakest. And I was a mess at that point, I was the most vulnerable wildebeest in the whole damned jungle.

Ben: Okay, this has been helpful. Thanks, Dave.

Dave: Is that the sort of thing you wanted to know?

Ben: In the vicinity, anyway. I hope you didn't mind my asking about this.

Dave: No. Uh-uh. It was so long ago, it feels like it happened to somebody else. I don't mind.

Ben: I appreciate it.

Dave: I just hope someday you'll tell me what this was all about.

Ben: Yeah, I will. Give my love to your family, okay? And let's talk again soon.

Dave: Right. About something stupid *you* did, next time.

Ben: [*laughs*] It's a deal. There are lots of examples to choose from, God knows.

I WAS STRUGGLING WITH A DRAFT OF THE AFL-CIO SPEECH— and it *was* a struggle; since it was hard for me to stay awake writing it, it was hard to imagine anyone else staying awake to hear it— when the president phoned me in my office. I still wasn't inured to these calls, but they were no longer quite so exciting as they had once been. Nor so welcome. On balance, I would have been much happier never hearing from him again. Still, this one proved to be a doozy.

"Working hard?" was how he greeted me.

"Earning my salary, Mr. President."

"Anything especially pressing?"

"The AFL-CIO speech."

"Oh yeah, right. Ho hum. Can you finish it fast, do you think?"

"Nothing would make me happier, believe me."

He laughed. "Well, then do it, even if you have to pull a couple of all-nighters. There's something I need you to do for me, and it won't wait."

"And what is that, Mr. President?"

"Go to Paris."

"Excuse me?"

He laughed again, obviously enjoying my reaction. He loved these sorts of surprises, loved to play puppeteer. Then, suddenly earnest, he continued, "It's the Africa business, Ben. The feelers are getting serious. But a couple of the parties—the major players— want assurances we're not just dicking them around. A personal envoy from the president should help accomplish that. So we've proposed a meeting in Paris. If these two groups sign on, the others are certain to fall into line."

"But—"

He rode right over me. "I don't want to use anyone from State or the NSC. They hate this whole business, they've been against it from the get-go. I wouldn't put it past them to sabotage it, just to prove that they were right all along. I have to let a few key people know what's happening, no way around that, but at this stage I prefer to use a back channel. When the time is right I'll present the bureaucracies with a fait accompli, they won't be in a position to kick."

"Okay, but—"

He still wouldn't let me get a word in edgewise. "It's advisable for me to use someone who isn't a total ignoramus about the issues involved, just in case the chitchat wanders into those regions. And crucially, someone whose presence won't attract any unnecessary press attention. And you happen to qualify, my friend. So write the labor speech pronto, then pack your bags."

"Except I'm not really in a position to, to—"

"Negotiate? You certainly aren't. Nor would I permit it. That isn't your franchise. This'll just be one of those bullshit rituals to get the process started. Preprocess atmospherics, you might say. I'll have some vapidly friendly letters for you to give to them, they'll probably have something similar for you to convey to me. Token gifts are likely to be exchanged. Everyone will say nice things. That's about it. If anyone tries to bring up matters of substance, you get the hell out of there immediately. Understood?"

"Yes, sir."

"Good. Call Alice's office, talk to Allan, he'll work out the details with you. Tell me how it went when you get back."

I didn't bother to tell Gretchen that night. I assumed she already knew. I even assumed—was I becoming so cynical so quickly?— that one of the reasons I'd been chosen was to get me out of the way so the president could have a clearer field of operations or perhaps an opportunity for a little after-hours action. Since in hindsight it was clear such a calculation had gone into his sending me to Camp David the previous spring, it was also a reasonable inference to draw now. But it wasn't a *pleasant* inference; it made me feel like Uriah the Hittite, sent into battle so that King David might have an unimpeded shot at Bathsheba. But at least I was going to Paris rather than Rabbah. And for a cause I believed in.

Anyway, regardless of my preference, I had no choice; a presidential request of this nature is indistinguishable from a command. So I hammered out a draft of the AFL-CIO speech that night, delivered it to Randy the following day, and left by commercial carrier for Paris the day after that.

My instructions were to check into my hotel and then proceed to the George V, where the Africans were staying. It was amusing that the representatives of these two warring factions were both at the same hotel. If they found themselves together in the elevator, were they polite to one another? Did they even acknowledge each other's presence? Well, that wasn't my problem. I was scheduled to meet with them separately. It was almost refreshing to contemplate a problem that wasn't mine.

In the event, everything went smoothly, without untoward incident, exactly as planned. Handshakes, exchanges of letters, exchanges of pleasantries, exchanges of gifts, exchanges of sincere good wishes, and a concluding set of handshakes. Indeed, so smoothly did everything go—and so resolutely devoid of content were both meetings—that I began to reconsider the nature of the whole enterprise. Did it have any real point at all, or was its purpose solely to get me out of town? The latter seemed an inconceivably petty motive for a trip such as this, but then again, everything else that had been happening to me lately was inconceivable too. When a president chooses to do something, even if it's simply to act selfishly, he does it, willy-nilly, presidentially.

The business part of the trip, if you could even call it that, was accomplished by noon. So I had almost twenty-four hours for myself. I was determined not to waste them wallowing in self-pity. This was my first trip to Paris, and it obviously merited something grander than a cuckold's brooding, even if I had to drag myself around by the scruff of the neck to achieve it.

Gretchen had urged an old dog-eared Paris guidebook on me before I left. I'd had funny qualms about accepting it, but since they made no rational sense, I ended up ignoring them. "This is a great book, I'm sure it'll come in handy," she told me as she located the musty paperback on the top row of our bookshelves and grabbed it down. "God, Ben, I'd just love to be with you on your first visit to Paris. To see your reactions. I wish I were going too."

"Oh," I said, "I'm sure you'll find a way to while away the idle hours."

But I took the book. And now it did prove useful. I transformed myself into Super Tourist, pushing to find out how many sights I could jam into one day. The Tuileries and the Louvre—I was in such a rush that after I located the Mona Lisa I immediately turned around and hightailed it out of there—Les Invalides and the Arc de Triomphe and the Eiffel Tower and the Rodin Museum, and so on and so forth. It was more like gorging than fine dining, of course, but I opted for quantity over quality. To savor one fine thing slowly might be preferable in the abstract, but given the practical circumstances, this orgy of gormandizing seemed the better strategy.

And it was glorious. I don't know how much of my pleasure came specifically from being in Paris on a gorgeous autumn day and how much derived simply from being out of Washington and away from my obsessions, a prisoner out of jail on a weekend furlough. But for whatever reason, I felt more carefree than I had in months. So carefree, indeed, that for the first time I realized just how much emotional stress I'd been under. It was as if an immense weight had been lifted, however briefly, from my shoulders, and the enormity of the relief described the enormity of the burden I'd been carrying.

All that sight-seeing was exhausting, though. By about five I thought I was going to drop. I hadn't slept in close to thirty hours, and I'd been in almost constant motion since my plane had landed early that very morning (a morning that seemed a lifetime ago).

But I wasn't ready to call it quits. I took a taxi back to my hotel, showered and changed, and held a brief debate with myself about the advisability of an early room service dinner and bed. It was, if I were being sensible, no contest at all: that option clearly *was* advisable. But I knew I wasn't going to do it. It was very unlikely that I'd be in Paris again anytime soon, and I was determined to take full advantage of the experience, to have fun whether I enjoyed it or not.

So I set out in the direction of Les Deux Magots. A corny choice, I admit, a sort of Disneyland existentialism, but I didn't know enough about Paris to come up with a better idea, and silly or not, the resonance appealed to me. Like many adolescents of literary bent, I'd read my share of Sartre in high school, and I'd been force-fed a sampling of Simone de Beauvoir by a college girlfriend.

And—not to be excessively existential myself—my current predicament seemed to vibrate in sympathetic rhythm to Les Deux Magots' emanations. I even had my own personal Nelson Algren to contend with. Who just happened to be the president of the United States. Top that, J.-P.!

I took a table and ordered a glass of wine. I suppose absinthe might have been a more romantic beverage, but it didn't occur to me at the time. And as I sat there, an odd and oddly pleasant melancholy began to settle over me. Part of it was simple fatigue, of course, and part of it was a feeling of peculiar but profound isolation; the café was plenty crowded, but the noisy people around me were all strangers, and chattering in a language I didn't understand. It seemed piquantly wrong—wrong in the manner of a romantic ballad—to be in Paris for the first time all by myself, wrong to be here without the woman I loved. But the woman I loved…Well, you get the idea. My thoughts were inexorably heading back to square one, and my melancholy was fast becoming less pleasant.

It was during this transition from melancholy to outright depression that a woman approached my table and said in perfect, although heavily accented, English, "Excuse me, aren't you Benjamin Krause? President Sheffield's speechwriter?"

To say I was startled is a mammoth understatement. That sort of thing hardly ever happened to me, even in Washington; that it should have occurred in Paris was dumbfounding.

I looked up. She was about forty, I'd say, not especially pretty, but she had a neat figure, and lustrous shoulder-length chestnut hair, and was very stylishly turned out. The presentation was reasonably attractive, and her demeanor, her bearing, suggested she regarded herself as *more* than reasonably attractive. Some French thing, I suppose. And right now she was looking at me with a frank stare, waiting for an answer. When I didn't come up with one—I was too busy trying to figure out how she could possibly know me—she said, "I must be mistaken. Please forgive me for troubling you."

"No, no," I said, "you aren't mistaken, I am Ben Krause. And you're not troubling me at all. But...?"

I must have looked thoroughly befuddled, because she suddenly laughed. "You are wondering how I recognized you, yes?"

"Well, yes, absolutely."

"This doesn't happen to you in Paris very often?"

"It doesn't happen *any*where very often."

She extended her hand. A surprisingly masculine gesture, palm vertical rather than horizontal. "Denise Charpentier." As I took it and shook it, she added, "From *Le Monde*. I write about American politics, among other things. Which perhaps explains how I recognized you."

I stood up, an awkward thing to do behind the small table at which I was seated. "It doesn't, really," I said. "I'm pretty low on the food chain. Even in the White House, I'm often asked for identification."

"That can't be true, surely. You wrote the inaugural address, did you not? And the speech about Africa?"

"Speechwriters never tell," I said. "The speech is always the president's." But I can't deny I was delighted at this unexpected recognition in this unlikely setting. Anonymous labor is intrinsic to the speechwriting business, but that doesn't mean a little acknowledgment is unwelcome now and then. Especially now.

"Both of those were extremely good," she said. "They received a great deal of...you say 'play'? They received a great deal of play here in France." The smile she gave me then—it was very knowing, and slightly patronizing, and perhaps for both reasons terribly sexy— vanquished my melancholy on the spot. But also made me feel impossibly young and callow. She seemed so *grown-up*.

"I'm sure the president would be delighted to hear it," I managed to say.

Her smile broadened further at that. "As the putative author, you mean? And the actual author? Would he be delighted as well?"

"How could he fail to be?" And then, emboldened by her smile, I said, "Listen, would you like to join me?"

"You mean here? Now?"

Which made me feel unsure of myself all of a sudden, and not a little gauche. Something in her tone seemed to suggest I was being unwarrantedly forward. But there was no graceful way to retract the invitation or make the awkward moment disappear. So I stammered, "Well...yes, I did mean here. And now. Here and now. For a drink...or...whatever. But if it's a bad time—"

"Well, why not?" She raised her eyebrows interrogatively, as if she actually expected an answer to the question, and sat herself down across from me.

After she gave the waiter her drink order, I said, "May I ask you something?" She didn't answer but instead inclined her head slightly, an invitation to proceed. "I was just wondering...why did you continue to address me in English? I mean, after you decided you were wrong about who I was."

"Oh," she said with a laugh, "young man, please! It would be quite impossible to take you for anything but an American. The look is unmistakable."

I didn't know what to do with that one. I also didn't know what to do with being addressed as "young man." It made me feel even younger than I was already feeling, which was approximately seventeen. So I just sort of gaped.

And then she said to me, "So, Ben...for how long are you in Paris?"

The use of my first name was unexpected, and almost as disconcerting as being called "young man." The frank way she looked straight at me made it very hard to look back; I felt transparent under her gaze. Transparent and entirely out of my depth. "Just the day," I said.

"You mean to say you arrived today?"

"That's right."

"And you're leaving tomorrow?"

"Uh-huh." I was already cursing myself. She was a reporter, for God's sake! My little mission, pointless as it may have been, was also supposed to be highly secret. It was crazy of me not to have been more guarded. But she had shaken me up, dislodged my brain from its moorings.

"So that must mean you are here on official business of some sort."

"Must it?" Just stalling.

"Yes, Ben, I believe it must." Another one of those smiles, reminiscent of the famous one I'd examined in the Louvre just a few hours ago.

"Honestly, I've spent most of the day seeing the sights," I assured her.

"And when you weren't?" She left only the briefest of pauses—not really enough for me to answer—before saying, "Yes, I thought as much." As if my tongue-tied silence was confirmation. Which of course it was, but if she'd given me a little more time, I might have been able to invent something. "Well. This is all very intriguing. A speechwriter on a secret mission. Is he an emissary for the president, perhaps? I can only wonder."

"Yes. That's all you can do."

"Unless you choose to tell me."

Now her smile was unambiguously flirtatious. But given the context, given the fact that she now wanted something from me, the overt flirtatiousness wasn't nearly as sexy as her previous mysteriousness. Still, I was enjoying her company a lot more than I'd been enjoying my own, and I savored the low-level radioactivity that seemed to be pulsating between us. It was a while since I'd experienced anything along those lines. The fact that she had the upper hand, the fact that I felt like a schoolchild in her presence…somehow that part was fun too. It accentuated the exotic perturbation of being in a foreign country for the first time, of not quite understanding the game, of having to intuit the rules as I went along. I liked the challenge of being on my uppers this way.

"Oh, I couldn't do that," I said. "Even conceding for the sake of argument that you're on the right track."

"I believe we've established that I am."

"Not at all, I might just be enjoying your interest and not want to lose it."

"And why would you be enjoying my interest? Conceding for the sake of argument that it exists."

I recognized the land mine she'd planted well before I stepped onto it. "Listen," I said abruptly, "would you like to have dinner with me?"

It was her turn to be taken aback. We were setting each other some knotty problems, no question about it. "Tonight?"

"Tonight's the only one I've got. And for a suspected presidential envoy, my evening is surprisingly free. Entirely free, to be precise."

"How sad for you."

"Downright pathetic. Have pity on a lonely traveler?"

"I can't help wondering why he's traveling in so lonely a fashion."

My wineglass was empty. I thought of trying a joke about her getting me drunk to loosen my lips—it seemed to have the right level of flirtatiousness, a "what kind of boy do you think I am?" quality— but it seemed inadvisable to suggest, however jocularly, that I might eventually be persuaded to tell her what she wanted to know. It didn't seem right, somehow, to dangle such a possibility in front of her. So instead I said, "Shall I signal the waiter? We can order some food."

She wrinkled her nose. "Certainly not." The refusal seemed categorical. But then she sat back and looked at me speculatively for a few moments and went on, "There are much better places. If this lonely traveler is going to eat only one meal in Paris, it ought to be memorable."

"Well, if you lead, I'll follow."

Another long pause, another speculative look. "I have to phone somebody," she announced. "Wait for me."

We took a taxi to a small restaurant in the cramped basement of a building that seemed to be centuries old. The ceilings were very low, the exposed timbers looked ancient, and the language of the menu was beyond my rudimentary French. Even if it had been in English, I might not have recognized much; a glance at neighboring tables told me the fare was pretty exotic. She noted my confusion, seemed amused by it, and announced, "Don't worry, I'll order for both of us. The less you know the better. The food here would not meet American dietary requirements."

"My arteries are at your disposal."

"And in the meantime, I shall try to get you drunk, and perhaps that way I will manage to extract some information from you."

So she had the courage to make the joke I'd balked at. But I was still craven, I declined to up the ante. "So this is an interview, then? Not purely social?"

"Not at all, not at all. Purely social. However, I would not refuse any information you should happen to proffer. That is reasonable, no?"

"Where did you learn your English, Denise? It's flawless."

She flushed. An unexpected exposure, a locus of vanity. "I went to school in London," she replied. "And I lived in Washington for several years. My husband was in the foreign service." She suddenly burst out laughing. "Don't look so alarmed! I'm not married anymore. The marriage was a youthful mistake, subsequently rectified. Am I to assume there is no Mrs. Krause in your life?"

"Only my mother. But—"

"That's all right, Ben," she interrupted. "Regardless of what you were about to tell me. This is your one night in Paris, we're simply having a pleasant dinner, I have no need to know your domestic arrangements."

And I thought to myself: Ah, but if you did, you'd no longer give a rat's ass about why I'm in Paris. You'd have the story of your career.

Which was a sobering thought. Or would have been, except the bottle of wine she had ordered as soon as we were seated quickly reversed the effect. Did she have an ulterior motive, was she really trying to get me drunk? I'll never know the answer to that question. It's certainly true that we both became freer and more open with each other as the minutes went by, that we shared some confidences and retailed our life stories. But I was never in danger of divulging anything sensitive, and she never appeared to lose control of the conversation, let alone herself. Indeed, she was as focused as a homing pigeon, she kept adverting to the mysterious nature of my trip every ten minutes or so; whether she thought I'd break under repeated questioning or whether it was intended simply as an amusing mode of flirtation is anybody's guess.

There was an awkward moment over coffee, when she started praising Sheffield, assuring me how lucky I must feel to be working for such an excellent president, telling me how popular he was in Europe, and then waxing rhapsodic about what an attractive man he was, how sexy and appealing and *sympathique*. If her intention was to soften me up further, this was definitely *not* the best way to go about it, although there was no way for her to know that. I confess I became a little taciturn; all the painful thoughts I'd been keeping at bay since meeting her came rushing back. In a torrent.

But the moment passed. Typically, it passed when she essayed a too cute transition: "But you must know all this better than I," she suddenly said. "If he trusts you with a sensitive secret mission, then I assume you and he must be on fairly close terms."

"Give it up, Denise."

Which won me another of those provocative smiles.

When the check came soon after, she grabbed it. I started to protest, of course, but she peremptorily cut me off. "No, Ben, you are my guest, I must insist."

"But there's no reason—"

"There are several reasons, in fact. First, since this is your only dinner in Paris, it gives me great pleasure to be your host. And second, the meal will go on my expense account whether I get a story out of you or not, so in fact it is *Le Monde* who is buying your dinner, not I. And third...well, to be candid, I wouldn't object if you feel you are in my debt."

"I do."

"Good."

"But not enough to tell you what you want to know."

"Ugh!" She laughed. "Is it really so earthshaking?"

"Nope."

"So you are teasing me?"

"I just like the mystique it seems to confer upon me."

When we got out of the restaurant, there was an another awkward moment. But this one was unavoidable, inherent in our situation. We were both somewhat drunk, the sexual tension between us had been gathering imperceptibly but steadily, and neither of us knew what the other was thinking. I didn't even know what *I* was thinking.

"Well...," I said. I was about to launch into a thank-you-and-good-night speech and then look for a taxi. I was attracted to her, goodness knows, and stirred by the whole episode, and sufficiently consumed by rage and self-doubt that I permitted myself to think a sexual encounter might actually do me good. But my life was already so complicated and compromised, and my motives were so impure, and besides, she scared me half to death....It seemed wise not to push it. Better to wonder what might have happened and warm myself later with the memory of unexplored possibility.

"Let's take a walk," she said. It wasn't an invitation, it was a direct order. "We're near the Quartier Latin, you should see it at night when there aren't so many people about. A thousand years disappear."

Once we got off the boulevard St.-Michel, I understood what she meant. Without people and without cars, the narrow winding streets seemed medieval in the frail moonlight. We walked side by side in silence, occasionally bumping against each other. Wine and fatigue and uncertainty and the strangeness of the setting were doing interesting things to my mood. Good things. A feeling of exhilaration was ballooning in my chest.

"This is really beautiful," I finally said.

She stopped and turned toward me, smiling. "Yes. I thought it was something you ought to see."

And then, impelled by…well, impelled by *everything*, I took hold of the lapels of her cashmere coat, gently pulled her toward me, and kissed her. After a startled moment, she kissed back. And what began tentatively turned into something not at all tentative. The sensation was vertiginous. After we separated, while my head was still reeling, she looked me straight in the eye and announced flatly, "I'm not going to sleep with you. It's quite out of the question."

"Okay."

"You're not upset with me?"

"I honestly hadn't thought that far ahead."

"Or disappointed?"

"Oh, I'm probably disappointed. I'll survive."

"It's not because you're keeping secrets. You do understand that?"

"The idea hadn't even occurred to me, Denise."

She nodded, and after a moment of indecision we resumed walking. Everything felt different now, though; it wasn't because of her announcement, not directly, but rather because the delicious ambiguity surrounding us had been so abruptly banished. I suppose I *was* disappointed, and simultaneously relieved. But the antique shadowy streets had undeniably lost some of their magic as a result.

About ten minutes later, as we rounded a corner, she said, "This is where I live."

"It is?"

"Mmm. The building dates from the thirteenth century."

"I hope the plumbing's more recent."

But this was the wrong side of the Channel for a joke about plumbing. She didn't even acknowledge the attempt. "Come up, we'll have one last glass of wine before we say good night."

I started to demur—it had been almost two days since I'd slept, and I had an early flight the next morning—but she overrode my objections, bossily insistent. "You're really being quite rude, Ben, whether you intend it or not. If you thought we were going to go to bed, you wouldn't hesitate. We both know that. You know it as well as I. So if you refuse to come up, I can only take it as a serious insult."

Well, what could I say to that? Her premise was inarguable, and her logic was unassailable.

The apartment was quite large, the decor was thoroughly modern. The effect was jarring, since the place was situated in the middle of one of the oldest parts of the city. But it was attractive enough if you ignored the setting. As she sloughed off her coat and dropped her keys on a little table, she said, "Why don't you check out the vintage of the plumbing, and I'll open a bottle of wine."

When I came back into the living room, Denise was seated on the sofa, her shoes off, her feet tucked under her tweed skirt. A bottle of wine and two glasses, already filled, were on the table in front of her. Borodin's string quartet was on the stereo. It was the perfect mise-en-scène for a seduction. I wondered idly why she was bothering as I sat on the sofa beside her. Not too close. I didn't want her to worry there might be a wrestling match in prospect.

She handed me one of the glasses and clinked hers against mine. "To secrets," she said with a smile.

I smiled back. By now I found her persistence sort of winning. "Listen, Denise, I'm so utterly exhausted, you make me feel as if I'm being interrogated in the Lubyanka. Wasn't that a KGB technique, not letting prisoners sleep? But you must realize by now I'm not going to break."

"Yes, I accept that. It isn't why I invited you up, to *break* you. I'm enjoying your company."

We drank our wine and talked inconsequentially. The mood was much less flirtatious now, and my mind was wandering to other things: to the difficulties of finding a taxi back to my hotel so late at night, to the unappealing prospect of repacking as soon as I returned so I could check out without too much of a rush tomorrow morning, to the inevitable depression consequent upon returning to Washington. It was late, well past one, and I was also beginning to wonder how soon I could leave without giving offense.

Denise excused herself for a moment. I tried to use the opportunity to make my own exit, but when I attempted to prepare the ground, she shushed me and gently pushed me back down. "I shall only be a moment," she said. After she left the room, I leaned my head back against a cushion at one end of the sofa and slumped down, twisting my body into a semireclining posture. My eyes seemed to close of their own volition, and lulled by the music, I was asleep within seconds.

I don't know how long I remained that way. But I do know that I woke up to discover her on the floor, on her knees, with her mouth locked tight around my exposed erection. When I opened my eyes they met hers, twinkling with amusement. I stirred and groaned, and she slipped off me, smiled up at my bewildered face, and said, "Do you think the KGB did *this* to keep their prisoners awake?"

I was confused. I was too confused even to be surprised. I was confused on about twenty different levels, starting with where I was and proceeding rapidly to what was happening and how come. But I didn't say anything, and when she murmured, "Come, we're going to bed," I followed her dumbly down the hall to her bedroom.

BEFORE I FELL ASLEEP FOR THE SECOND TIME, SHE INSISTED ON leading me back into the living room. She brought an alarm clock and a couple of blankets with her. "We'll say good-bye now, Ben. I like you very much, and this was perfectly lovely. But not lovely enough for me to wake up at five o'clock. Nothing is lovely enough for that." So we kissed and embraced—the lovemaking had been good, the tenderness felt genuine—and I spent the few hours of night remaining to me alone on her couch, deep in a dream-rich slumber. I was asleep too fast even to wonder what had changed her mind. I wish I had thought to ask her when I'd had the chance.

Back at my hotel—it had been a miserable half hour trying to find a cab so early—two messages from the previous evening were waiting for me. One was from Gretchen. Well, fine, I thought a little nervously, let her stew. The other was from one of the African delegations. They needed to see me. It was imperative.

Since it was so early—still shy of six—I showered, changed, and packed before I phoned the George V. Nevertheless, I obviously woke the person up. But when he heard who it was, he invited me to come by as quickly as I could.

The immensely tall, lean man who greeted me at the door of the suite at the George V was not the one I had met with the previous day. This one was all business, making no attempt to be gracious. Another letter had been prepared for the president. It was vital I take it to him. The hand-off was made without ceremony, and I was out of my own hotel and in a taxi to Charles de Gaulle Airport less than an hour later.

The flight back was a bad six hours. Unable to sleep in my cramped coach seat, I obsessed about the previous twenty-four hours instead. Not much satisfaction there. I felt ill used by the president—no, worse, deeply affronted—sent off on a fool's errand for no reason other than his sexual greed. And the memory of my night with Denise made me positively writhe. I tried to put a brave face on it, telling myself the usual macho things guys say in these situations: So, you dog, only one night in Paris and you managed to score, etc. But it didn't work this time. Is there a person alive who has ended up feeling good after a revenge fuck?

About midway through the flight I recalled a relatively brief, even fleeting moment from my dinner with Denise, and it kept me occupied for the remainder of the trip. She had said something about my domestic arrangements, and I had thought to myself how amazed she'd be if she had even an inkling of what they really were. And now, suddenly, the idea started to appeal to me. It wasn't real, it wasn't any more real than my assassination fantasies during the summer doldrums, but I began to spin out scenarios involving my leaking to the press the fact of Gretchen's affair with Sheffield. I could do it anonymously. What a ruckus that would cause! For an hour or two, as I flew over the Atlantic, the punishment struck me as appropriate to the crime. But I came to my senses before the descent into Dulles. The pain I was suffering was purely private, but the repercussions of such a course would be public, and historic.

An official car met me at the airport and took me directly to the White House. I handed Sandra the various letters and gifts to give to the president—he was in a meeting and couldn't be disturbed—and then proceeded to Gretchen's office. I usually avoided the East Wing these days; the place was such a hotbed of gossip, there was at least a remote chance someone there might be aware of my situation. But coming home from a trip to Europe, even a trip as short as this one, seemed to justify enduring a little bit of uneasiness.

I stuck my head into her cubicle and said, "Honey, I'm home."

She looked up. The smile she gave me was so warm that I felt a sharp stab of guilt. "How was it?" she asked.

"It was okay. Utterly pointless, but okay." Reminding her—and myself—of why I had been sent helped ease my conscience slightly.

"I called you last night. You were out."

"Yes, the hotel gave me the message."

"Where were you?"

"Notice I haven't asked what *you* were up to while I was gone?"

Her smile disappeared. "Does that suggest that you were up to *some*thing?"

"It might."

"But I shouldn't ask about it?"

"Seems fair."

She nodded. She couldn't really argue, but she didn't look happy. And all at once I felt as if the wall between us had suddenly grown thicker. "Well...no matter what, it's good to have you back," she said. It was hard to tell whether she meant it. An unfamiliar state of affairs as far as Gretchen was concerned.

I SLEPT FOR OVER FIFTEEN HOURS THAT NIGHT. WHICH WAS a good thing, because the very next morning I got a call summoning me to the office of Alice Hahn, the president's chief of staff. It wasn't advisable to deal with Alice when you weren't well rested. She was fat, efficient, and brusque to the point of rudeness, and she prided herself on what she called a "zero tolerance for idiots" policy. She ran true to form when her assistant told me she was ready for me and I should go on in to see her. She didn't get up from her desk, she didn't offer me a chair, and she didn't say hello. "Two things, Ben. First, the president is very disappointed in your AFL-CIO draft. He thinks it's way below your usual standard. A total yawner. He wants you to start over from page one. From sentence one."

I felt the anger rising. I had rushed to complete the thing at the president's express insistence. That his assessment was completely justified didn't make the criticism any more acceptable. How much shit was a guy supposed to eat? "And point two?" I said.

"No, I want you to acknowledge point one first."

"I heard you."

"I'd like a little more acknowledgment than that."

I suppressed the urge to tell her she was pushing her luck, she was baiting a dangerously short-tempered bear. I also suppressed the urge to whine about being sleep deprived and jet-lagged. "I'll take another pass at it, Alice. But I can't say I like the way you've delivered this news."

"You want sugarcoating? I'm giving you a message from the president. Be a mensch about it."

"And second?" If I had no choice other than to swallow my pride in my dealings with the man himself, I'd be damned if I was going to be bullied by his minions. I'd reached that stage, at least.

She gave a little chuckle. Maybe she liked my feistiness. She reclined in her chair, pushing it back a little from her desk. It emitted a little sigh as it absorbed her full weight. "Okay, second. Randy is being transferred. It's a lateral move. His title will be 'Adviser to the President.' He'll still be reporting to the director of communications. But he won't be in charge of speechwriting any longer."

Some lateral move. She told me all this without any change in her expression, but it was obvious Randy was being demoted. And of course everyone would understand it that way. One additional decisive humiliation in the face of hundreds of small professional humiliations he'd been absorbing since joining the Sheffield campaign almost two years before.

"Does he know?" I asked.

"Yes, I had him in here a few minutes ago."

"Did you exhibit the same delicacy with him you just employed in telling me my speech sucks?"

Another low chuckle. I was apparently worming my way into her good graces. "This isn't sensitivity training, Ben. I gave him the news without any window dressing. That's my job. And he took it like a grown-up. You'd do well to emulate his example."

"Yeah," I said. "Look where it got *him.*"

She laughed outright, then said, "I don't think it had much impact one way or the other. But I admired his composure."

His composure. I wondered how much composure he'd displayed right after he'd left her office. And I wondered what his secretary would have to say about his composure when she talked to her co-workers about it in the basement cafeteria later that afternoon.

"Has it been decided who's going to replace him?"

"Uh-huh. You are."

I was too stunned to speak. After a couple of moments she added, "The president's wanted to do this for quite a while, frankly. He feels the time is finally right. We'll be releasing both announcements this afternoon. So congratulations."

"Yeah...thank you."

"You're certainly taking *this* news with composure."

"I have to absorb it, Alice."

"The president's extremely pleased about all this. So...don't make him regret it, Ben. Do a good job on the AFL-CIO speech. He'd like a draft on his desk by tomorrow, if possible."

"Right."

The interview was clearly over. I went back to my office and tried to figure out what I felt. There *was* some elation in there somewhere, I couldn't deny that. It would mean a welcome raise in salary and a sizable bump in status. And it was a sign of presidential approval.

Or was it?

It occurred to me that this honor might not have come my way except for the president's doings with Gretchen. Just like all those White House social invitations we'd started getting the previous spring. By some peculiar operation of feudal logic, because she was under his protection, I was as well. At bottom, this promotion might merely be a pimp's payoff.

That thought, once it arrived, tended to take the edge off whatever elation I might have felt.

Not that my elation was exactly in distillate form before that. Helping the president look good, which is what in essence my job was all about, wasn't something I felt a burning desire to accomplish anymore. A large part of me wanted the man to fall on his ass. And this new position would require me to spend even more work time in his company; in the last couple of weeks I'd discovered what an ordeal it was to deal with him as if this immense personal issue between us didn't exist. I didn't anticipate its getting any easier with time. (I also started to imagine how I'd feel if, as I was heading into the Oval Office, I happened to encounter Gretchen as she was coming out. What a horror!) I gave some thought to the possibility of declining and even revisited the notion of quitting altogether.

But I knew I wasn't going to quit, and if I wasn't going to quit, it would be stupid not to accept the new position. The duties weren't so radically different from what I was already doing, but at a higher salary and with increased prestige. And the prospect of more face-time with the president...well, if it was once or twice a week instead of once or twice a fortnight, the difference was hardly vast. Besides, whatever my personal feelings, face-time with the president was the executive branch coin of the realm; this would make me a more significant player. Why I should care about that now I don't know, but everybody who worked in that environment cared dreadfully, and I was no exception.

And after all, nobody else needed to know I was simply collecting my pimp's reward. Except maybe the person who had put Gretchen at the head of the rope line the day Sheffield returned to Washington from his summer vacation. Could that person have been Alice Hahn?

"Be a mensch," she'd said to me. Only now did it occur to me that her use of the Yiddish word might have been intended, in some subtle way, as a palliative, a small token of tribal solidarity, a subtextual consolation. But consolation for what? For the president's displeasure with my speech or for his sexual relationship with my girlfriend?

It's some indication of my emotional state during those days that I hoped it was the latter almost as much as I dreaded it. The idea that another person might know of my situation was horrible, but, contradictory as this may seem, the possibility that another person sympathized with and understood what I was going through also held some appeal. Alice Hahn was as unmaternal as any woman I could think of, ample bosom notwithstanding, but I found myself imbuing her words with a slight ephemeral wisp of motherly concern. Ridiculous, of course. She was famous for riding roughshod over anybody who crossed her path, from interns to cabinet secretaries, trampling personal feelings with oblivious abandon. And aside from that, she had worked for Sheffield for over a decade, she'd been his Senate AA before following him to the White House. Her loyalty to him was beyond question, and one could even reasonably surmise she had been his procuress, or at least amatory enabler, on many occasions.

She did *not* intend to provide a shoulder for me to cry on. The very idea was foolish, and my desperate hope that I had discerned such an impulse totally absurd. "Be a mensch," regardless of the ethnicity of the vocabulary employed, is not a sympathetic piece of advice. It's pretty much the diametrical opposite, in fact. But since there was a speech due on the president's desk the following day, I also realized it was advice I'd be well advised to take. I managed to pull myself together somehow, at least sufficiently to make a plausible start on the AFL-CIO speech.

There was another dark spot later that afternoon. I had gone across the hall to use the men's room and found Randy standing at one of the urinals. He couldn't run, and once we'd made eye contact, I didn't feel I could either.

He grimaced. "Well," he said, "I guess congratulations are in order."

"I don't know, Randy."

"Of course you do. You've been scuffling for this right from the start. And you finally made it."

"Believe me, it came as a total surprise."

"Yeah, right. Ingratiating yourself, sucking up…no ulterior motives there, uh-uh, no sir."

"Well now, Randy," I said, getting a little pissed myself now, "I suppose everyone tries to ingratiate himself around the president. Seems to come with the territory. It's just, some of us are better at it than others. Or maybe it's even simpler than that, maybe some of us are just more naturally likable."

By now he was washing his hands, and I was at a urinal. He looked over at me. "In any case, you're exactly where you want to be, right?"

"If only you knew," I said.

He tossed his paper towel into the trash and left, not even bothering with a parting shot. It was a relief in a way, having the friendship officially over. From the moment I'd joined the Sheffield campaign, relations had been difficult. And the truth is, we'd only considered each other friends in earlier campaigns, back before we'd gotten to know each other.

When I got home that night, Gretchen had a bottle of champagne waiting.

She seemed surprised when I showed my displeasure, walking right past her into the bedroom to change out of my suit without saying anything. She followed me in a few moments later, the bottle still in her hand. "Is something the matter?" she asked. "I thought you'd be feeling pretty good tonight."

"Your boyfriend told you about my promotion, did he?"

One aspect of my resolve not to obsess about the details of Gretchen's affair with Sheffield was to try not to think about, and certainly never ask about, the calendar of their encounters. I didn't know the frequency of their meetings, I didn't know at what time of day or in what location they occurred. I wondered about all that; indeed, there were times when I could think of little else. But I always tried to suppress such questions.

Now, though, it was obvious they had seen each other. Of course I assumed they had seen each other while I was away, but assuming and knowing are two very different things. Or perhaps he had seen her again today? For some reason, that seemed to compound the insult. It didn't make any practical difference, of course, but it made things *feel* different. And the fact that they had discussed *me* in the course of their concupiscent doings was another unwelcome bit of intelligence. I could barely force myself to look at her.

"He's wanted to do this for a long time, Ben."

"Yeah, that's what Alice said."

"It doesn't have anything to do with me, if that's what you're thinking. He wanted to do it before...before he and I..."

"Go on, just say it."

"You know what I mean. It's your work that got you this. Not my relationship with him."

"You and he had a nice long talk about it, though?"

"He told me he was going to do it, yes. And he told me why."

"Has it occurred to you he maybe tells you what he thinks you want to hear? That politicians do that?"

"You don't know anything *about* what he tells me."

"That's true, I don't."

"You have no idea what the tone is, what the level of candor is, how much or how little bullshit there is."

"How could I? You don't tell me anything."

She hesitated. She looked at the bottle of champagne in her hand. Then she said, "Nothing I say is going to make this okay, is it?"

"Nonsense. I glory in the idea of my girlfriend and her lover discussing me in their quiet intimate moments. Praising me in a patronizing way during afterglow. After sending me out of the country so they can have more time together. Who wouldn't appreciate that?"

She nodded. "I miscalculated," she said, very simply. "I see your point, Ben. I understand how obnoxious this must seem to you. But I honestly thought…Aw shit, it doesn't matter what I honestly thought. Just don't let my stupidity ruin the good news. Please? It's a great thing, you earned it on your merit, and I only wish it was something we could celebrate together. But even if it isn't, even if we can't, for God's sake, Ben, find a way to celebrate."

She turned and left the room. I was aching. Everything I loved about her had been evident in that little speech. And everything I hated had occasioned it.

The condo suddenly felt too small for the two of us. Any further conversation seemed pointless right then, but hiding out in the bedroom wasn't an attractive option either. In addition, despite everything, I felt hungry. The misery had been with me too long and too persistently for it to affect my appetite anymore. So I quickly changed into jeans and a sweater and went out for a bite. That's how I celebrated becoming the president's head of speechwriting, alone in a funky trattoria with a pizza and a pitcher of beer. A far cry from my Parisian dinner two short nights ago. After finishing, I strolled over to a bookstore and looked at books and CDs for a while.

When I got back home it was barely ten, but the lights were all out, and Gretchen was in bed. At first I thought she was asleep, but as I began to undress in the dark, she said, "I am sorry, Ben."

"Yeah, I know."

"Do you wish he'd lost?"

"The election, you mean?" It was an interesting question. I pondered it for a moment. "Jeez, I don't know. Am I supposed to pull a Bogie? Say, 'The problems of three little people don't amount to a hill of beans in this crazy world'?"

She exhaled with amusement and said, "You really love that movie, don't you?" At my insistence we'd seen it several times in succession when it was playing at AFI.

"Yeah. But I can't emulate Rick. Not in this case. That kind of nobility is totally beyond me right now."

"'Cause *I* do. I wish he'd lost."

"Really?"

"I just don't know what I should do in this situation. I wish I'd never gotten into it. But I can't honestly say I feel I should get out of it."

"Yes, you've made that pretty clear."

"That's aside from not knowing how to." That one sat there for a few moments. Then she said, "I just wish there was some way to convey to you what this signifies for me. Maybe that would help you accept it. I mean, it doesn't even feel like a sexual relationship, really...it's more like, it's like, it's like having some special sort of intimacy with, with American history. And I keep asking myself— I hope this doesn't make you feel worse, but I'm just going to be honest—I keep asking myself, When I'm eighty and I look back on this period in my life, which would I regret more: doing it or deciding *not* to do it?"

And while she spoke I was thinking, I can't stand this forever. It's a totally peculiar situation, and I love this woman more than I've ever loved another human being, so I'll try to do what I can for as long as I can. I've put up with it for a month or two, and maybe I can put up with it on a day-to-day basis for a little while longer, but I realize now that I'm never going to get accustomed to it. Sooner or later it's going to destroy everything.

"Tell me something," she suddenly said, interrupting my elegiac little reverie. "Is it worse for you that he's the president? If I were having an affair with just some guy—not that that would ever happen, believe me—but let's say it did, would that be less difficult to deal with or more difficult?"

She sounded as if she really wanted to know the answer. "God, Gretch...I'm obviously not one of those people who handle these things well under any circumstances. I'm quite tolerant of human frailty when I don't have a dog in the fight, but...I don't deal with betrayal well. I take it personally."

She started to protest the word "betrayal," but I rode over her. "But I think this is worse. Ultimately, it's worse. It's so...forgive the cliché, but it's so *unmanning*. I mean, if it were anybody else, I could at least compete. But if you're looking for a boyfriend they play 'Hail to the Chief' to when he enters a room, then only one guy fills the bill. And I'm pretty much out of contention."

"But doesn't that make it *less* terrible? I mean, he's not *really* my boyfriend. Nobody's my boyfriend but you. I'm not interested in anybody else. And it's not a judgment about you. Comparisons aren't relevant. He's, he's...he's this figure on a stage. It isn't personal. It doesn't even *feel* personal. Not even when he talks personally. And it isn't like, I don't know, like his conversation is more interesting— it mostly isn't very interesting at all—or that he treats me better, or he's more attractive, or he's a better lover. It's just, the position he occupies makes the whole thing unique. Irresistible. Irresistible as a bizarre once-in-a-lifetime opportunity. I realize there's no equivalent for you, but if there were, if you can somehow imagine one... Can you be certain you wouldn't do exactly what I'm doing?"

She was letting slip a little more about all this than she had seen fit to reveal up to now. I suppose she felt still guilty about what had happened when I first got home. There was a tone in her voice— you could almost call it *pleading;* she wanted me to see things from her point of view.

But I'd already tried hard to do that. And succeeded as far as was humanly possible. Seeing it from her point of view wasn't, finally, enough to make it okay. "Look," I said, "you asked a question, and I tried to answer it as truthfully as I could. Both situations would be dreadful, and this one is probably the dreadfuller of the two. It's pointless to try to argue me out of it. It isn't susceptible to argument or logical analysis. It's just there."

"I know," she said.

"Besides...do you think *he* believes it's only a matter of the position he occupies?"

"Maybe we shouldn't get into this."

"We're already in it. You led the way. And left the door ajar."

She sighed. "Yes, okay, fair enough." This was the sort of thing she'd tried all along to declare off-limits. "No, of course he doesn't. He thinks it's about him. Or maybe it would be more accurate to say, he thinks his position and his person aren't so easy to separate. He thinks...you know, he thinks that he isn't president by accident. And he thinks the qualities that got him where he is are also qualities that make him sexy."

"He told you this?"

"Not in those words exactly. But something along those lines. He did say...God, I really shouldn't be telling you this....He said he thought men found him sexually threatening. And he quoted Henry Kissinger to me."

"'Power is the ultimate aphrodisiac'?"

"You know the quote?"

"Oh yes. It's quite famous. Largely as a specimen of narcissistic self-deception." I gave my anger a chance to bank a little and then went on, "I don't suppose you bothered explaining to him that he'd got it wrong?"

"Noooo...it didn't seem the right thing to do in that situation."

I knew in advance what her answer would be, of course, but nevertheless my anger flared anew, and I rounded on her: "Do you have any *idea* where this leaves me? Do you know how utterly humiliating this is? And what makes it even worse...God, I'm sure he says nice things about me. I'm sure he's really quite fond of me. But every time he looks at me, he thinks, Poor sap, I've got his girlfriend in my pocket. Every time he thinks about me, he thinks, Nice guy, but hell, I'm the alpha male, no one can blame his girlfriend for finding me irresistible. It's a lovely position you've put me in, don't you think?"

"Oh Ben, what difference does it make? He's going to think what he needs to think. Anyway, what's happening between him and me isn't about you."

"That's where you're wrong. It may not be about me as a person—it's not about *you* as a person either—but it's certainly about his sense of entitlement, and his sense of entitlement extends to me. If he sees I have an attractive girlfriend, then he needs to demonstrate he can have her too if he wants her. The only way a guy like that knows he has enough is when he's got more than anybody else."

"I don't think he's like that."

"No, well, you wouldn't, would you?"

"Besides, your hands aren't exactly clean anymore."

It was inevitable, I suppose, that my Paris escapade wouldn't remain unmentioned forever. But regardless of any misgivings I had about it, and there were plenty, in this context it seemed to me to be an irrelevant distraction. So I said flatly, "If you want to talk about that some other time, fine, we'll do it. But the situation isn't remotely comparable."

There was a long pause. I think she was debating with herself whether to open hostilities on that front. She finally elected not to. She sighed and said, "It's not very flattering to me, you know, this notion of yours."

"Well, look at it this way: At least you made the cut. I'm sure someone like Alice Hahn didn't merit a second glance."

I climbed into bed beside her. But we managed to keep some distance between us.

THE NEXT DAY AN INTERN CAME TO MY OFFICE TO DELIVER a handwritten note from the president:

Dear Ben,

Congratulations are in order! In case you were wondering, your trip to Paris was a success. The second letter the Masai representative handed you may unravel the Gordian knot for us. It's quite possible we have, if not the basis for a settlement, at least the basis for *negotiations* for a settlement. Believe me, that's a giant step forward.

Many thanks for your help. I know it must have been a stressful trip, but if peace is the outcome, it will have been well worth it. Please be assured of my deep respect and appreciation.

With all my best wishes,

Chuck

Talk about your pimp's reward. Here's a little something for yourself, my good man. Disgusted, I crumpled up the note and threw it in the wastepaper basket.

And then it hit me: What if it were true? What if my trip to Paris had actually made some sort of difference? The notion seemed absurd on its face, but what did *I* know about such things? Perhaps the empty charade I'd gone through was a necessary precursor to peace talks. If so...Jesus, it was unthinkable, but if so, the son of a bitch was on the brink of achieving something genuinely noble. And in my own small way I had helped him.

I reached into the wastepaper basket and fished out the note and then tried to uncrumple it, rubbing my forearm over the heavy paper in an attempt to smooth out the creases. For all I knew, this might just prove to be a historic document. Something, God help me, I might want to have framed and hanging on my wall.

THIS WAS THE BACKDROP, THE EDGY STATE OF PLAY, WHEN Gretchen's father decided it was time to pay us a visit.

I had met Arnold Burns once before, during inaugural week, but only very briefly. A quick hello when he arrived at some function just as Gretchen and I were leaving. Nevertheless, for all its brevity, our encounter was a classic case of mutual loathing at first sight. This time, though, it figured to be much worse. For one thing, I wouldn't get off with just a snarl and a fast handshake; there was an entire dinner on the schedule. And he was bringing his inamorata. And my mood wasn't anywhere near so benign these days.

Gretchen took it even harder than I did. "*Why* does he feel it necessary to do this to me?"

"He probably doesn't think of it in exactly those terms," I suggested.

But she was irked beyond reason. She had a lot of unresolved problems with him, of course, but she also didn't like him very much as a person. And goodness knows I wasn't unsympathetic. He was narrow-minded, bigoted, a bit of a blowhard, and sure of himself and his beliefs as only an ignoramus can be. But I think he probably also loved her and was bothered by the frosty relations between them. And just possibly wanted to make amends.

When I mentioned this last possibility, she was unimpressed, even dismissive. "Who cares?" she said. "I'm sure he'd like everything to be nice and cuddly now that he's old and feeling needy. But where was he when *I* was needy and *he* was riding high? Sorry, I don't feel I owe him a damned thing. You ain't done your chores if you wait till noon to milk the cow."

A Gretchenism. They still made me melt.

"So you plan on being rude to him?" I asked with some apprehension.

"No, no, I'll do my best. I always try, you know. Although it isn't exactly the ideal time for something like this."

"Tell me about it."

"And then there's poopsie to contend with, too. God help us all."

Poopsie, aka Beryl, was Arnie Burns's girlfriend. Gretchen hadn't met her yet, but hadn't let that get in the way of forming an opinion. "I don't *have* to meet her," Gretchen assured me. "Rehoboth Beach widow—probably sold their main house after her husband kicked and moved into the vacation home—sixty-eight years old, left a comfortable chunk of change by her late husband, and now she's snagged a former congressman. What more do I need to know? I can tell you what color she dyes her hair, how tight her pants are, what size boobs she bought herself. I promise you she plays a little tennis and a lot of golf. I know how she votes, I know what she thinks of…she'd probably call them 'the colored,' I can guess what TV she watches and what she drinks at cocktail hour. And trust me, she and Dad *do* have a cocktail hour."

"It's good how you're keeping an open mind. This should be a fun evening."

"Well, at least I managed to limit it to a *single* evening. Dad was agitating for more."

We met them at the bar of their hotel, the Washington Hilton, and from the look of things, they'd already had a few. They were quite jolly and seemed to have a bit of a buzz. Arnie was smaller than I remembered him, compact, wiry, and spry. And Beryl…well, I have to admit Gretchen wasn't far off. Her hair was a brilliant yellow not found in nature, she had a deep tan, and the skin of her face was stretched taut, giving her eyes a startled look. She had a loud laugh and a braying voice, and she made the error of calling Gretchen "honey" from the moment Arnie introduced them.

But then, I was seeing her through Gretchen's eyes. The fact is, for a sixty-eight-year-old woman she was impressively well preserved, attractive even, and there was a liveliness in her vulgarity that wasn't devoid of charm. And it was obvious that she and Arnie were having a great time in each other's company. The way he treated her, you'd think he was an adolescent in love for the first time. It led me to suspect she might be the first sexual enthusiast he'd ever encountered, and he simply couldn't believe his good luck. So if one were inclined to be charitable, it was possible to silently congratulate them on their having found each other so late in life and to consider them…well, almost *cute*.

If one were inclined to be charitable.

"This is the hotel where they shot Reagan, you know," Arnie announced after the introductions.

"*'They'?*" Gretchen said with a decided edge in her voice. That's when I knew we were in for a very bumpy night. Of course, she had known Arnie all her life, she was certainly more attuned to his sub-text than I, she doubtless discerned hidden significance where I noticed none, but still...she could have let this one go. But she obviously wasn't in a state to let *anything* go.

She had made reservations for us at Ruppert's, one of our favorite places, a tiny restaurant in a dicey neighborhood not far from Capitol Hill. But right after I'd found a parking place, while walking from the car to the front door, I suddenly recognized the mischievousness behind her choice. The food at Ruppert's was aggressively nouveau and the service staff unapologetically gay; Arnie and Beryl were *not* going to feel at home here.

"Maybe we should try someplace else," I said as we neared the door. "This restaurant is a little...I don't know, a little *quirky.*"

"Oh, that's sweet of you, honey, but don't you worry about us," said Beryl. "We eat everything. Don't we, Arnie? I tell you, when my late husband and I went to Japan one time, you should have *seen* the crap we ate. Raw stuff, slimy stuff, parts of things you didn't know they even had. It was all fine with us. Just as long as the portions were big."

"The portions are very small here," I said.

"The portions are fine," said Gretchen. In any case, we were already at the door and obviously not going to turn back now. She added, toward me, "You know you like this restaurant."

"Yeah, I mean I do, but—"

"Worried about the check?" said Arnie. "Don't you worry, Ben, dinner's on me."

Trust Arnie to try his luck with a veiled bit of antisemitism. Maybe I was being paranoid, but I don't think so; I believe I caught the intended subtext, this time without Gretchen's help. "Yes," I said flatly, "I assumed it was." I wouldn't give him the satisfaction of rising to the bait or even of letting on that I recognized what he was doing. Gretchen took my arm and gave it a squeeze, a wordless expression of solidarity. She was unquestionably on my side and authentically offended on my behalf, but I think she also liked it just a little bit when Arnie spewed some venom in my direction; she thought it made clearer to me what she had to put up with.

Once we were seated, Gretchen and I were treated to the predictable jokes about the place's preciousness, and after our waiter came to our table and walked us through the menu's obscurities, Beryl proclaimed, a little too loudly, "Isn't he just the most *adorable thing!*"—not sarcastically, you understand, she actually did like him—and Arnie, just a bit too broadly, mimed a limp wrist. Ugh. Gretchen was suffering visible paroxysms of discomfort—self-imposed, but no more bearable for that—and my smile was, shall we say, rather pasted on.

But still, all this was pretty much a standard-issue evening out with the visiting folks, boasting the expected, almost ritualized embarrassments and provocations. Gretchen reverted, predictably, to sullen college student surliness, and Arnie became a classic sadistic teasing dad, determined to bully a rise out of her. So it was bad, but bad in a familiar way and relatively manageable.

But then I made a mistake. My intentions were good: I wanted to divert him from the subject of the restaurant, on which his deliberately philistine commentary was causing Gretchen such grief (and attracting uncomfortable attention from neighboring tables). I thought my best bet was to get him talking about himself. So after the wine was poured and sipped, I asked him how the day had gone.

It hadn't, as it happened, gone well. He had taken Beryl to the House of Representatives to show her where he had served his country for so many years. He no doubt expected to be made much of, to be welcomed back by his erstwhile colleagues with a show of great good fellowship. He no doubt also expected to make a terrific impression on his new love. But it hadn't worked out that way. None of it had worked out that way. Many of the people he had known during his time in office were gone—members and staff alike—and those who remained had probably never much liked him in the first place.

As a consequence, it had been one humiliation after another. A leery guard had prevented the two of them from going onto the House floor for close to fifteen minutes while he had Arnie's bona fides checked. And of course Arnie didn't take it well, he made the sort of scene a loudmouth makes in that sort of situation. They encountered similar difficulties getting into the members' dining room, where they went for lunch, and once seated they found themselves totally ignored by the other diners there. He approached a few older members with whom he had served, and they responded without much interest or warmth. He even thought he descried something contemptuous in the way they greeted Beryl when he introduced her.

As he recounted all this to us, he started to get worked up. He had already polished off his first glass of wine and was making a serious dent in the second. On top of the drinks he and Beryl had had at the hotel bar, the alcohol must have loosened what few inhibitions he might otherwise have possessed. I noticed Beryl seemed to be getting apprehensive, which was interesting in itself; she didn't seem the type to suffer from self-consciousness or social discomfiture. Nevertheless, she even made one or two small efforts to calm him, but he waved her off unpleasantly. Not that she tried very hard. I think she must have seen him in this mode before and knew it was useless to try to stop him. He quickly generated a full head of steam and progressed effortlessly from the poor treatment he and Beryl had received to the various ways in which Washington was going to hell in a handbasket.

Crime, mismanagement, the incompetence of the school system, the corrupt indifference of the police, the ubiquity of "the colored" (chalk one up for Gretchen), ignorant foreigners driving all the taxis, rotting infrastructure, impossible traffic, gross rudeness. From there it was all too short a hop to politics. The stupidity of the House and Senate leadership, the obnoxious ubiquity of Jewish lawyers and lobbyists, the idiotic direction the country was taking... well, he finally got where he no doubt had wanted to go from the moment we all said hello in the hotel bar. He intended to spritz the administration, and now he had the requisite momentum and nothing was going to stop him.

He passed over policy questions lightly. A quick scornful dismissal sufficed. No, it was the personal failings of Charles W. Sheffield that engaged him. A charm boy, a lightweight, a pushover, an interloper who had no business in the Oval Office. A smooth-talking used-car salesman, a bald matinee idol, a mealy-mouthed lying son of a bitch. Not even a rogue, because a rogue at least had the good grace to wink at you while he was picking your pocket. Etc. He started from there and kept building.

Well, it was damned awkward, hard to know where to look. But I, the nonrogue's new head speechwriter, didn't really particularly care what Arnie thought of the president, except for the fact that he was talking much too loudly and starting to attract the attention of strangers. Gretchen, on the other hand, was beside herself. I couldn't tell whether she was angry because Arnie was saying bad things about her lover or because he was intentionally, provocatively belittling the administration for which both she and I worked; but either way, she was getting *very* angry. She didn't try to argue with him—it was impossible to get the floor away from him in any case—but I recognized the significance of her body language, and the look in her eye, and the color in her cheeks.

And then, just as I was wondering how we would ever get past this and manage, after he finally wound down, a semblance of a normal conversation over dinner, we were unceremoniously asked to leave. Just like that. It had never happened to me before or, I'd wager, to anyone else at the table. A man in a white shirt and dark pants came up to us and told us we weren't going to be served and he would appreciate our vacating the premises immediately. My guess is, he was a Democrat and that played a role in the ukase he issued, although Arnie's ravings were certainly loud enough and bellicose enough that they might have gotten us thrown out regardless of their political tendency. I doubt it, though.

Well, this certainly shut him up. And it may have been the only thing that could have. We were all dumbstruck for a moment, totally flummoxed. Arnie might have been tempted to make even more of a scene, except Gretchen murmured, "Thank God," stood up abruptly, and started out. I quickly followed, and at that point Arnie and Beryl really had no alternative but to do the same. Behind me I heard him saying something about "faggots," but I was on my way out the door and didn't turn around.

And you know what I was thinking? I'm not proud of this, but I was thinking, Well, there's a favorite restaurant we're going to have to scratch off our list.

We reassembled outside on the sidewalk. Everybody else looked shell-shocked, and it's safe to assume I did as well. Beryl was the only one who had the nerve to speak. "What do we do now?" she asked.

"Let's go someplace else," Arnie growled. "Someplace normal. The Old Ebbit's Grill or Blackie's, something like that." He was trying to put a brave face on things, but he looked a little crestfallen. He knew he had screwed up major league, whether he copped to it or not.

Gretchen wheeled on him. "Are you out of your mind?" she demanded. "Are you fucking crazy? Do you honestly think I'm going to go to another restaurant with you? I'm not going *any*where with you! I refuse to spend another *minute* in your company! This has been a complete nightmare!"

"Honey," said Beryl, "you're upset."

"Me? Upset? What in the world ever gave you *that* idea?" Just then, across the street from where we stood, a taxi was speeding by, and Gretchen, reacting with startling alacrity, hailed it. When it screeched to a stop, she turned to her father and Beryl and told them, "Take it. The driver's probably 'colored,' but I'm sure he can figure out how to take you where you want to go, back to your hotel or wherever the hell you want. Ben and I are going home."

"You're being unreasonable," said Arnie. But he was extremely subdued.

"Yeah," said Gretchen, "that's the problem. That's always been the problem. I'm so very, very unreasonable." She took hold of my arm and squeezed hard. "Come on, honey, take me home, *please.*"

As we walked toward our car, Beryl called out, "Good night." And Gretchen said to me in an urgent, humorless whisper, "Don't you dare!" I knew what she meant and resisted the powerful urge to say "Good night" back.

When we got in the car, as we were buckling up, Gretchen muttered, "Maybe now you can understand why I...I mean, you don't have to be Sigmund Freud to figure out why I might have some issues around authority figures. Not that I'm making any excuses." I had no answer. We drove home in silence. Then, as soon as we got through the front door, Gretchen began to cry. Standing there in the entrance foyer, still wearing her raincoat, still holding the key to our front door in one hand, her purse in the other. Great racking sobs.

My heart bled for her, but the tenderness was somehow blocked, paralyzed. I just couldn't make the effort necessary to overcome the internal resistance and take her in my arms. I could hear a mean little voice inside me saying, "Listen, since your boyfriend's such hot shit, get *him* to comfort you."

I stood there beside her for a moment, unsure what to do, and then gave up and went into the bedroom to undress, leaving her crying uncontrollably in the foyer. I had no solace to offer. Even though I knew she was crying for herself and me at least as much as for her father.

A COUPLE OF DAYS LATER GRETCHEN AND I WERE INVITED TO go to the Kennedy Center with the Sheffields to see a new production of *Don Giovanni*. I wanted to beg off, but since the evening was explicitly presented as a celebration of my new job, and since the social office—which in this case meant Gretchen herself—let me know we were the First Couple's only guests that night, there was really no way to decline.

And I was dreading it. But oddly enough, when the evening arrived, my mood took a reasonably good turn. Don't ask me to explain why, because I can't. Sometimes, perhaps, when you dread something enough, it's almost a relief when it finally happens. But I also think Gretchen may have had something to do with it. When she came to my office to fetch me, there was some subtle hint in her manner that suggested she and I weren't in an adversarial relationship tonight, we were stuck in the same foxhole, we were allies.

"Well," she said brightly, "a night at the opera!"

"If only Groucho and Harpo were along," I said.

"Nope, it's just a cozy foursome. We don't even get Gummo."

We actually giggled. I don't know what Gretchen thought about Claire Sheffield, I don't know whether she felt competitive or admiring or jealous or cattily critical or apprehensive or absolutely nothing at all. But regardless of her attitude, I imagine she must have felt somewhat exposed in this situation. Which tended to level the playing field a little as far as she and I were concerned.

"Are they going to feed us first?" I asked as we strolled across West Executive Avenue to the White House. "Some of them tasty White House victuals?"

"I wouldn't count on it," she said.

"I was afraid of that." And produced two granola bars, which I had carried in my pocket just in case. "It would be wrong to let our rumbling stomachs drown out Mozart." I handed her one, and she took it with a smile. For the first time in weeks we seemed to be on the same side, edgy about a social evening with the boss.

It was good I'd brought those snacks, too. When we arrived at the residence—a very rare occurrence for me, although I can't say whether the same was true for Gretchen—the Sheffields greeted us warmly but wasted no time. Down we went to the limousine, followed by a very quick hop to the Kennedy Center—it's amazing how fast you can travel when they stop traffic for you—and then up to the president's box. We sat in the comfortable anteroom before the overture and made conversation. Sheffield's valet opened a couple of splits of champagne from the little refrigerator and poured for us, and then the president of the United States raised his glass and offered me a short but gracious toast. This would have been a pretty heady experience under normal circumstances. Even as things stood, I found I could tolerate it. Maybe, I thought, over time you can get used to anything, especially if the recompense is sufficient. Ben Krause, shake hands with Dr. Faustus.

It really didn't seem too bad. The conversation flowed smoothly and innocuously enough. Of course, Charles Sheffield was an old hand at sustaining conversation under adverse conditions; it was part of his professional equipment. He'd had to campaign in Iowa, for God's sake! So he managed to keep things lively (if you regard self-referential monologues as lively). There was one odd moment when Claire Sheffield said something about the friendship Chuck had formed with Gretchen, about how much he enjoyed talking to her, and I didn't know where to look. What was the First Lady telling us? She wasn't a stupid or naive woman, not even slightly— on the contrary, she had a Manhattan-honed sophistication that was downright intimidating and left many a Washington wife daunted and stammering—so this was a difficult statement to deconstruct. Was she being mischievous? Did she know about the affair and assume I must as well? Or had the president simply told her that he and Gretchen talked occasionally, making it sound innocently mentoring, and she had accepted his version of events? It was impossible to say, and curious as I was about both Sheffield's and Gretchen's reactions, I was sufficiently concerned about my own that I avoided looking anywhere other than at my champagne flute.

Then President Sheffield brought his heralded political skills to bear, gracefully extricating us from the awkward little cul-de-sac into which Claire Sheffield had, intentionally or not, led us. He said how isolating his job was, how alienating in some ways, and what a lovely surprise it was to have been able to make two new good friends under such unpromising conditions. This time I did risk a glance at Gretchen—I was honestly curious about how she was taking this shameless bullshit—but now it was *her* turn to stare in fascination at a champagne flute.

So all in all, I wasn't sorry when we got up to go out to the box.

We were greeted by a standing ovation. I say "we," but I don't actually believe it was intended as a salutation to the president's new head of speechwriting. Nevertheless, it was exciting to be on the receiving end of such a demonstration, regardless of how incidentally. The president and First Lady waved at the crowd—Gretchen and I hung back—and he milked the applause for a little while, then made a silencing gesture with his arms, after which the two of them took their seats. But the applause didn't stop. There was no denying his popularity. This was no pro forma ovation, it was the real thing. These people wanted to show him they loved him.

I looked at Gretchen. She didn't look back at me. She was staring at Sheffield, and she was glowing, basking in the reflected glory. Damn! The stab of jealousy was intense. Here was my problem—or at least *one* of my problems—in a nutshell. Meanwhile Sheffield made a little show of laughing at the ongoing fuss, shook his head apologetically in our direction, then stood up and waved at the crowd some more, bringing renewed cheering. His approval ratings across the country were in the high sixties, but among this crowd they must have approached one hundred. He eventually gestured for silence again and resumed his seat. After a few more moments the applause finally died away.

So I was in quite a state when the overture started. Quite a state. Not knowing what the hell I felt, let alone what I *should* feel. Pride in my association with such a popular president? Pleasure at being part of his entourage? Outrage at his hypocrisy? Jealousy at Gretchen's manifest admiration? Helplessness at my inability to command a standing ovation when I entered a public space? Embarrassment at my pettiness? Probably all those and more. I was roiling.

But I somehow managed to settle down enough to enjoy the show. Good old dependable Mozart poured oil on my troubled waters. Until about halfway through the first act, that is. It's funny: opera has rarely had any effect on me as drama. The multiple levels of artifice have just been too great an obstacle for me to get past. But in this case I can say with confidence that without supertitles— without, in other words, my being able to understand and thus be affected by the drama—the remainder of the evening would have been far less troublesome than it was.

Because, you see, without warning I came face-to-face with scene three.

The situation is this: Don Giovanni's lustful eye has fallen on the peasant girl Zerlina. But, awkwardly for him, her fiancé, Masetto, is also present. During the recitative, Don Giovanni makes their acquaintance, then instructs his buffoonish servant, Leporello, to take Masetto somewhere else so that he will be free to have his way with Zerlina.

Don Giovanni: ...Is there a wedding?

Zerlina: Yes, I am the bride.

Don Giovanni: I am happy to hear it. And the groom?

Masetto: I am he, at your service.

Don Giovanni: Well spoken. At my service—this is the way a real gentleman speaks....

Zerlina: Oh, my Masetto has a very good heart.

Don Giovanni: As do I. I want to be your friend....My dear Masetto, and my dear Zerlina, I offer you my protection. [*To Leporello, who is flirting with some girls*] Leporello, what are you doing, you rascal?

Leporello: I, too, dear master, am offering my protection.

Don Giovanni: Hurry, go with them. Take them to my villa. See that they are served chocolate, coffee, wines, and smoked meats. Keep them amused, show them the garden, the pictures, the rooms, the furniture. Be sure my dear Masetto is happy. You understand?

Leporello: Oh yes, I understand....

Masetto: Sir...Zerlina cannot stay here without me.

Leporello: His Excellency will take your place. He will fill your shoes very well....

Soon, and heartbreakingly, Zerlina too urges Masetto to accompany Leporello; dazzled by Don Giovanni's position and glamour, she has succumbed to his blandishments and is eager to be alone with him. And then, in a short aria, "Ho Capito, Signor, Sì," combining farcical rage and real poignancy, Masetto, who understands perfectly what is happening but has no recourse in the matter, is forced to express his acquiescence. And he doesn't merely acquiesce, but feels compelled to do so in the servile and obsequious manner appropriate to his station. The music—this is Mozart's genius—tells us of his rage and anguish, but his language is thoroughly deferential:

Masetto: I understand, yes, sir, I do. I bow my head and go away. Since this is the way you want it, I make no objections. No, no, no, no, no objections. After all, you are a cavalier, and I really must not doubt you. I am reassured by the kindness which you show me.

It was during this aria that I stood up and stumbled out of the theater and into the anteroom. I just couldn't take it anymore. Believe me, that last sentence isn't merely a conventional expression. You don't walk out on the president in the middle of an opera while sharing his box (unfortunate choice of words!) unless you literally feel your life depends on it. I couldn't breathe, I felt dizzy, my heart was beating wildly, my vision was clouded, I felt faint. None of those are conventional expressions either.

I staggered into the empty anteroom, plopped myself down onto one of the red sofas, and tried to normalize my breathing. I was gasping for air as desperately as if I'd had the wind knocked out of me. It occurred to me—as a hypothesis I immediately rejected, mind you—that this might be some sort of heart attack. Even in my confused and panicky state, the odds struck me as close to nil, but my condition felt desperate, and I'm not usually given to hypochondria.

Why, I found myself wondering even while gasping for breath, why hadn't any contemporary composer written an opera about Masetto? He seemed like a perfect postmodernist subject. And I was available for free consultations to interested composers and librettists.

No one came to check on me. They probably just thought I had to use the bathroom. Still, it was distressing that Gretchen succeeded in mastering her concern, remaining in her seat until the end of the act. Was it that she didn't understand what had happened, or that she did?

Well, I poured myself some of the champagne left in an already open bottle, I closed my eyes and concentrated on my breathing, and I waited. There was no way I was leaving the theater without the others, not unless it was in an ambulance. So once my respiration and my heart rate returned to near normal, the most serious problem I had to confront was simple embarrassment.

Once again, it was the president who came to the rescue. He was awfully good at defusing difficult situations. When he, Mrs. Sheffield, and Gretchen came into the anteroom after the first act ended, he said jocularly, "So this stuff puts you to sleep too, eh, Ben?"

I have to admit it struck the perfect note. And he knew it; he exuded satisfaction at his own facile charm. That joshing tone, that implicit shared masculine disdain for the fine arts, masked any embarrassing problem I might have been having, from narcolepsy to a diarrhea attack to…well, to having Mozart and da Ponte rub my nose in my own pathetic cuckoldry.

Still, I felt a need to defend myself. Despite everything, I didn't want him to think me a philistine. "Nothing of the sort, Mr. President. I just suddenly got…It was a kind of claustrophobia. I couldn't breathe. It's never happened to me before."

Gretchen gave me a little look signifying that she understood. A small consolation. Had Masetto's plight passed by without her noticing how it seemed to comment on our situation, my sense of irrelevancy would have been even worse.

But Sheffield was still intent on defusing the tension his antennae were picking up. "You know, that happened to me once," he said. "During Bellini's *Norma*. A regular code blue, it was. My doctor prescribed two football games and a six-pack."

It was at this point that I noticed Claire Sheffield looking at me strangely. She had a very penetrating stare on those rare occasions when she let herself use it. "Perhaps you should go home, Ben," she said. Her tone was kindly, but her glance unwavering.

"No, no," I said. "I'm fine now. Honestly. And I'd never forgive myself if I missed the part where the statue drags Don Giovanni down to hell."

"Shit," said the president, "you just gave away the ending."

At which we all laughed. And after that, conversation resumed as if nothing out of the ordinary had occurred.

He had skills. There's no denying he had skills.

IT'S HARD TO CONVEY WHAT THOSE AUTUMN WEEKS WERE LIKE. Recent as they are, they seem impossibly distant now. The experience was nightmarish, but also, most of the time, strangely placid. I got up, I went to work, I came home, Gretchen and I had dinner, we went to bed. Once a week or so there might be a White House event we'd attend, and those never got easier for me. Other nights we often went to embassy receptions or book parties or some other of those countless festivities with which Washington keeps itself entertained. On weekends we tended to see friends the way we had before all this stuff happened. I don't know if the strains between Gretchen and me were visible to outsiders, but we both tried to keep them hidden.

You could even say we were getting along pretty well; the emotional temperature around our home wasn't what you'd call warm, but we maintained a level of affection that went beyond mere politeness. Our sex life was pretty minimal, which can be laid at my door rather than hers; she was the one who usually made the overtures, and I tended to demur. Not to be punitive, but because the constant spectral presence of Charles Sheffield in our bedroom tended to have a dampening effect on my ardor. I could function sexually, rather to my own surprise, but there wasn't much satisfaction in it, before, during, or especially after. I no longer felt that urge to *meld* with her that had once been so overpowering. On the rare occasions when we made love, I almost felt like a kid taking his medicine, awful as that is to say: doing what's required, but trying to distance himself from the experience and minimize the taste as much as possible.

And we were talking to each other much less—almost any topic eventually touched on areas that were out of bounds or fraught with anxiety, so it was easier not to try—even though our exchanges weren't especially acrimonious. We usually stuck to very concrete subjects, however: dinner plans, our social schedule, anecdotes from our workday (with great gaping lacunae, of course), things like that. Those lovely tender nights when we tried to convey our most personal and elusive feelings, when we shared and jointly analyzed the previous night's dreams, when we talked about the future, when we were open to each other without hesitation or reservation, those days were assuredly over. But for all that, it still wouldn't be inaccurate to say we remained each other's best friends.

Nevertheless, the whole situation felt profoundly unstable. There was no way we could live like this for too many more months, let alone for the remainder of Sheffield's term. We both knew it. Without admitting it, either to ourselves or to each other, we were both aware our relationship was moving into the endgame phase. The psychic toll was just too damned great.

Which was one of the things we didn't talk about.

One afternoon in late September while I was moping around my office, trying to assemble a draft of the president's comic speech for the Senator MacMillan roast, I got a call from Chris Partridge, my British reporter friend, asking if I was free for a drink that evening. He suggested meeting at the Jefferson Hotel.

"Is something up?" I asked. I hadn't seen much of him since the campaign, just cordial greetings in passing, so the invitation struck me as odd.

"Ah, Krause, you see right through me."

"No great achievement."

"Actually, there *is* something I'd like to ask you about, yes. But candidly, there may be some sort of good-fellowship phenomenon operating here as well. I've rather missed your company. Please keep that to yourself if you don't mind."

"Your reputation's safe with me."

"Can't say the same, of course."

"Of course. Seven?"

"Splendid."

Something to look forward to. Any diversion would be welcome today. The MacMillan roast was proving to be a major headache. Was it George S. Kaufman who said, "Comedy is a serious business"? He should have tried writing it in the White House.

Not that I was crazy enough to try it the way Randy had insisted on doing it, gathering the humorless drones on his staff (myself included) and ordering them to write something funny. No, I knew there had to be a better way, although I wasn't sure what it was. So I phoned the head of speechwriting from the previous administration and asked him how he'd handled the problem. (One of the things that drove Sheffield nuts during the spring was having his efforts unanimously declared inferior to those of his predecessor, so it seemed worthwhile to try to learn from the other guy's success.) The fellow had gone back home to South Carolina to write his novel, but the White House switchboard located him in seconds rather than minutes. And although he was a Republican, and so presumably wished us anything but well, he turned out to be the soul of good-natured collegiality. In fact, he began by fulsomely praising the inaugural address and the Africa speech and telling me what a good job our shop was doing. That's how he referred to the speechwriting office: "your shop." I in turn complimented the work *his* shop had done on the humorous speeches and confessed my own bewilderment about how to approach them.

"Yeah," he said in his southern frat-boy drawl, "those things are a bitch, aren't they? But here's what I finally figured out. People get a call from the White House, they return it. Doesn't matter who they are, doesn't matter how busy. And when they call back, if you let 'em know the president would appreciate a favor, by God they'll do it. Happy to oblige. Tickled pink at the opportunity."

"Okay."

"So that's it. Find out which comedians and comedy writers and so on are on your side. Or at least, aren't on *our* side. The neutral ones'll probably help out too. Then call 'em and tell 'em you need jokes. I promise you, by the end of the day you'll have more fuckin' jokes than you know what to do with. Some of 'em'll even be good. And listen, it'll be a lot easier for you than it was for us. Don't repeat this, but... *Republican comedians?* I mean, Jesus wept."

It was good advice. Most of the people I called got back to me the same day, and a sizable majority were willing to help. For days our fax machines were awash in jokes. But selecting the right ones, assembling them in an order that made some sort of structural sense... the task may have been purely editorial, it certainly beat having to write the damned thing, but still, it was making my eyes cross. After several days of it I no longer could tell what was funny and what wasn't.

And of course, my heart wasn't really in it.

So anyway, meeting Chris Partridge for a drink that evening had some appeal. If the truth be told, the drink had appeal all by itself. Chris Partridge was a perfectly welcome addition, but in no way essential.

He was already at the Jefferson when I arrived, at a table, sipping a drink and munching on nuts. Immensely tall and rather portly, he was impossible to miss in any setting. "What'll you have?" he asked. "I'm drinking Maker's Mark. One of your country's few indispensable contributions to Western civilization. Jazz, Raymond Chandler, and good bourbon. That's about it."

"You're leaving out the First Amendment."

"Not in the same league, dear boy."

"I'll have whatever you're having," I said.

He caught the waitress's eye, pointed to his glass, and then held up two fingers. Learning how to deal with the help is certainly one of the great achievements of the British public school system; I could have been waving my arms wildly for minutes on end before I'd gotten any service.

We schmoozed desultorily for a while. Was my summer pleasant? Had Gretchen and I been able to get out of town for any of it? How was I enjoying my new position? Did I know anything about a projected state visit by the new Iranian president? Any word on the Supreme Court vacancy?

I think he was waiting for the bourbon to enter my bloodstream.

And then, when he judged the event must have taken place, he looked around the room briefly, lowered his voice, and murmured, "Off the record?"

As I believe I mentioned earlier, in a concentrated six months of wide-ranging and quite candid conversation he had never burned me, not even once, so I had no hesitation about agreeing. "What's on your mind, Chris?"

"There's a rumor flying about," he said. "We're not quite at the feeding-frenzy stage yet, but should that happen, I'd very much like to be at the head of the queue. First shot at the carcass and all that. You understand?"

"Of course. It's not an especially complicated notion."

"No…quite so. Now, of course I understand you work for the chap, so you may be disinclined to help me, but…" He lowered his voice even further, so that I had to lean forward to hear him. "Strictly *entre nous*…d'you happen to know anything about a presidential lady friend?"

I suppose I should have seen it coming. But I hadn't; I was completely blindsided. I felt my face get hot and hoped the effect wasn't visible. I took a slow sip of my drink. "Lady friend?" I echoed. Just buying time.

"A little something on the side? Oval Office playmate? Hail to the chief's willy?"

My official duty was to shoot this one down as quickly as I could, of course, but the task was made difficult by inconvenient emotions and about a thousand questions clamoring for answers. Where had he heard this? What exactly had he heard? Did he know more than he was letting on? Was he asking me because of my connection to Gretchen, or was it merely a coincidence, my happening to be a familiar and reliable source?

But how could I find out without giving something away?

"Jeez," I said.

"Should I take that as a confirmation?"

"Good God, no."

"Not that you'd necessarily be aware of it, of course." He was giving me a searching look. Very disconcerting. "But you haven't picked up any buzz? Or seen anything?"

"Do you know who the person in question is supposed to be?"

He shrugged. "Some trollop. I don't have a name."

Was he lying? I decided, finally, that he wasn't. We weren't particularly close, but we were at least friendly enough so he wouldn't be torturing me like this just for a giggle. Nor was it in his interest to alienate me.

"I can't help you, Chris."

"Because you don't know, or won't say?"

"Does it make any difference? I can't help you."

He took a long time before nodding. "No, I suppose it doesn't really make any difference. And of course there's no reason for you to answer regardless. This was a shot in the dark. And not the primary reason for seeing you. Just thought I'd combine a little business with the pleasure."

"You do know," I said, "that there's going to be talk whatever the truth might be. There was talk during the campaign too."

"Oh," he said quite casually, "but it was true during the campaign. That's established."

"It is?"

"You mean to tell me you don't know?"

"Was it…are we talking about the same woman?" Since Gretchen had never traveled with candidate Sheffield, this was a little test to see if Chris's information had any credibility at all.

"No, no, a different situation entirely." I could see he was debating with himself whether to tell me more. Then he gave in to the impulse. "Liz MacMillan. You know, the senator's wife. Went on for quite some time. Years. We all had it, but…well, it's almost impossible to double-source something like that. And in any case, nobody had the stomach for it. Even the tabs blew it off."

I was shocked, I admit it. Perhaps I should have been unshockable by now, but I was shocked. "Are you certain of this?"

"About as certain as one can be in these situations. It was pretty generally known."

"But…I mean, Jared MacMillan's supposed to be his best friend."

"Mmm."

"Was he supposed to…That is, did he know about it?"

"Was he *complaisant,* you mean? You see, we English actually have a word for it, the situation being so strangely common among our upper classes. However, in MacMillan's case, I'm afraid I don't have the answer."

We looked at each other for a short while, each thinking his own thoughts. Finally, I was the one to flinch. "Where'd you hear about this?"

"About Liz MacMillan? Or the current one?"

"Either. The current one."

He shrugged. "Now, now, old boy, you don't actually expect me to reveal that sort of information, I'm sure. You know I won't. It's why you trust me. Because I've demonstrated you *can.* Which also means, should you hear anything, or have a change of heart…"

"I'll definitely keep you in mind, Chris."

"Good lad. The story is ripening like a fine old Stilton, and if someone has to break it, why not your amigo Chris? D'you see what

I mean? I'm not asking you to be*tray* the man exactly, merely to give me a leg up if the ladder's already been put in place. It may even be in his interest for you to do so."

"Oh yes? How do you figure that one?"

"Well, after all, if shit and fan are on a collision course, wouldn't it be better for your fellow if he gets his version of events on the record as quickly as possible? Before the story has been told by, *defined* by, those who wish him ill?"

"Yeah, right, I'll bear that in mind."

He was enjoying himself hugely now, enjoying my evident discomfort, and enjoying the sound of his own voice. "It may not be Pulitzer material, I'll grant you that. But still, being first out of the box with it would be quite a coup. Attention, as your Arthur Miller might say, would have to be paid. Quite a *lot* of attention, I daresay." He was practically rubbing his hands together in gleeful anticipation.

"You don't regard this story as beneath you?"

"Good heavens no! A good story is a good story. This would be a *great* story."

"Bloodsucker."

He thought I was joking and smiled malevolently. "Gives a whole new meaning to the words 'president johnson,' don't you think?" And with that little mot out of the way, he began asking me about whether I'd made my Christmas plans yet. He didn't encounter any resistance on my side; there was plenty I was desperate to know, but it would have been a serious mistake to show too much interest right then. He had, as they say, a reporter's instincts. I knew I had to be cagey, wait for the right opportunity. So it was only later, as we were leaving, that I asked, as casually as I could manage, whether anyone else he knew was pursuing the story.

"The saga of the Sheffield squeeze? A few of us. There's gossip being traded all over town, and some of us are working one angle or another....But it's a tough one to nail down. As you say, there's always going to be talk, so no editor's willing to rely on a single secondhand source. Or even several secondhand sources. A few Polaroids would do the trick nicely, of course." His eyes danced. "So how to describe it? There's this sort of *impending* feeling at large in the land. I suppose you could say it's the quiet before the storm. But why do you ask? Want to give your chaps a heads-up?"

"Something like that." I breathed an internal sigh of relief; at least my question had been timed right, at least he hadn't picked up my personal stake in the answer. But in a larger sense, I felt no relief whatsoever. What Chris had told me was a very disturbing development indeed.

"Well, then you're forewarned, but perhaps you needn't worry overmuch, despite my admittedly ghoulish enthusiasm. Historically, unless one of the parties sees fit to complain for some reason, these things don't usually go anywhere. And the way it works..." He shook his head. "Not that I understand it, mind you. The whole transaction is a total puzzlement to me. But as long as no one gets pregnant, there aren't usually complaints. I suspect presidential mistresses are the rule rather than the exception, we just don't usually learn about them. That Clinton business a few years ago was an anomaly. A fluke. The sex got caught in the onrushing headlights of a zealous prosecutor pursuing a financial scandal. In the normal course of events, people go into these things with their eyes open, they seem to understand the implicit bargain. The commander in chief gets his adoration and handy cooze, and the woman gets... well, that's actually the part I don't understand. What *does* she get? Hurried, furtive sex with someone who couldn't care less about her. Why is that attractive? What could possibly make that appealing? But there you are. It's the way of the world. She gets *proximity*. Or some sort of notch on her belt. And for a certain kind of tart, I suppose that must be enough. And since there usually aren't any complaints, the thing normally stays private."

There was a brief crazy temptation to voice my own complaint, but it wasn't too hard to resist. Whom would I be punishing, after all? And what would I accomplish, other than a brief catharsis followed by remorse, possibly a lifetime of remorse? So I just bade Chris good-bye and wondered instead whether I should report to Gretchen about this conversation.

I wanted to, and at first I thought my reasons were relatively friendly and well intentioned: if these rumors were more than idle journalistic speculation, it must mean that she had been a little incautious, in which case it seemed like a good idea to warn her about it. Had she confided in someone besides me, for example? Had her Oval Office comings and goings been observed by any East Wing colleagues? Had she openly displayed her affection in a setting where someone might have been able to observe her and the president?

But as I drove home, I realized my motives weren't nearly so friendly as I wanted to believe. In fact, I recognized I was furious with her. All over again. How could she do this to me? How could she do this to *herself?* There was obviously something punitive in my desire to let her know her secret was in jeopardy—I could easily find a way to slip in a generic warning without scaring her—and something vindictive in the urge to let her know about Sheffield and Jared MacMillan's wife. Once I understood that, I decided not to tell her anything. My intentions were too tainted.

After all, it had not been so long ago, on the flight back from Paris, when I was maliciously toying with the possibility of outing her myself. I would never have done it, but the thought hadn't entirely lacked appeal. Let Sheffield learn something firsthand about humiliation, let Gretchen see what it felt like to lose all self-respect. Of course, my own degradation would thereby be exacerbated as well, and would become public currency. And the real beneficiary of the resultant scandal wouldn't be me, certainly wouldn't be my relationship with Gretchen; it would be our political opponents, people I abominated. Perhaps the real victims wouldn't be Sheffield and Gretchen and I, but the people of East Africa, some of whom might actually have their lives saved if Sheffield retained his political predominance.

So okay, it was a bad idea. And examined closely, a terrifying prospect. I could only hope Chris was right when he said, toward the end of our little drinks session, that the story probably wouldn't go anyplace. But coming to that conclusion did nothing for my peace of mind.

When I got home, Gretchen was already there. That wasn't always the case these days. I didn't want to talk to her, though; the effort not to indulge my bitterness and my anxiety was too draining to leave energy for anything else. So I nodded a hello and went into the kitchen to nose around for something to eat.

She followed me in. "Ben?" she said.

So I was forced to look at her. And notice how solemn and how troubled she looked.

"What is it?"

"Something's come up. You won't like it."

"For a change." My first thought was, She's heard about the rumors too.

"Just listen, okay? The president's going on a trip to California and the Pacific Northwest next month."

"Yeah, you're right. That breaks my heart."

"Please, Ben. The thing is...the thing is...They just told me this afternoon. I'm on the trip. I'm scheduled to travel with the presidential party."

IN *THE RAGMAN'S SON*, KIRK DOUGLAS DESCRIBES ONE OF HIS early Hollywood experiences. He had recently arrived from New York, had just gotten his first good movie part, and, to celebrate, had finagled an invitation to his first fancy Hollywood party. He had even managed to arrange a date with an attractive young woman. When they arrived at the party:

"People were laughing and having a good time....I didn't know anyone and I was rather shy. But I was enjoying it, especially when I looked up and, my God, there was Jimmy Stewart! Then, a man with his back to me turned around—Henry Fonda! All happy and laughing. I just took it all in, a kid from Amsterdam, New York, gawking at the stars I had seen on the silver screen.

"It grew late: the party began to dwindle. I asked my date if she wanted to go home. She said, 'Yeah, sure.' Just then, Henry Fonda's wife motioned to her. The two women moved away a bit and chatted. I watched, wondering what they were giggling about....

"My date came back. I said, 'Shall we go?' She replied, 'Just a minute, I'm going to the ladies' room.' So she went into the ladies' room while I waited. I watched Henry Fonda and Jimmy Stewart, who had come alone, talking with Frances Fonda. They were all laughing. I thought how nice it would be to be a part of it. Maybe some day I would be. Quite a few minutes went by. There was a general exodus. Everyone was leaving, and I was still waiting for my date to come out of the ladies' room. I became concerned; perhaps she was ill. I asked one of the waitresses to please see if everything was all right. She obligingly checked and came out with puzzling news: 'The ladies' room is empty.'

"The musicians were packing their instruments, and the clean-up crew was moving in. I didn't know what to do. I was really perplexed. Then one of the waiters came up to me and said, 'Are you waiting for that blond girl you were with?'

"'Yes.'

"'Oh, she left a half hour ago with Jimmy Stewart and Henry Fonda. They went out the back door.'

"I couldn't believe it. My date had taken the proverbial powder....Finally, through my thick skull, I realized that Frances

Fonda had probably said, 'Why don't you dump this nobody and join us for a drink? We've got Jimmy Stewart with us—he's got no girl.' Of course, [my date]…jumped at the opportunity. Anything to be with a star. My evening of celebration had turned into a humiliating experience…."

The first time I read this passage, all I noticed was its awful unadorned cruelty, and that element certainly remains paramount. But the story says other things to me now as well. Among its points of interest is the degree to which, forty years and innumerable, unimaginable successes later, Douglas still obviously finds the memory of that night rankling. It's the sort of humiliation too profound for subsequent triumphs to eradicate. The way he was treated said to him, in the kind of brutal terms that permit no alternate, anodyne interpretation, You're nothing, you don't count at all, you're such an utter nullity that your feelings don't merit even the most minimal consideration.

Perhaps even more interesting is the obvious although unstated fact that, had he attended the same party a mere year later, the very woman who ditched him would have cheerfully ditched whoever she was with in order to be able to go off with him instead. He would have been the exact same person he had been the night she noticed nothing but his thoroughgoing insignificance, but he would have looked completely different to her. What counted, in other words, wasn't whatever *star quality* he may have possessed, it was the less ambiguous imprimatur of *stardom;* and although neither she nor he knew it, the world was in fact about to confer that seal of approval upon him. Which would, of course, have changed everything. All his charismatic qualities, the same ones that somehow eluded his date on the night in question, would have been blindingly evident to her and to everyone else only a few short months later.

Context is everything. And these days context was my worst enemy.

★

"YOU CAN'T GO," I SAID. GRETCHEN HAD PICKED THE WRONG
night to tell me about the jaunt to the West Coast. In the brief time
since I'd left the Jefferson, my conversation with Chris Partridge
had had an increasingly corrosive effect; those questions he had
posed stirred emotions I had been trying too hard to tamp down
for too long. To add to such a volatile mix this new prospect, of
Gretchen going along on a presidential junket in the role of traveling comfort girl... Something finally snapped. I didn't even experience it as rage. It felt colder and calmer and more certain. There was
almost a kind of pleasure in it.

"I didn't *expect* to go," protested Gretchen. "I didn't *ask* to go. No
one consulted me. They just went ahead and included me on the
flight manifest."

We were at the kitchen table. I was picking at some cold chicken
and sipping from a glass of white wine. "Who told you? Alice
Hahn?"

"Yes." She looked surprised. "How'd you know?"

"Just guessing," I said. Being a mensch. "Anyway, it must be
thrilling for you, the prospect of flying on Air Force One. What a
fabulous induction into the mile-high club."

"I just found out, Ben. Please believe me."

"It doesn't matter whether I believe you or not. Just like it doesn't
matter when you found out about it. You're fixating on irrelevancies.
What I'm saying is, I'm not going to roll over this time. If you go,
you're coming back to a different apartment. I'll buy your share of
the condo from you and that'll be that."

She thought about it for a few seconds. "Is this so different for
you? From what's gone before, I mean."

"I don't know whether it's that or whether I've just finally hit the
wall. At long last. But there's only one reason you've been included
on this trip. You know it and I know it. And we both know it isn't
to arrange social events aboard Air Force One."

"Yeah." She sounded thoughtful. "It's really awfully presumptuous of him, isn't it?"

"Well, I'm sure you've given him ample reason to believe it would be acceptable."

She didn't rise to the bait. Something else was on her mind. "I mean, he might at least have asked first, don't you think?"

"I really don't care to discuss his manners," I announced, sounding distressingly prim even to myself. But I didn't let the distress break my stride. "That isn't an issue that engages me."

She looked up at me, then down again. "It isn't his manners I'm complaining about exactly," she said. "You've misunderstood me. I mean, it *is*, but it goes beyond that. It has to do with…it has to do with the way he treats people."

"Gretchen—"

"I mean, I know that *is* manners, in a way. But it sort of goes deeper too, doesn't it? It's about something more fundamental than just observing the niceties, saying 'please' and 'thank you' and so on."

"Gretchen. Please. I want you to listen carefully. This is important."

Her eyes slowly rose again to meet mine. "Okay."

"Remember I once asked you what you would do if I gave you an ultimatum? And you said you didn't know? Well, I want you to focus on what I'm telling you now. The time has come. I'm giving you an ultimatum."

"Because of this trip?"

She still seemed to be taking things calmly. Which may well be what pushed me decisively over the edge. What right did she have to be so calm when my whole life had become a bubbling cauldron of self-doubt and misery?

"No, not just the trip. Everything. The whole deal. The whole demeaning, insulting deal. Being treated like, because I'm not the president of the United States, I don't count, I don't have any rights. I can't take it anymore. I won't take it anymore. It's him or me."

Then I recalled the distinction she had once made. "Or if you prefer, it's the situation or me. Whatever. I can't live like this. It's ripping me up. I can barely stand to get out of bed in the morning."

She left a very short space of time before saying, "So we finally got there."

"You don't sound too surprised."

"By the timing, maybe. A little. I thought there might be more of a buildup first. But I assumed it was going to happen sooner or later."

"Does that suggest you have an answer ready?"

"I do, in fact." She reached across the table and touched my hand. "You can consider it over. Between him and me, I mean."

I waited for some big emotion. This was a moment for which I'd been hoping over the course of several miserable months. But it felt anticlimactic, unsatisfying, not really settled. So I issued no war whoops, did no victory dance. All I said was, "That's it?"

"That's it. Case closed."

"Did you know that's how you were going to respond?"

"Well, I wouldn't say that, exactly. But…as soon as you put it to me, I didn't have any doubts this was the right thing to do. It feels like a burden's been lifted, to be honest."

It all seemed too easy. "What's the catch?" I asked.

She laughed. "There isn't one, honey." Then she ruined the moment by adding, "Not really."

"I knew it."

"No, honestly. But…look, I've thought quite a lot about the possibility of this happening, as you can probably imagine."

"I've tried to keep my imaginings to a minimum."

"And I just…Please try to understand it from my point of view. I mean, I know I've asked you to do that too many times already, but just this once more, okay? The thing is, it's not going to be easy. I mean, ending a relationship is hard under the best of circumstances, and he's…he's…you know, he's who he is. *What* he is."

"Maybe you should have given a little thought to that in advance."

"You're right, I should have. I should have done a lot of things. I made a big mistake." She reached for my hand again and insisted on holding it. I wanted to pull away, but somehow that seemed too definite and hostile an act, so I compromised by leaving it loose, not returning her grip. "What I want from you is, is…what I'd like from you is some *time*. Not to stop sleeping with him. I won't do that anymore. That's over. And I won't go on the trip. Okay? I'll tell Alice I can't, I'll say there's some sort of conflict, I'll figure something out. But let me finesse this thing for a little while, let me wait to confront him till the time's propitious."

"Why?"

"Honey, I know him. I know how unpleasant this could be. Or how easy. He could get vindictive and vengeful, or he could feel avuncular and generous. It all depends on his mood, and on circumstances that have nothing to do with me. Why risk ruining everything when it won't have any effect on the thing you care about? Let me pick the opportunity."

"Are you scared to do it?"

"*Yes!*"

I didn't expect that answer. It didn't seem like Gretchen. I always considered her fearless. "What are you afraid of?" It was curiosity, not argumentativeness, that prompted the question.

"What am I afraid of? *He's the president of the United States.* You don't just casually reject the president of the United States."

"So don't do it casually."

"Please, Ben. This is going to be the hardest thing I've ever done."

"Harder than betraying me?"

She didn't miss a beat. "Yes, even harder than that." Which was the kind of unblinking honesty, not always one hundred percent welcome, I had once taken for granted from her.

"Do you want *me* to do it?" Actually, as soon as I said it, I felt a shiver of fear myself. I still hadn't shaken free of his thrall. But I was willing. Some part of me was even eager. Damn the torpedoes.

"No!" Her vehemence was startling. She must have caught my eagerness. After the echoes from that single loud syllable finally stopped reverberating off the linoleum, she went on, "I don't want him to know you know. Know you *knew*. Ever. Anyway, it isn't your problem. I got myself into this, I should be the one to get myself out."

"When?"

"I don't know. In a day, in a week, in a month. Does it matter? The important thing is, it's over. Whether he knows it or not, it's over. That *is* the important thing, isn't it?"

"I suppose."

Perhaps it should have been. But for some reason it didn't feel like it.

THE FOLLOWING COUPLE OF WEEKS WERE REALLY PECULIAR. Gretchen acted as if the chapter were closed, but the whole situation seemed to me to shimmer with ambiguity. I wanted closure. I *needed* closure. Something definitive and incontrovertible. I tried not to ask her if she'd done the deed—tried not to ask on a daily basis, that is—but I have to admit I woke up every morning hoping that this would be the day she finally took care of it.

Should it have mattered?

I don't know. I'd kept this secret so close to my vest that I had no reality check, no way of determining if I was being reasonable, or even rational. All I knew was, the business felt unfinished. Now, I admit there was a practical aspect to this: Gretchen had lied to me about her relationship with Sheffield over the course of almost two months, so there was no guarantee she wouldn't do it again, wouldn't tell me she was no longer sleeping with him while continuing to do so. But I didn't really believe that was likely. Not after what we had just been through. My occasional fleeting suspicion wasn't the real reason the situation felt so incomplete.

It was more, I think, a matter of knowing what Sheffield saw when he looked at me. This feeling wasn't about Gretchen at all, really, it was about him and me. When he looked at me, he saw someone he had bested, someone over whom he had decisively established his personal supremacy. An area of social geography he had effectively colonized. And as long as he saw it, I felt it. Regardless of the situation on the ground. I felt like a whipped cur. It wasn't a pleasant feeling.

Gretchen, as I say, tried to reestablish our relations on their old footing. And I was amenable in principle. But you can't restore trust by simple fiat, not after it's been abused like that. And not when there was this great unexplored landmass, this terra incognita, this island of Atlantis, lying there between us. If in the past our late-night discussions had been characterized by total unfettered candor, well...that option just wasn't available to us anymore. She had declared too much off the table. I found it impossible to open myself up to her unreservedly when I knew how much she was keeping closed.

I occasionally let myself ask her whether she'd seen the president. Usually the answer was no, a couple of times yes. If I managed to stop myself from saying anything at that point, she often found the pressure of the ensuing silence too great to cope with and would offer some small fragment of information. "He sent for me, but I said I had a doctor's appointment, and I left work early just in case he checked up on me, so the lie would have some credibility," she told me once. On another occasion she said, "Yes, but when he started to get...you know, to get friendly, I told him I had my period, and when that didn't seem to slow him down much, I said I had a blinding headache. That did the trick."

After a few of these, I asked whether she thought he might be starting to notice that something had changed between them.

"I don't think so. You have to understand, Ben, we never did get together with any regularity. Even at the height of it, it wasn't like a daily occurrence. It was pretty catch-as-catch-can. When he had the time and the inclination, I'd get a summons. So two or three misses, which is all it's been, wouldn't constitute a pattern in his mind."

"Didn't you ever find this demeaning?"

"No. Yes. What can I say? It was *sui generis*. I didn't judge it by normal standards."

"Lucky Chucky. How wonderful to be granted that sort of indulgence. Dispensation unavailable to the rest of humanity."

Something else was happening to me during those weeks. It may sound paradoxical, but I was finally getting *angry*. Really angry, I mean. Angrier than I'd been when the affair was going on. Maybe the anger was a luxury I couldn't afford before. Or maybe, now that the smoke had cleared, I was no longer afraid that it would drive Gretchen away from me and toward Sheffield. Or it might have been that I needed the immediate threat to the relationship to be ended before I could experience clearly the sheer humiliating injury to which I had been subject, purified of the anxiety and jealousy and neediness that were clamoring for pride of place. Or maybe it was the threat of exposure hanging over my head like a sword of Damocles ever since my last conversation with Chris. Whatever it was, Gretchen's implicit attitude that everything was now all right further stoked the fire.

Now, I still didn't want to do anything that might drive her to change her mind, so I didn't yell and scream and galumph around the apartment. Not my style in any event. But I was usually smoldering, in a pretty constant state of emotional oxidation. I didn't express it much, and when I did, my outlets tended to be passive-aggressive. I just couldn't find a toehold for anything direct. So, for example, I finally told her about the conversation with Chris Partridge.

She was gratifyingly disturbed. "You mean there are rumors about the president and me? Why didn't you tell me this before?"

"Well, it was all pretty vague. Chris asked me if I knew anything. He didn't know it was you, I'm pretty sure he was being honest about that. He didn't have a name. But he had heard *some*thing. He said people were talking."

"Jesus." Her face had darkened noticeably. "I don't know how this could have happened. We didn't flaunt anything."

"Sometimes flaunting isn't required."

The corners of her mouth came down. "It would be just awful if it came out. For *every*body."

"Well," I said, aiming for airiness, "you know what they say around here: Never do anything you wouldn't want to read about in *The Washington Post* the next day."

After a little interval she said, "Liz MacMillan? Really?"

"That's what Chris said."

She shook her head, whether with disapproval or disbelief or dismay I can't really say. But she seemed abstracted and preoccupied the rest of the evening. Which I took—such was my mood—as a victory. There was so little else available to me in the way of satisfaction.

I mean, constantly haranguing her wasn't a viable option. No discernible purpose would be served by simply reiterating the same old complaints, no matter how pervasively and constantly they demanded expression. She could legitimately ask me what more, other than telling Sheffield it was over, I wanted from her. And I wouldn't have had an answer. I did desperately want her to tell Sheffield it was over—I hated the fact that she still hadn't—I wanted it more than words can express. But that only scratched the surface. Nevertheless, beyond that, I couldn't have even said what I wanted. I wanted her somehow to be able to wave a magic wand that would cause the whole affair never to have happened. Apologies were all she could offer, but they didn't begin to equal in weight the distress I had suffered and was continuing to suffer. The scales weren't in equilibrium.

A few months ago there was a terrible accident in some small midwestern town, one of those horrible meaningless catastrophes in which a drunk truck driver ran a red light and rammed a school bus, killing several children. It happened when not much else of note was going on in the world and so got a lot of coverage for a little while. One of the town's local ministers was all over the news shows during the following seventy-two hours, urging the bereaved parents to search deep in their hearts and find forgiveness. And I remember turning to Gretchen in bewilderment and saying, "What does that *mean?* Do you understand it? What does forgiveness consist of in a case like this? Does it mean you stop grieving for your children? Or that you no longer blame the driver for drunkenly ramming their school bus? Does it mean you shake hands with him and say, 'Oh well, these things happen'? You can say those sorts of words, but what do they signify?" I did feel indignant, I suppose, at the minister's sanctimoniousness, but it wasn't indignation I was expressing. I was expressing honest ignorance.

I don't mean to equate my trivial domestic misadventure with a tragedy of that magnitude. They occupy different universes. I'm just noting for the record that you can't always will yourself into letting go.

WHEN CHRIS PHONED ME AGAIN, IT DIDN'T COME AS MUCH OF a surprise. I'd been dreading the other shoe dropping since our last conversation. The threat he posed had never been totally absent from my mind, even if there were occasional days when, through an effort of will, I managed not to contemplate it too closely.

"Jefferson Hotel, seven o'clock?" he said. No malarkey about good fellowship this time.

"Is something up?" It's surely unnecessary to describe the sinking feeling in the pit of my stomach.

"Ah, dear boy, have a little patience."

A little patience proved to be necessary. He kept me waiting this time. I sat at a small table, nursing my bourbon, contemplating the horror in store, while the minutes ticked away. He arrived almost a half hour late.

"Dreadfully sorry. Awash in mortification. A problem arose at the office, I extricated myself as quickly as I could."

I suspected something more sinister and calculated: give the prisoner a chance to stew in his own apprehensions before you initiate the third degree.

"Well," he said after ordering, "I suppose you have some inkling of what this is about." Ominously, he extracted his reporter's notebook from the inside breast pocket of his jacket as he spoke.

Playing it too cute would only be a red flare for someone like Chris, so I didn't bother acting dumb. "Seamy Oval Office sexual shenanigans?" I hoped putting it that way would disturb some residual sense of journalistic high-mindedness—he worked for the *Guardian,* after all, not some Rupert Murdoch rag—although it wasn't too likely it would have any significant effect.

"There's my headline," he said with a beatific smile. "Thank you." He cleared his throat. "Now listen, young Krause. I've reached a point—I realize this isn't pleasant for you, but please, hear me out— I've reached a point where I have most of the story. This thing *is* going to happen. So the decision you need to make is whether to try to influence the way it's told by cooperating."

I finally understood the meaning of that sentence beloved of second-rate thriller writers, "His blood ran cold." No amount of emotional preparation braced me for this moment. And here's a peculiar psychological datum: I suddenly thought of Arnie Burns, how he would react when the story appeared and what Gretchen's first conversation with him afterward would be like. Jesus. Details like that…there would be thousands of them before this nightmare was over.

So I gave it one last shot. "What if I were to tell you I've nosed around and I can say unequivocally the story is untrue? That if you publish, you'll just embarrass some innocent people and get egg all over your face?"

He regarded me sadly. He took a sip of his drink. He shook his head. "Ah, Krause, I expected better of you, I must say. I don't believe we've ever outright lied to one another, even on those occasions when we both knew we were *using* one another. If you had simply offered a 'No comment,' you might not have helped your boss, but at least your honor would have remained intact. Whereas now…" Another sigh. "Unlike some of my colleagues, I actually take such matters seriously. Perhaps you haven't noticed, but I do."

I *had* noticed, which was why his words drew blood. No matter how many other concerns were driving me, it was galling—worse than galling—to think that I was compromising my integrity in order to protect President Sheffield, especially since what I was protecting him from were the consequences of the injury he had done me. Could there be a more painful demonstration of my marginality?

Chris's tone was gentle when he said, "Let's start over, shall we?" He hadn't intended to wound, he'd wanted merely to goad, and the look on my face must have revealed that he'd hit something far more vital than what he'd been aiming for. "Why don't we try this? I'll tell you what I have and what I don't have, and you can choose to respond to it in any way that's comfortable for you."

Comfortable for me.

"Right off the bat—an appropriately American choice of expression, no? unless the bat in question is a *cricket* bat, of course—in any event, right off the bat, let me say, I don't have the bint's name."

A relief on two counts. One of them is obvious. The other concerned my relationship with Chris. I was now free to believe that, had he known of my connection to the story, he wouldn't be subjecting me to this ordeal.

"I'm confident I'll get it eventually, but I don't have it yet. Here's what I *do* know about her." He opened his notebook, flipped past several pages, and consulted it before continuing. "She's romantically linked to someone who works in the White House. Besides the POTUS, I mean. She's around there all the time, she's either a volunteer or she might even have some low-level job. She's a lot younger than Sheffield. She's extremely attractive. You know, great heaving tits and all that sort of thing. The standard package of dealer extras. She's supposed to have invited his attentions, to have made her availability pretty clear to him."

He looked up from his pad. "In a way, you can't even really blame the fellow, can you? I suppose there are quite a few men out there who would have found it difficult to resist, given the circumstances. A pretty girl makes adoring cow eyes at you, shows you what she's got, throws herself at you, aggressively offers all manner of exotic fleshly delights... one needn't be some species of perverted sex fiend to succumb."

"In theory," I said. My voice came out as a dismayed croak. But through the awful pain of hearing Gretchen's behavior described in those terms—and the excruciating pain of assuming the description had to be more or less accurate—something else occurred to me. Chris had a source in the White House itself. He had to. There was no other way he could have gotten hold of some of this information. And it had to be someone who didn't have a policy job, it had to be a nonpolitical staffer of some sort, a career person; that was the only explanation for the lacunae in what Chris had learned.

He looked up at me, a little surprised by the choking sound I'd made. But then he went on, "On the other hand, once Liz MacMillan is factored into the equation, one is rather less inclined to be charitable. This hardly appears to be an isolated occurrence, does it? We're not exactly talking about the president as innocent victim. In fact, in a case like this it's a bit of a challenge to distinguish predator from prey."

Even though I had nothing to say to that, he held up his hand, as if to forestall me. "Old boy, I simply *must* visit the gents'. Whatever wisdom you were about to impart, I trust it will wait. Shan't be but a moment."

He rose laboriously and left the room in a funny sort of loping waddle.

That's when I did something unforgivable, the memory of which still makes me twist about in self-loathing and will probably torment me right up to my dying day. Something unforgivable and indefensible. Although—without asking for absolution—I will still say in my own defense that the danger facing me seemed sufficiently extreme to justify extreme measures. But I wouldn't feel very confident if I had to rely on that argument at the Pearly Gates admissions office.

What I did was, I waited until Chris rounded the corner, watching him until he was no longer visible from where I was sitting, and then I reached across the table and snatched hold of his reporter's notebook. I hated myself even at the moment I was doing it, but I didn't give myself time to weigh the ethical ramifications. I couldn't let the opportunity pass.

His handwriting was unexpectedly clear, almost girlish in its rounded legibility. I flipped through the pages quickly. The early ones had nothing to do with Sheffield at all. Then there were some notations about the president's answer to a question about Iran at his most recent press conference, a couple of other notes about aspects of the administration's domestic policy. And then I came to a page with the word "NOOKIE" written in large block capital letters at the top, underlined twice. Underneath, and for several pages thereafter, were notations and more or less random jottings about the president's affair. Much of what he had just been telling me about Gretchen was there. And plenty of other things. There was one particular page that contained more jottings than any other:

SS—Jfrsn Htl 3 Oct:
2–3 X week
Summons! = lk srvnt w/bell?
Lnch
Cktl hr
Sndys aftr Chrch
Xpsed brst
Nrvs gigl
BJ OO. Fk flr & sofa OO + little room
Mstly day—Nts, wkends = special trt
"Chuck"
1ˢᵗ ldy call during Bj
1nce at Cong. Pcnc

I couldn't make sense of everything on the page, although I stared hard at it, trying to commit it to memory. What I did understand was painful in the extreme, however, and that last notation gave me an especially sharp twinge. There had been a picnic supper for the Congress on the South Lawn of the White House in the late spring, and Gretchen and I had attended. As was our custom, we'd spread out and mingled separately during the evening. It wasn't a very interesting event—its main purpose was to provide House members and senators an opportunity to bring their families to the White House—and I became antsy pretty quickly. But when, at a certain point, I felt it was probably okay to leave, I couldn't locate Gretchen. I searched for her for about fifteen minutes, wandering from group to group, before I noticed her coming out of the mansion. "Just had to use the bathroom," was her explanation when I caught up to her.

But evidently, at least according to Chris's notebook, her explanation was far from constituting the whole story. Did she regard me as
particularly gullible that evening? I wondered now. Did she and
Sheffield have a hearty laugh at my expense, as well as the expense
of all those congressional families, while the two of them frolicked
in the Oval?

But other than exacerbating my misery, none of this had any
practical use that I could see. It made me hot and sweaty with ret-
rospective jealousy, and it confirmed my sense of impending
calamity, but it didn't give me a clue as to what to *do* about the danger. Had I violated one of the fundamental tenets of civilized behavior with only *this* to show for it?

I put the notebook back on Chris's side of the table, making an
effort to situate it in exactly the position in which it had lain before
I picked it up. I felt like a two-bit thief. No, I felt worse; after all,
Chris had been questioning my sense of honor only a few minutes
before, and now I had surrendered the last pitiful shreds.

And I hadn't even accomplished anything.

He was back soon enough so that I was glad I hadn't dawdled
over the book. He evinced no sign of suspicion. I'm sure his opinion of my character, even if it had taken a recent downward turn,
still didn't encompass the possibility I would do something as contemptible as read his private notes.

"Well," he said after he'd eased his bulk back into his chair. He
took a sip of his drink, looking at me levelly over the rim of his glass.
"I've given you some time to think about all this. Or perhaps I
should say, my bladder has extended you that courtesy. Now I'm
wondering whether there's anything you might want to tell me. It
can be mitigating, it can be exculpatory, it can be anything. Additional information would certainly be welcome, but any reaction at
all might prove useful. We can go on deep background if you'd prefer, we can go entirely off the record. But it would reassure my edi-
tors no end if I had a second source."

"No comment," is all I said.

He nodded. "Okay, fair enough." He smiled at me, his first friendly smile of the encounter. "That's certainly preferable to your lying, speaking personally rather than professionally."

He apparently thought my honor had been restored. It was touching how much this seemed to please him. Touching and acutely distressing.

As if this weren't enough, on my drive home a new source of anxiety occurred to me. Just what I needed.

I was already contemplating the sheer awful horror of Chris's story appearing. Headlines everywhere, stretching out over the horizon. Gretchen's picture on the covers of all the newsmagazines, with, no doubt, a snide sidebar about me inside. Interviews with Arnie and Beryl and everyone else she'd ever known, going back to kindergarten. TV news specials devoted to the story. Inquiries from Barbara and Diane and Larry and Katie. Late-night talk show hosts devoting their entire opening monologues to our situation. Reporters camped out on our front door. The phone ringing constantly. Friends unable to talk about what was happening but unable to talk about anything else either. Sidelong glances from strangers, with accompanying obbligato stage whispers, wherever we went.

And that aspect of things would never really end. If anything either of us accomplished in the years left to us merited an obituary at our death, the first paragraph would inevitably mention our participation in this scandal. That was guaranteed.

And then there were the political ramifications. My dislike of Sheffield didn't extend to wishing his opponents well, but his opponents were the only ones who figured to benefit from the story's becoming public. The president was popular now, and some of that popularity might survive something like this, but there was no question his effectiveness would be damaged and his detractors energized. Among the most likely immediate victims would be the Kenyan people; if we were successful in negotiating a peace treaty that involved some U.S. participation, it would require Senate approval. Should Sheffield be perceived as seriously weakened, it might well be dead on arrival.

These were things I already knew, had already agonized over on countless occasions. But as I say, something else struck me during the short drive home. Something selfish. Something relatively trivial, at least compared to these other things. And, given the circumstances, something terribly ironic. But no less troubling for all that: If Chris's story appeared, *I was the one who would be blamed.*

It was so fucking unfair. I had lied, I had surreptitiously read Chris's notes, I had resisted every opportunity to be vindictive (tempting though some of these opportunities had been). I had done everything in my power to prevent the story from appearing. But none of that would do me a lick of good. People knew I was friendly with Chris, they knew I had been a good source for him in the past, dating all the way back to the campaign. And they would have to figure that, as the injured party, I was feeling aggrieved, and therefore I had a motive to want to expose the affair. There wasn't a thing I could possibly say that would convince a soul I'd had nothing to do with it. Not a soul. No one in the press corps, no one in the White House, not the president, and not Gretchen.

Benedict Arnold Krause.

Whatever minuscule hopes I still had of salvaging my relationship with Gretchen would be over. My White House employment would be over. My employability anywhere in politics would be over as well, since no one could ever trust me again. I'd be poison. Persona non grata. A rat. Even the journalists willing to kiss up to me to get an interview would regard me as a contemptible turncoat, would feel like washing their hands after they were done exploiting me. Now, it's true that my lifelong love affair with politics had become a pretty tattered thing over the past couple of months, but politics was all I knew, and I had achieved some success in it. I sure as hell wasn't fit for anything else. But no avenue in politics would ever be open to me again. They probably wouldn't even let me lick envelopes.

The view through my windshield that night was one of utter desolation.

I had to find a way to stop the story. There was no way to stop the story. Christ. I was dead meat.

I DIDN'T SAY A WORD TO GRETCHEN WHEN I GOT HOME. I DIDN'T eat dinner. I simply went to my desk and played solitaire on my computer until eleven. Then I got into bed with no expectation of sleep. Expect nothing and you won't be disappointed.

Sometime around two, I got out of bed quietly, put on my robe, went back to my computer, and booted up the solitaire game again. It was during that game that inspiration struck.

I suddenly recalled the first line on that awful page of Chris's notebook:

SS—Jfrsn Htl 3 Oct.

And felt like Archimedes in his bath. All at once I understood what it must mean. Since Chris's source figured to be some career employee in the White House, "SS" must be shorthand for Secret Service. Some Secret Service agent must have been talking to Chris; it was the only possible explanation. The two of them must have met for drinks in the Jefferson Hotel bar (Chris's favorite meeting spot, as I had every reason to know) on October third, and the agent in question must have taken the opportunity to divulge all that hot information, all those OO BJs and so on. Chris had dutifully recorded every salacious detail.

It wasn't much, perhaps, but it was an opening. Now I had to figure out how to find a wedge.

I waited out the dawn sitting at my desk. I dozed off a few times but always awoke with a jolt after a few minutes. When the clock read six-thirty, I reached for the phone. I knew it was still too early, but I'd been as patient as I was able.

Joe Burton answered on the second ring with a gruff hello.

"Did I wake you, Joe?"

"Hell no, I've run six miles already. Who is this?"

"Ben Krause."

He expressed no surprise. "What can I do for you, sport?"

Joe was the closest thing I had to a friend in the Secret Service. Not that we were close. But we occasionally chatted and joked around a little, and the feeling between us was always amiable. A very dark, very tall black man, built like a linebacker, Joe had a face that glowered menacingly at rest, but if you said something that amused him, he would break into the broadest, most infectious grin imaginable. Often, when I was at some White House function where I felt awkward or out of place, I would gravitate toward him and shoot the breeze for a while. It was always comfortable, a port in a storm, and he seemed to appreciate the company too, even though his eyes never stopped surveying the room.

"It's very sensitive, Joe."

"This a private matter?"

"Not exactly."

"How sensitive?"

"Very."

"Sensitive like…? You mean Pointer sensitive?" "Pointer" was Sheffield's Secret Service code name.

"That's what I mean."

There was a long pause. Then he said, "Not on the phone, sport."

"You think you're bugged?"

"Probably not. Probably you're not either. But if it's sensitive…"

"Why take a chance?" I said, finishing for him.

"That's my thinking." Another long pause. "You don't want to talk at work, obviously."

"Why take a chance?"

"We may just talk ourselves out of talking at all."

"No, that isn't an option."

"Yeah, I figured." I heard his tongue tapping moistly against the roof of his mouth for a few moments. Then he said, "You a religious fella?"

"No."

"You know the Greek Orthodox Church near the National Cathedral?"

"Yeah."

"That work for you?"

"Just don't tell my parents."

Well, I have to admit I was spooked. It had never occurred to me that my phone might be tapped, and I certainly never thought I would have to engage in this cloak-and-dagger stuff, skulking about like a spy, in order to talk to anybody about anything. I tried to reassure myself: excessive caution went with the man's job. But still, seeing as how he was involved with security, he also might just know something the rest of us didn't.

Anyway, as a result of his infectious wariness, I didn't park on Garfield, right near the church, even though there were spaces available, but drove an extra couple of blocks and parked down on 34th Place. I even waited in my car for a minute or two to see if there were any signs I'd been followed. There weren't, of course.

As I walked back up to the church, I tried to steel myself for the uncomfortable conversation that was about to ensue. I was on pretty shaky ground, I knew that much, and in addition, if Joe was aware of what had been going on between Gretchen and the president— as seemed likely—he might regard my role in all this with withering scorn. I, Ben Krause, acting as the special security detail for my own cuckolding. The OIC, no less. But concerns like that had to be secondary now. If he lost respect for me…well, I'd already gone through the same experience. Welcome to the club, Joe.

I entered the church. It was empty. His choice had been shrewd, clearly; any eavesdropper would be glaringly obvious in this setting. I wasn't sure what sort of behavior was appropriate—my experience of any church, let alone a Greek Orthodox one, was pretty meager—but I took a seat in a pew somewhere in the back and waited, staring down at my knees. After a few minutes I heard footsteps, and then Joe sat down beside me. He was so large, his presence seemed to alter the gravitational field around me.

We looked at each other. The expression on his face was neutral, but his eyebrows went up expectantly.

"Morning, Joe," I whispered.

"Got a feeling this is worth my time," he whispered back. "But do me a favor, don't take no more of it than you have to."

"Okay," I said. "There's a reporter. English guy. Christopher Partridge. Know him?"

"*Of* him."

"He has a story about…about Pointer. About Pointer and a young woman. Probably gonna appear in the next few days or so."

"About carnal relations between 'em, you mean?" His voice remained expressionless. There was no hint of what he knew and what he didn't.

"Yeah." I felt myself flushing and was glad the room was so dark.

"Go on."

"The thing is…the reason I'm talking to you…I have reason to believe his source is somebody in the Secret Service."

I finally got a reaction out of him. He turned slowly until we were facing each other again, and then, when our eyes locked, he said, "You shittin' me, sport?"

"I'm pretty certain."

"Who?"

"Well, I don't know that."

He expelled some breath. "Wish you did."

"Would it help to know he or she met with Chris Partridge at the bar at the Jefferson Hotel on October third?"

"Might."

"Is there anything you can do, Joe?"

He broke the stare. "Listen, Ben. Our job is to protect the president and his family. Don't mean diddley what the courts say, we don't just protect his *body*, we protect *him*. Period. If I told you the sorta shit we've handled over the years, the sorta messes we've cleaned up after, you'd be amazed. Not that I'm going to. We keep what it is we do to ourselves. That's the unspoken rule. And we don't ever talk to no fuckin' reporters."

"Should I take that as a yes?"

"Take it as an I'll-do-my-best." He gave me the barest hint of a smile. "Fact is, what you tell me, I'm *pissed*. Which is another way of saying, I'm *motivated*."

There was something reassuring about the man, no question, about his strength and his clarity. And he sounded determined. But still, I didn't leave the church feeling a whole lot of reassurance. There was so little time, and he certainly didn't make it sound as if his determination was matched by any commensurate confidence of success.

But at least it was out of my hands. There was some small relief in that, along with huge frustration at the enforced passivity.

I didn't phone Joe for the rest of that day, although it was an ongoing struggle not to. But the next day, Friday, which also happened to be the day of the Jared MacMillan roast, I phoned him just before lunch. Since we were both at work, I chose my words with care. "That matter we discussed, Joe. Have you made any progress?"

"Not enough," he said. "But I haven't given up. Still working on it."

I had a meeting with the president in a couple of hours. It wasn't going to be easy to focus.

THE FORMAL OCCASION FOR THE JARED MACMILLAN ROAST WAS a fund-raising dinner for the Spina Bifida Foundation, of which the senator was that year's honorary chair. The event was to be held that night, Friday night, and President Sheffield had scheduled a run-through of his speech for the afternoon. The participants, other than the president himself, were a theater director flown down from New York to provide coaching, the director of communications (my immediate superior in the White House hierarchy), and I. I was in no mood for comedy, but participation wasn't optional. And to be honest, even with all my anxiety about Chris's story, some part of me looked forward to the meeting. I felt good about the work my office had done.

You had to be able to compartmentalize if you worked in the White House. A capacity for denial was one of the prerequisites for success.

Sheffield loved the speech. He greeted the three of us at the entrance to the Oval Office with the speech in his hand, and he was laughing out loud. "This is great stuff, Ben. Hilarious. I knew you'd come through for me. The biggest challenge for me tonight will be trying to keep a straight face."

It *was* a good speech. No particular credit to me, except for gumption. I had asked fourteen or fifteen of the best comedy writers in the country to write jokes for me without any recompense, and most of them had gone ahead and done it. I then had the luxury of culling the very best of their best. The result was pure gold.

The rehearsal session, which was conducted at the table in the private little study just off the Oval Office, went smoothly enough. It was the director's first experience with the president, his first experience with any president, his first time in the White House, so he was a little awed at first, somewhat hesitant and apologetic about offering suggestions. But Sheffield was so receptive, and in this context such an accommodating performer, that the man quickly got over his nervousness. Soon he was giving the president line readings, explaining how to time a punch line, telling him how to stand and how to calibrate his facial expressions, even letting him know, quite harshly, when he was making bad choices. At one point he even said, with undisguised impatience, "Jesus Christ, you just fucked up the funniest line in the speech," although a fraction of a second later he realized what he'd said and to whom he'd said it, and he looked pretty abashed. But Sheffield's casual, "Sorry, let me try it again," got us past that potentially awkward moment in jig time.

Sheffield was usually obstreperous and resistant when told what to do (George Bush used to grumble to overzealous subordinates, "If you're so smart, why ain't you president?" so maybe the attitude comes with the office). But in this case he was sufficiently worried about the speech, and sufficiently unsure of his ground, that he uncomplainingly did precisely what he was told. And it worked. The director had adopted a shrewd approach; he didn't try to transform the president into a polished comedian, which would have been hopeless, but rather found a way to use Sheffield's customary oratorical style, his well-known, frequently parodied dry detachment, for comic effect. "Just forget you're being funny," the director told him. "That's absolute *death* to comedy. By all means have a good time up there, but tell yourself you're giving a straight speech."

Sheffield nodded. "Yes, good, that'll also keep me from laughing." He was a pro, after all, good at internalizing that sort of direction. And indeed, although he had broken into giggles several times during his first two read-throughs, he had no difficulty controlling the impulse from then on. In general, his next go-round was much funnier.

I was awfully glad the director was there. Not so much for the service he was rendering, but because he did so much of the talking and demanded so much of the president's attention. I still had the problem of finding it hard to look at Sheffield, hard to talk to him, hard to know how to behave in his presence. One-on-one with him was torture. It was a relief to have someone else occupying his line of sight. Especially now, with the time bomb of Chris's story ticking away. The president apparently didn't know about it, but I did; it was impossible not to think about it while pretending to focus on this other matter. And hard not to do my duty and warn him about it, although, under the gruesome circumstances, that wasn't an option I considered seriously.

There was only one *overtly* odd moment during that afternoon meeting, and it came at the very end, as we were leaving. Sheffield thanked us all, the director particularly, and then turned to me and said, "You'll be there tonight, won't you, Ben?"

"Yes, sir." I tried to return his level gaze, but I just couldn't. I looked down at the carpet. And when I forced myself to look back up at him, I saw something quizzical in his eye. Rather like the look he had given me at our first meeting after he had returned from Cape Cod, when he'd asked me if I was ill.

But this time he didn't say anything, other than, "Well, good, see you there."

"Break a leg, Mr. President."

Which provoked another quizzical glance. This wasn't my own imagining. The look was evident enough so that the director felt obliged to offer, "That's a show biz expression, Mr. President. It means good luck."

"Yes," said Sheffield, "I know what it means."

It occurred to me only later that he hadn't asked if Gretchen was planning to attend as well. An untypical omission. But just as well, since she had announced that morning that she planned to stay home.

"Why?" I asked. Not because I was so eager for her to be there, but it wasn't like her to skip a big evening like this.

"Oh, I don't know…I've kind of had it with those formal events. And if you think the speech was a success, well, I can catch it on C-Span later."

"It doesn't have anything to do with being around the president?"

She colored slightly. "I don't think so. I've been around him a few times. And anyway, there'll be lots of people there. I can handle it."

"Or Liz MacMillan?"

She colored more deeply. "I just don't want to go, all right? These big Washington events...they're not fun anymore. And they're all exactly the same. The same people, the same conversation, the same food. I don't want to get dressed up, I don't want to do my hair, I don't want to put on makeup. I'd rather stay home and watch a video. If you really want me to come, I will. But it isn't my preference."

"No, I don't mind going alone. The vibes figure to be crazy enough regardless."

She didn't argue. I took her silence as tacit acknowledgment that the situation might feel a little more awkward than she had wanted to admit. God knows it was hard for me to imagine it being anything but. The president was going to give a speech ridiculing the man he'd apparently cuckolded, and was going to do so in front of both their wives. And the speech had been written by another man he had cuckolded. That the speechwriter's girlfriend chose not to attend seemed like a sound decision, on the whole.

And she didn't even know that Chris's story was an imminent threat. I hadn't told her. On balance, I couldn't see the point. If it happened, it happened. There was no way you could prepare yourself for something like this. Advance warning would accomplish precisely nothing.

I phoned Joe at about six-thirty. There was no answer.

At seven I pulled on my Armani and presented myself to Gretchen. "So...how do I look?"

"Yummy," she said. "Maybe you should stay home tonight and let me prove it."

Which immediately made me uncomfortable. It was a habit I was trying to break, God knows, but my thoughts ineluctably went to Sheffield, fastened on to how *he* must look in his tuxedo, and I couldn't help wondering if she'd ever told *him* he looked yummy, in that same seductive drawl.

FROM *THE TWELVE CAESARS* BY SUETONIUS (TRANSLATED BY Robert Graves):

> "...[Caligula] made advances to almost every well-known married woman in Rome; after inviting a selection of them to dinner with their husbands he would slowly and carefully examine each in turn while they passed his couch, as a purchaser might assess the value of a slave, and even stretch out his hand and lift up the chin of any woman who kept her eyes modestly cast down. Then, whenever he felt so inclined, he would send for whoever pleased him best, and leave the banquet in her company. A little later he would return, showing obvious signs of what he had been about, and openly discuss his bed-fellow in detail, dwelling on her good and bad physical points and criticizing her sexual performance."

I CHOSE TO WALK TO THE WASHINGTON HILTON, TO AVOID parking hassles. It was an uncomfortably warm night, but the distance was only a few blocks, and I thought the exercise might even help me rid myself of some of the suffocating tension I was feeling. It didn't. I quickly realized that the avoidance of parking hassles was the only satisfaction this walk was going to provide.

About a block from the hotel, I heard a nearby car horn beeping insistently. No great rarity in Washington, but when I looked over, I saw a blue Lexus alongside of me with a dinner-jacketed Chris Partridge at the wheel. Not a welcome sight. I waved a hello, hoping that would cover it, but he shouted peremptorily through the window, "Get in," and then pulled over a few paces ahead of me. He wasn't in a parking lane; he was blocking quite a bit of traffic behind him. Considering the circumstances, it didn't make sense to have an argument about whether on the whole I'd just as soon walk, so I slid into the passenger seat. The horns of the cars behind us were blaring cacophonously. He shifted into first and we started to move.

"Well, hello, Chris," I said. "You're awfully dapper tonight."

He didn't look at me. He hadn't looked at me since I'd climbed into his car. "You bastard. You fucked me good and proper, didn't you?"

This sounded encouraging, but I wasn't quite ready to breathe a sigh of relief just yet. "I beg your pardon?" I said instead.

"Gave me a bloody great buggering. I only wish I knew how you managed it."

"Do you care to explain what you're talking about?" I couldn't tell yet whether he was really furious or just peeved.

He finally deigned to glance over at me. "You may remember, there was a story I was working on? I asked you about it once or twice?"

"I dimly recall."

"I'm sure it will come back to you if I jog your memory slightly. A certain powerful personage involved in an illicit sexual dalliance?"

"Oh yes."

"Well, there's another interesting new development. That is, it's a development *I* find of interest, and perhaps you will as well. It concerns my source. I had a superb source, you see. Only one, mind, which was a little worrisome. But a uniquely good one. Perfectly situated, you might say. And absolutely unimpeachable."

"Sounds excellent." My heart was beating faster, and I was saying a silent prayer: Please let this go where it seems to be going.

"Yes, excellent indeed. Except for one small problem. One which has arisen very recently. *Very* recently. That's the new development to which I referred a moment ago. Would you like to guess what it might be, or shall I just tell you?"

"Just tell me."

"This superb source of mine phoned me not an hour ago. And he had the most dreadful confession to make. Covered in ignominy, he was. It seems he had invented the entire story. Fabricated it out of whole cloth, if you will. And now, for some reason, he was having an attack of conscience. He felt obliged to admit his wrongdoing to me, and felt it necessary to withdraw his remarkable tale before either he or I found ourselves in hot water as a result of its appearing in print. He told me he was not merely disavowing the story, but was prepared to denounce it publicly if it were published. And to initiate legal action. To claim I had misquoted him and twisted his words to mean the opposite of what he intended."

We had reached the hotel entrance. "I'll get out here," I said to Chris. I didn't fancy finding myself in an underground parking garage with him in his present mood.

He pulled to a stop and offered me a grim smile. "Any theories as to what might have happened?" he asked.

"Perhaps he had one of those born-again experiences?"

"No, Krause, you don't seem to understand, although I see how you might be confused. His recantation isn't credible. He was telling the truth before, he's lying now. That's my sincere belief. So what do you make of that?"

"Just a bad break, I guess." I was out of the car. I shut the door and inhaled deeply. I felt as if a death sentence had just been commuted.

He lowered the passenger-side window in order to be able to continue the conversation. "I wonder if... that is, someday, I wonder if you'd expend a little intellectual energy and see if you can explain to me how this sort of thing might have happened. Who knows? You might come up with a provocative hypothesis. What do you think?"

"No comment."

"Ah, Krause, fuck you and your entire clan," he said, and without another word drove off in the direction of the parking garage. It was that parting shot that assured me our friendship wasn't irreparably damaged. I was pleased. It was a small and—I admit it—a completely unmerited bonus.

ONCE IN THE HOTEL, I WENT STRAIGHT TO THE MEN'S ROOM. MY heart was beating so fast, I felt a little faint. I washed my face and tried to dry it with one of those stiffly abrasive but nonabsorbent paper towels, I combed my hair, I took a couple of minutes to steady myself. The arrival of the cavalry had been timed just a little too closely, at least for a nervous system like mine. I wasn't built for that kind of excitement.

I took the escalator down to the basement level, where the banquet room was located, and made a beeline to the bar. The whole situation was beginning to catch up with me. I really needed a drink. Using my sharp elbows—well whetted after so many months of White House employment—I managed to secure a gin and tonic. While standing at the bar, I greeted a few people I knew, said hello to a few people I didn't know but who had greeted me, and then bumped into Chris. Literally bumped into him. The crush around the bar was so great that when I pivoted to move away, I slammed right into him, spilling some of his bourbon. He took it in stride. He occupied so much space, mishaps like that must have been a way of life for him.

"No harm done, old boy," he said. "I'll just give the dinner jacket a good suck when I get home." He busied himself with a napkin for a few moments and then, guiding me away from the bar, said, "The word on the street is, Chucky's speech tonight is all *your* doing." As if our earlier conversation, now all of ten minutes old, were completely forgotten, mere ancient history. The fellow was a pro. "True or false?"

"Only if you think it's good."

"I have every confidence."

"Actually, Chris, I hate to say it, but your sources have led you astray yet again." It was gratuitously mischievous to put it that way, but my mood was so expansive, I couldn't resist. "The speech was basically a cut-and-paster. If you want to praise me afterward, don't bother saying anything about the content, just tell me the structure was seamless. That's all I can claim as my own."

"Much too modest, I'm sure." He glanced around, then lowered his voice. "Strange business altogether, wouldn't you say? Chucky roasting MacMillan while the poor berk's wife is right up there on the dais looking on. The pressing question is, which of the three will be squirming the most?"

"It's different at those elevations," I said, my tone flat. I wanted to discourage further palaver on the subject.

"Only if one lets it be." My tone hadn't discouraged him in the slightest. "In any event, I'd hazard Mr. Sheffield will manage more comfortably than the other two. He's the one who emerged unscathed from their unpleasant little *folie à trois,* or so I'm given to understand. But then, he never *is* scathed, is he? Other people get scathed in his stead. The designated scathees, you might say. He leaves great trains of *mutilés de guerre* in his wake as he blithely follows his bliss. Perhaps it's because others are unaccountably willing to do his dirty work for him."

"He's fortune's darling."

"Yes, Lucky Chucky. It's not his nickname for nothing." Then something else occurred to him. "Damn me, Krause, this almost slipped my mind! I was so preoccupied with my source's perfidy that I…It's related to that business, you see. The one we were discussing outside. You know the one I mean?"

"Oh yes, Chris, I haven't forgotten."

"Good. You see, in my recent annoyance with you—yes, I freely admit I was feeling annoyance, although I'm pleased to report affection is slowly returning—but in my annoyance with you, I neglected to tell you something I'm quite confident you'll find rather interesting."

I had really hoped we wouldn't be discussing any aspect of the story anymore. But no, he was like the Little Engine That Could. Or maybe it was the Little Engine That Couldn't Help Itself.

"Why bother, Chris? What's the point? If the story's dead, why not just let it lie? What more is there to talk about?"

"Well, the song may have ended, but the melody lingers on. And it *is* damned interesting, don't you agree? I mean, the amorous goings-on of the great and famous…who can resist that?" This last was accompanied by a furtive glance around and a conspicuous lowering of his voice. As if, by being discreet every tenth sentence or so, he was defended against any accusation of indiscretion.

Sighing inwardly, I said, "*I* can."

But he wasn't having any of that. "Bosh. Don't pretend to be highfalutin with me, old boy. Your mind's in the gutter just like everybody else."

"But not that particular gutter."

"Please, you've killed my story, no hard feelings, you were doing your job and you did it damned well. I'm still puzzled how. But the point is, now that you've done it, there's no call to float above the fray. Enjoy the passing parade. I'm in possession of a fascinating new piece of information. And since I can no longer publish it, I'm prepared to offer it to you gratis. Well, perhaps gratis overstates the case. As an investment. Someday you may find a reason to share with your dear old friend Christopher again. Someday there may be a story you won't consider harmful to your hero."

"A new piece of information?"

"Yes. Yes indeed. Crucial information, you might say."

What could that mean? Nothing good, that was certain. "Crucial information?"

"Mmm. I have the name, old boy. I have the name. Curious?" He smiled at me, and I saw an image of malice incarnate. "You *must* want to know this."

Oh Christ. This was really sadistic of him. Not that I didn't have it coming, I'd screwed him six ways to Sunday, but he was certainly getting his own back now, with interest. To be toyed with in this manner was awful, to be carefully set up just in order to be knocked down. He'd obviously been saving the moment for when it would punish me the worst. My stomach started to churn, and a hot wave of nausea washed over me. I took a deep breath and extended both arms outward from the elbow, gin and tonic in one hand, the other an open palm. Not asking for information, just offering surrender. I tried to brace myself, but you might as well try to prepare yourself for the dentist's drill. Some things you just have to take like a man.

At least it wasn't going to become public knowledge, so I could take comfort from that. I'd accomplished the main thing, and so the humiliation in store would remain personal and intimate, just him and me. Sure, he might share it with a few colleagues over drinks at the Jefferson Hotel bar in the course of the next year. There would be talk, unavoidably. But compared to my worst imaginings, this was a gas pain rather than a heart attack.

"All right, go ahead, Chris," I said. "I'm ready. Tell me all about it. Have your little fun."

He smiled with pleasure, raised himself up to his full height. "Okay, then. Here we go. Although I feel we should have a drum roll or something, you know what I mean? Well, anyway, try to use your imagination…tara-diddle…The bint in question is…Judges, the envelope, please…tara-diddle…Ladies and gentlemen, may I present to you the lovely, the charming, the talented…the world-class presidential strumpet…Please put your hands together for… *Ms. Jennifer Sloat!*"

It was one of those split seconds—they frequently occur during automobile accidents, I'm told—that feel as if they're stretching out to eternity. I could hear the reverberations of the name slowly fade and decay while I stared at him, openmouthed and stupid. I finally managed to stammer out, "What...what did you say?"

"Jennifer Sloat. Why? D'you happen to know her?"

"Jennifer Sloat?"

"What's the matter," he demanded with a laugh, "are you rogering her too, is that the problem?"

"No, I...no. I mean, I don't know the woman. I've never met her. Never even heard of her, I don't think. Should I have? Does she work in the White House?" I leaned against a nearby table to steady myself.

"From what I gather, she does not, except for some occasional volunteer work. I suppose we can now safely surmise what tasks she volunteers for. Her husband *does* work in the White House, however. He's an attorney in the Counsel's Office."

I tried to ignore the rushing sound in my ears. "Does he have a name?"

"Stephen something."

"Sloat?"

"No, it's one of those modern marriages. Stephen...something. A name that sounds Jewish, but then again might not be. You know the kind I mean? Most offputting. You never quite know where you stand with people like that."

"People with names like 'Krause'?"

"Well, yes, rather like that. Although there's never been much doubt about *you*, old boy. Mmm...Could it be 'Rossner,' perhaps?"

"Steve Rossner. Yes. I don't know him, but the name unquestionably rings a bell." Which of course made Chris's story more plausible. "This is supposed to have been going on for a while?"

"So I understand."

The way he was looking at me, I knew a response was expected. "Interesting," was the best I could come up with. I was in shock. This whole business had been a fucking shaggy dog story. I'd lied, schemed, cheated, I'd even involved the Secret Service for God's sake, and the story had never been about Gretchen at all. I was reeling.

"I wonder if this Rossner fellow is aware of it," Chris was going on. "You know, like Burt Bacharach when Angie Dickinson was having it off with JFK."

"'The most exciting seven seconds in a girl's life,' is how she described it." I'm afraid my smile looked pretty sickly. Perhaps I can claim credit for simply *attempting* a smile. An A for effort.

"Yes, but it's what *Bacharach* said that might be relevant. He professed himself to be pleased about the whole business. 'It's like going to bed with a little bit of history,' is how he's quoted." Chris shook his head. "Bizarre, the whole thing. All this ruler worship you Americans indulge in. While my people contemplate establishing a republic, you treat your presidents like kings. No, *pharaohs*, direct descendants of the gods. Didn't you chuck us out to get away from that sort of nonsense? One can admire the chap without wanting to present him one's testicles on a silver salver."

"So you think Rossner *is* aware of it? Complaisant, as you say."

"I have no idea. Just speculating out loud. The whole business intrigues me, rather. Your Mr. Sheffield *does* seem to have a weakness for other men's women, doesn't he?"

"Assuming this is true."

"Yes, assuming that, of course. I do make that assumption. Do you not?"

"Well…you *did* say that your source retracted the story."

"Please, Krause. I'm just starting to tolerate you again, you don't want to interfere with the process." This made me laugh, and my laughter in turn made him laugh. "No, really, I'm quite serious. You must have gone to fairly extravagant lengths to protect the egregious Mr. Sheffield. And I suppose your loyalty's admirable from a certain point of view. But there *are* other ways of looking at it. Would you have been so loyal if it was *your* girlfriend the president was skewering? You might want to think about that."

And then again, I might not. I didn't say anything.

"And honestly...don't you find the other-men's-women aspect of the story awfully provocative? Something distinctly odd is going on there."

"You have an interpretation?"

"You know, I believe I do. This whole thieving magpie business ...I think it's a way for him to demonstrate to his own satisfaction that he's better than the other men around him. Better, bigger, more magnetic, just...more. He needs that, I expect. So it's a way of establishing superiority. Dominance. You'd think the presidency would be enough, but I suppose for the sort of fellow who covets the presidency, *nothing* is enough. The concept doesn't exist."

This was similar to my own analysis. Which led me to think him very astute, of course. "Maybe," was all I said. Because suddenly something else, something blindingly obvious, hit me. Why had it taken till now? Probably no other reason except emotional overload; it had been quite a night so far. But I suddenly realized that if Chris's information were true—and I didn't doubt it was, not even for a moment—then Sheffield had been seeing this Jennifer Sloat person at the same time he'd been involved with Gretchen.

Before I could even ask myself what I felt about that, Chris's eyes suddenly narrowed and he said, "Are you feeling all right, Ben? You look a bit greenish about the gills."

It was all just too much, this roller-coaster ride I was on. Too much misery, too much excitement, too much suspense. With no end in sight. I was starting to feel like one of Dostoyevsky's protagonists, suffering from the sudden onset of brain fever. Or maybe it was something less grandiose, maybe more like a Victorian heroine succumbing to an attack of the vapors. Well, whatever, none of this was anything I planned on explaining. And Chris, rather sweetly, was looking sincerely concerned. So I forced a smile and said, "No, no, I'm fine. Just prespeech nerves. Remember, for a White House ink-stained wretch, this is opening night."

"Ah yes, of course, I did forget. How thoughtless of me. The most exciting seven seconds in an ink-stained cutter-and-paster's life."

I shook free of him and headed into the banquet room. I needed solitude in order to return to my earlier ruminations, to try to think my way through the emotional labyrinth. According to Chris's information, Sheffield had been involved with another woman at the same time he'd been sleeping with Gretchen. What was I to make of this? Did it have any impact on my own situation?

My reactions were just too damned complicated for me to disentangle. I was upset, of course, almost independent of the specific information; anything that reminded me of Sheffield in conjunction with sex guaranteed grief. But was I distressed on Gretchen's behalf, or did it have some other source? Somewhere deep inside myself I thought I detected a new level of anger. But directed at whom? At Sheffield, for his carnal gluttony? Or at Gretchen, for letting herself be sullied by somebody whose interest in her was so manifestly impersonal and exploitative? I felt like a high school nerd, listening in the locker room while the captain of the varsity football team boasts to his friends about his crude casual conquest of the girl the nerd worships from afar.

Maybe all I felt was disgust, trapped in everybody else's games, a relatively innocent bystander whose well-being, even while they disported with it, was a matter of indifference to all of them. A plague on the whole tribe, on the president and the First Lady, on Senator and Mrs. MacMillan, on Jennifer Sloat whoever she might be, and yes, on Gretchen too. I was heartily sick of having to think about any of it. My own feelings had become as confused and corrupt as everybody else's.

I found my table, glanced at the name cards to figure out who my dinner companions were going to be—the predictable combination of journalists and officials, but reasonably acceptable representatives of both breeds—and took my seat.

Let the games begin.

That evening, as had happened so often in his life, Sheffield was lucky. His astrological chart must have been something to behold. Because he spoke last, and because the other speeches were so utterly lame, so labored and unfunny, almost anything he said would have been judged a success. Although it's also true that, even without benefiting from comparisons, his speech would have qualified as a triumph; the lines really were good, and he delivered them flawlessly, blandly satirizing his own professorial style in a deadpan manner he never allowed to slip. He even added a bit of stage business of his own devising, taking the director's final piece of advice and carrying it further than anyone would have dared suggest: whenever he got a big laugh, he feigned mild surprise, as if he hadn't realized his comments were in any way barbed. He did it well, always underplaying the reaction, and it worked wonderfully. He brought the house down. Every line he uttered got a laugh, and the laughter kept building as the speech proceeded. And no one laughed harder than Jared MacMillan. The quintessential good sport. An inspiration to us all.

When the president finished, the room erupted in a sustained standing ovation. It didn't feel obligatory, this ovation, it seemed to be a genuine expression of appreciation and enthusiasm. Up on the dais, MacMillan jumped up and laughingly embraced the president, then Mrs. MacMillan shook the president's hand (I wondered if anybody else noticed the coolness of the gesture), and then everybody up there began slapping him on the back and congratulating him. At my table, I was experiencing a modest version of the same thing; word was out that the speech was my handiwork. And I accepted the praise without demurral. I was guided by something my mother had once told me, after I had won some sort of academic award in junior high school and had, perhaps, milked the occasion a little more than was seemly: "Ben, when someone pays you a compliment, don't offer elaborate explanations and don't argue. Just say thank you and shut up." Sound advice.

After the guests on the dais filed off, the event began to break up. I planned on walking home rather than catching a cab—after all I'd been through this evening, the night air, fresh or not, figured to do me good—and was standing near the exit, trying to extricate myself from the people who approached me to pay their respects. Since I'd been named head of speechwriting, this wasn't unheard of when the president gave a speech in Washington, even though very little about my work itself—either the nature of my duties or the quality of what I produced—had changed. But the new title seemed to confer a literary distinction upon my efforts that had previously been lacking. It would have been foolish and perverse to resent this phenomenon now that I was its beneficiary; after all, when Randy used to receive praise for stuff I had written, it bothered the hell out of me. So this wasn't exactly an ordeal. Nevertheless, it had been an emotionally arduous night, and I was pretty eager to get the hell out of there.

But just when a pathway to the door seemed to have opened, permitting me to make my escape, one of Alice Hahn's assistants—collectively known around the West Wing as "Alice's little peons"—approached me and tapped me on the shoulder. "Excuse me, Mr. Krause, but the president would like to speak to you." Which produced the kind of small splash I used to enjoy before the whole experience got contaminated.

I assumed Sheffield wanted to thank me for the speech. He was punctilious about things like that. I would have been perfectly content—would have preferred it—if he had chosen to wait until Monday to convey his appreciation, ideally through a note rather than in person; but he evidently felt the success of the speech merited some immediate expression of gratitude. So once again wishing with all my being that Gretchen had already told the president their affair was over, I steeled myself and followed the staffer back across the banquet room and through a door leading to the smallish backstage area. I wasn't wearing the kind of badge required to gain admittance, but the Secret Service agent guarding the door (it wasn't Joe Burton, alas; I would have welcomed a chance to talk to him) recognized me and nodded me through.

As I entered the little room, the person nearest the door was Senator MacMillan. He noticed me, grabbed me in a bear hug, started to laugh heartily, and said, "You son of a bitch, *you* wrote those damned insults, didn't you?"

"Will you hit me if I say yes?"

"You bet! Beat you black and blue. No, seriously, Ben, fabulous work. Not that I'll ever speak to you again." And he laughed a great booming "har-har-har" to show he was joshing. Then he introduced me to his wife, a reserved, handsome woman I'd never met before, who was just polite enough to pass muster but seemed less than overjoyed to make my acquaintance. Perhaps the evening had been emotionally arduous for her as well.

Then I caught a glimpse of Sheffield, surrounded by a small handful of well-wishers. When our eyes met, he beckoned me over.

The little group around him parted to let me get near. "Great job, Mr. President," I said, extending my hand. I was still finding it hard to look him in the face. The compliments from the people around him helped in that regard, gave me a pretext to avoid doing so.

For all that, I expected a friendlier, jollier greeting than I got. "Yes," he said quietly, "it went fine. Listen, I want to talk to you. Can you come back to the White House?"

"Tonight?"

"If it isn't too much trouble."

"No, of course it isn't." I was taken aback by his tone, which seemed to occupy that zone lying somewhere between neutral and downright unfriendly. "I don't have my car here, but I'm sure I can—"

"You can come with Claire and me," he interrupted. "We're leaving right now."

Sheffield was taciturn in the limousine during the short ride back to the White House, all but silent. Perhaps he was distracted, or simply recouping after the rigors of his speech, but it nevertheless felt oppressive. The First Lady took up the slack, telling me how much she enjoyed the speech and how happy she was that I had taken charge of the speechwriting office.

"That's very kind of you, Mrs. Sheffield."

"You know, Ben, I'd be very pleased if you called me Claire."

This was a surprise. She'd always been cordial, but our relations had never been particularly personal. "I'll try."

"It'll get easier with practice."

I snuck a glance at Sheffield, but he was looking out the window, apparently lost in thought. Well, it didn't matter; in my household I wasn't the one who would ever call him Chuck.

When we arrived at the White House, Claire Sheffield gave me a kiss on the cheek—another surprise—and bade us both good night.

"Good night, Claire," I forced myself to say.

"See? You're getting the hang of it already." She patted my arm before turning and heading toward the family quarters.

Sheffield said a couple of words to one of the stewards, then turned to me. "Let's go out on the balcony. It's a nice night."

I followed him out. I wouldn't have called it a nice night exactly, since the air was heavy and humid, but it was certainly warm. Uncomfortably warm: I was sweating heavily. And there was a full moon; the view across the Mall was strikingly beautiful, the illuminated Washington Monument staking its customary squirrel monkey claim on the city's attention. When the president removed his dinner jacket and loosened his bow tie, I gratefully followed his lead and did the same. We sat ourselves down in adjoining chairs. I was acutely conscious of the falsity of my position, extraordinarily discomfiting even by the exacting standards of that period of my life. Immediately after we took our seats, the steward arrived with a bottle of cognac and two snifters.

"This is very good stuff," Sheffield said. "Over a hundred years old. A gift from someone, I don't remember who." Which made it a wasted gift, I remember thinking. And another example of Sheffield's casual, almost oblivious acceptance of other people's generosity. The opposite of noblesse oblige: *noblesse mérite.* He nodded to the steward, then turned his gaze back in my direction. "You know," he said, "when Nixon entertained here, he used to tell the stewards to reserve the good bottles of wine for himself alone, and pour quasi swill for the guests. Pretty shoddy, no?"

"Very shoddy."

"I think his working hypothesis was that most people couldn't tell the difference anyway. But that's not really the point, is it?"

"No, sir."

"Besides, he probably couldn't either. It was just label snobbery."

The steward had poured the brandy and now handed the president one snifter and me the other. "Well," Sheffield said, "cheers."

We each took a sip. It just tasted like brandy to me, but I offered some generic appreciation—something about its being smooth, as I recall—which seemed pretty much obligatory considering what he'd just said about it. And after that, neither of us uttered a single word for a minute or two. A minute or two that felt like an eternity. It was eerie, to be honest, sitting alone with him out there so late—it was getting on toward midnight—in total silence, without a clue as to why he wanted me there. There had been a time, not so long before, when this arrangement would have felt like nirvana. Now it was almost intolerable.

Finally he spoke. "That first time we played chess...on the campaign plane, you remember?"

"Of course."

"I noticed something. When I realized I was going to lose...to my chagrin, I don't mind admitting. Anyway, I looked up at you, and you were studying the board, but you looked up for a second, right at me, and then you looked back down. And in that second, you looked right through me. As if I weren't there at all. I don't know if you remember it."

"I don't."

"It's the sort of thing politicians notice. And don't forget. Even stupid politicians. The stupid ones might not put it into words, the whole thing might occur beneath the radar of their consciousness, but if somebody reacts to them that way, it registers all the same. We need to know where we stand with people. It's second nature, assessing that. When we can't tell, it makes us nervous. Now, I have no idea what you were thinking at that moment...."

"I was probably thinking that your king side was inadequately defended and a couple of pawn moves would crack it wide open."

"Yes. Exactly. Something like that. But I had to wonder. See, the thing is, Ben...that was at a time when...I mean, *nobody* looked through me that way. I was going to be president."

"I meant no disrespect."

"No, no, I didn't take it that way. I was impressed, in fact. Impressed, and also a little...not miffed, but...disconcerted, maybe."

I waited. Where the hell was he going with this? He took a slow sip of cognac before continuing. "And the thing is...Lately, I've had the distinct impression you've started looking through me that way again. When you look at me at all. Which you frequently don't."

Jesus, he did notice things. At least when they concerned *him*. And I wasn't looking at him now, that's for damned sure. Even in the darkness, it felt safer to stare out at the Mall, despite that unavoidable Washington Monument mocking me with its simian assertion of the perquisites of power. But Sheffield's subsequent silence felt expectant; I knew I had to say something. "My mother taught me it's rude to stare," I said. Pretty pathetic, but I was under the gun.

There was another long silence. Intended, I think, as a rebuke for my evasiveness. He finally broke it by saying, "There's a story about

Winston Churchill. This is supposed to have happened between the wars, well before he became prime minister. You have to understand he always treated his assistants and his household staff very badly, very high-handedly. He wasn't what we'd consider a good person to work for. If he lived now, there'd probably be lawsuits and grievance hearings and things. Well, anyway, there was one time he must have really gone too far, or maybe he just picked the wrong day to browbeat this particular servant, because the fellow finally decided he'd taken quite enough abuse and answered Churchill back. And it got out of hand, it turned into a real shouting match. And when the dust finally started to settle, Churchill said, 'You were very rude to me, you know.' I guess he expected some sort of apology. And the servant—still standing his ground apparently, he must have been quite a brave sort of guy—the servant still wouldn't give way, he said, 'Yes, but you were rude too.' And Churchill said, *'Yes, but I am a great man.'*"

This was the moment at which something akin to dread joined all the other miserable emotions contending for the upper hand within my central nervous system. My shirt was drenched with perspiration, and the humidity was only partly responsible. But once again, some answer was obviously required. "The fact that you're telling me this story, Mr. President...does it suggest you think Churchill was in the right?"

"That isn't the point, really. The point is...Listen, Ben, Winston Churchill saved civilization. He's probably the greatest figure of the twentieth century, all things considered, he's just an immense personage, a paragon to those of us in public life. And he used his greatness almost entirely for good. At least when the chips were down. So whether I think he was in the right or not, it's almost irrelevant. It isn't the right question. The right question is, do I have any difficulty balancing his incredible achievements against his rudeness to a manservant? And I don't. I really don't. Not a scintilla of difficulty. Sure, it would be nice if he'd always been the soul of graciousness, sweet tempered and gentle with everyone who worked for him, everyone who crossed his path. But as tradeoffs go...well, this one's kind of a no-brainer."

"So he's exempted from the ordinary demands of human decency, you mean? At least as a practical matter?" This came out sounding argumentative, and I realized I didn't mind. I still hoped the conversation wasn't going where I was afraid it might be going, but I'd be damned if I was going to let myself be bullied.

Sheffield exhaled with displeasure. He must have thought I was being willfully obtuse. "No, not *exempted,* exactly. Nothing so definite. Nothing so categorical. I'm just suggesting that with a man like Churchill, maybe he needs to be judged on a different scale."

"So...wait, let me get this straight. This was before World War Two, right? He wasn't...that is, was he even a member of Parliament at the time?"

"Yes, but just a back bencher. He'd resigned from the government."

"So when he called himself a great man...I mean, it hadn't exactly been demonstrated yet, had it?"

"He knew who he was. He knew *what* he was."

"So do lots of people who don't turn out to be Churchill." I felt Sheffield's gaze on me. "Is it okay for *them* to be rude? Should *they* be judged on a different scale? I mean, according to your thinking. On the off chance they might be right."

Sheffield shook his head and sipped his cognac. Congressional Republicans might occasionally be bold enough or unfriendly enough to challenge him this way when major differences were being argued over, but never members of his staff. He didn't seem to like it. There was an edge in his voice when he said, "Do you have any idea what I'm dealing with these days, Ben? I mean, of course you don't, and I really shouldn't be telling you what I'm about to tell you. I'm going to have to ask for your complete discretion."

"Of course."

He took a breath. "There's a right-wing group in Eastern Europe that's come into possession of a fairly large quantity of biological weaponry manufactured in the former Soviet Union. The Russian government told us they'd destroyed the stockpile, but they were lying. And now, rogue Russian generals have been selling bits and pieces of it to the Russian Mafia, who in turn put it on the market and sell it to the highest bidder. And now we've got to try to find a way to forestall a terrorist attack and we don't know where or when it might happen. The DCI tells me the target is likely to be a major city in the continental United States, although the agency doesn't know which. And we aren't even sure if we should be looking at some large organized group or just a handful of skinhead crazies with financing. So that's one thing.

"And here's another. The new government in Iran has requested a fortune in military hardware from us. I'm not opposed in principle, they've been doing everything right so far, and they're facing a serious threat, they need to defend themselves. But meanwhile, the mullahs are back in control of large stretches of countryside, they may soon be in a position to attack major cities, including Tehran, the outcome of such an attack isn't at all clear, and what we do might tip the balance in favor of the good guys, or alternately, the whole fucking arsenal might fall into the wrong hands.

"And then there's the situation in Kenya. We haven't spoken about it lately, you and I, but we've been making genuine progress since your little jaunt to Paris. Our foreign policy people have finally gotten involved, we've been talking in secret with the different factions, and we may be quite close to brokering some sort of peace agreement. One that might hold. It's very, very complicated, and even if we get there, selling it on the Hill will be close to impossible, since it involves the deployment of U.S. ground forces, and besides—let's be candid—these are black people killing other black people. But we might actually have a chance to end a decade of butchery. And the negotiations are so delicate, I'm literally afraid to breathe when the NSC briefs me about them.

"And all that's not even *mentioning* our domestic proposals, since they're not exactly matters of life and death in the same league as this other stuff. But they're not nothing. People's lives can be improved in a significant way. We've already done a few good things, but if we don't find a way to deliver on the rest during this congressional session, we probably won't get another chance till after I'm reelected. Assuming I am. I think I will be, but of course my chances would be much greater if we get the programs passed. Which is another thing I have to think about, grubby as it some-times seems. Frankly, it mostly seems grubby when *other* people do it. When I do it, it just feels like another aspect of enlightened governance.

"And besides all that, I may have to…well, this is something I genuinely shouldn't be breathing a word about. Even more than everything else I've been telling you. Let me just say that the Justice Department has been giving me regular briefings about the vice president's husband. God knows where that one's going, maybe nowhere, let's hope and pray nowhere, but it's a headache, and regardless of the ultimate outcome, there's no way it's going to help with all the other stuff I've just mentioned."

He paused to take a sip of cognac. "So there you go," he then said. "A little *tour d'horizon*. The view from my desk. None of this is any-thing you should know about. As we speak, you may be the only person in the entire country, other than the president, who's aware of all of it. But I'm trying to make a point here."

"I think I get the point. You're not a back bencher."

He grunted. It was hard to interpret the grunt, but I didn't let that discourage me, and went on, "In fact, to hear you tell it, it's more like I'm Job and you're the Whirlwind. You know, where was I when you created Leviathan, that sort of thing."

Which actually made him chuckle, the last thing in the world I expected. Or even wanted. It was a dry, sour sort of laugh, but it was a laugh. "No, Ben, my grandiose pretensions don't go *that* far. 'Not a back bencher' is surely adequate for the purposes of this discussion."

His first outright acknowledgment that this discussion *had* a purpose. He was certainly taking a circuitous path toward it.

"Well, president of the United States goes way beyond 'not a back bencher,'" I said. "There isn't much argument about that. But I'm still...I mean, do you intend to suggest...that is, do you think it automatically confers all those rights and privileges Churchill was claiming? You know, that he was claiming as a natural concomitant of being a great man. Dispensation denied the rest of humanity?"

He sounded icy cold when he finally answered, "Maybe it's time we stopped dancing around these issues, do you think? Maybe it's time we stopped dithering and laid our cards on the table."

"By all means." My voice came out strong and confident, I'm pleased to say, despite the fact I was feeling anything but.

"There's something between us. It's affecting our relationship. I know it, you know it, and now I know you know it. So let's address it."

My heart was beating a mile a minute. Had such a conversation ever taken place on the Truman Balcony before? All I could say was, "Go on." It was all I trusted myself to say.

"I've slept with Gretchen. Either she's told you or you've figured it out. There. It's been said out loud. We're not pretending anymore. And so we now find ourselves in a situation. What are we going to do about it?"

"Do about it?"

"Either we find a way to cope with this, or...Well, let me put it this way. If for some reason we *can't* find a way to cope, I'm obviously not the one who'll be looking for other employment."

This was absolutely typical Sheffield in its aggressive seizing of the initiative, but it was also a tactical blunder. When you constantly get hammered the way I'd been hammered, one of two things happens: you either get totally whipped, or the anger keeps building until it eventually reaches the boiling point. I wasn't feeling totally whipped. I mean, who the fuck did he think he was dealing with?

"That's fine," I said. My shirt was sopping wet, I could smell my own rankness, but by God, my voice held nice and steady. "I understand. My resignation will be on your desk tomorrow morning."

"Now wait a minute, Ben." He sounded flustered. He wasn't prepared for this development. "I've obviously failed to make myself clear. I'm *not* requesting your resignation. On the contrary. I want you to stay. You're doing great work for me. I'm just saying we need to find a modus vivendi."

He was backpedaling. It was the oddest thing, but for the first time since his inauguration, maybe the first time since we'd first met, he didn't seem presidential. He just seemed like a guy who had screwed another guy's girlfriend and had been discovered and was trying to fast-talk his way out of it. It was ironic, really; by exploiting that odd extrinsic mantle the presidency had bestowed upon him, he'd also surrendered it.

"You mean like with Steve Rossner?" I suggested. It was a blind stab, a risky knight feint away from the center of action in order to menace his undefended right flank, but I was emboldened by his tentativeness.

And his answering silence confirmed the efficacy of the thrust. Interesting. Little did he know that I'd just spared him public exposure on that score. And now, for a very long time, neither of us spoke, or even moved. But I didn't find the silence quite so oppressive anymore. It was his move, and his clock that was ticking.

"Let's stick to you and me, if you don't mind," he finally said. Sternly, but I thought I heard an undertone of uncertainty in his voice. This may have been his first hint that the relationship with Jennifer Sloat was known to others. He pinched his shirt collar and held it away from his throat for a second. I wasn't the only one feeling the heat. "The thing is, I want you to stay on. You're an asset to this administration. But only if the air between us is clear. I can't tolerate those baleful looks of yours every time we meet."

"You're telling me to get over it?"

"I'm suggesting you be a grown-up. Certain types of people gain the presidency. And once they get it, whatever qualities they had in the first place are considerably enhanced. There's a sexual component to leadership. Some modicum of sexual appeal comes with the territory, and a sexual aura surrounds it. *Engulfs* it. You want to fight that? Why not try to command the tides while you're at it? I'm not the first person in this position, you're not the first, and Gretchen's not the first. These things happen. It's beyond our control. It's how human nature functions."

"So in other words, you're telling me to get over it?"

He sighed with impatience at my stubbornness, took hold of the cognac bottle, and refreshed his glass. "Claire and I are tremendously fond of you both," he said. "Gretchen's a great girl. You two make a terrific couple. This…this *thing* between her and me, it's just…Well, for me, it's just…I mean, she's so attractive, she's so energetic and positive and irreverent.…It's just *fun*. A diversion from all the burdens of the job. She makes me feel young, she makes me laugh, she keeps me from taking myself too seriously. I really do relish her company. And for *her*…oh, I'm sure you understand, Ben. Even if you don't like it, you must understand. It's an adventure. I mean, it isn't really about me as a person. Not *only,* anyway. Maybe not even primarily. I recognize that. I can accept it. Can't you? It's a…it's an escapade. A hoot. It isn't any kind of commentary on your relationship. Nor need it be a threat to it."

Smugness positively *oozed* from him. What a shithead. Not that I could tell him that, of course. I wasn't feeling intimidated anymore, there wasn't much awe left, but still, it wouldn't do to go calling the president of the United States a shithead. But I did hate the fact that Gretchen hadn't yet told him the relationship was over; hated it, I mean, even more than I had before he'd started talking this way. He might have been at least a *little* less smug if she had. And I might have had at least a *slightly* reduced sense of being, as Stephen Potter would put it, one-down. His self-satisfied complacency, and my sense of being at a colossal disadvantage, an irremediable disadvantage, probably contributed to what followed.

"In the past," he went on, "in this sort of situation, lots of marriages survived. Edward the Seventh, for example, had many married mistresses, starting back when he was Prince of Wales. We were mentioning Winston Churchill just now, and by coincidence Churchill's mother happened to be one of them. And the husbands of these women—it was almost a club—they often felt honored. Not," he added with a self-conscious laugh, "that I expect you to feel honored. I'm just saying, you can realize it's a kind of unique set of circumstances, you can make allowances you might not otherwise be prepared to make. And she's such a great person, Ben. I mean, I'm sure you're aware of that already, you hardly need *me* to tell you. But she's very special. I think she's *worth* your making some allowances."

"You know, Mr. President," I heard myself saying, "with all due respect, some of this isn't actually any of your business."

The snifter was halfway to his lips when I said that. He didn't complete the move; he started slightly and swiveled around to face me instead. But if he was provoked, he didn't lose control; he barely showed it. Sheffield had a temper—everyone who worked for him had seen it at one time or another—but he didn't lose it, he *deployed* it. And I guess he didn't judge this to be an appropriate occasion. After the briefest of pauses he said mildly, "Maybe you're right, maybe it isn't." And then, "Listen, would it help if I stopped seeing her? Would that maybe make things all right between us?"

As if this were a handsome gesture. He didn't realize the relationship was already ended, of course. And then it hit me that until he knew, it *wasn't* ended, not really. No line had been crossed, no decision announced or acted upon, nothing irretrievable had taken place. Her not telling him, just like her succumbing to him, was a response to the power he wielded. And that power remained his.

But leaving that to the side, what I found really offensive was the casual way he spoke of Gretchen, as if she were a plaything he was fond of but was prepared to jettison for the sake of his relationship with me. An issue we could negotiate between ourselves, leaving Gretchen to be informed of the outcome at some later date.

So I didn't answer him directly. My anger was rising again— reaching a new high-water mark, really—and I struggled to keep it in check. I took a couple of deep breaths before I let myself speak. "You know, Mr. President, the problem I'm having right now is with…with…I guess you'd call them the quasi-sovereign aspects of the presidency. I mean, you mentioned Edward the Seventh, and maybe that's sort of telling. I think you're doing a good job here, and I'm generally supportive of the policies of the administration. Not that you need my blessing, but…well, there it is, unsolicited. But with so much…so much power, or maybe it's just so much attention, focused on one guy…it becomes kind of difficult to distinguish the office, or occasionally even the country, from the person who occupies the office and heads the country. Do you see what I mean?"

"Yes, Ben," he said expansively, "I think I do. I sometimes have that difficulty myself, in fact."

"I'm sure you must. I mean, I've noticed. But still, I'm not convinced you *do* understand what I'm getting at. You see, the thing is…while I'd defend your policy choices, and I suppose I'd probably even vote for you again, it's just…I no longer respect you as a human being." And now, having uttered words that felt like an act of lèse-majesté, I didn't let myself stop to draw breath, but continued, "So if that matters to you, if the opinion of somebody like me matters to you, then you'd better hope you *are* a great man, you'd better hope you *are* some sort of Winston Churchill. I gather you'd regard that as redemptive. But frankly, I don't see any evidence for it."

I flatter myself that, for all my wussiness up till that moment, I at least burned my bridges with a certain panache.

I HAD TO WALK HOME. MY PANACHE DIDN'T QUITE EXTEND TO requesting a White House car—which would have sidled into that no-man's-land where panache gives way to chutzpah—and it was so late that there weren't any taxis out on the street. And it had started to... not rain exactly, but there was a warm mist in the air, a pervasive oppressive dampness that wilted everything it touched. Ordinarily it would have been frightening to be walking downtown at that hour all by myself, especially in an Armani tux. But after what I'd just been through, it didn't give me even a moment's anxiety. Even the tropical wretchedness of the weather wasn't much of a bother.

I had other things on my mind. I was horrified at myself. I was in a state of elation. And something in my aura must have told would-be muggers they'd be well advised to look elsewhere for victims tonight.

I compulsively replayed the little balcony scene we'd just enacted—so different from Romeo and Juliet's—silently rehearsed it as I walked up desolate Connecticut Avenue. It had already acquired some of the feeling of a dream. The funny thing is, I hadn't even been telling Sheffield the truth when I'd said I didn't respect him as a human being. I mean, I did in some ways and I didn't in others. He had his strengths and his weaknesses just like everybody else. It was my misfortune that one of his weaknesses happened to poke me right in the eye, but that didn't make him a monster. Despite what my wrath urged me to believe, he *wasn't* Caligula. He was simply a fellow with sexual appetites—not necessarily even excessive appetites—who found himself in a position where he had the wherewithal, along with the vanity and indiscipline, to indulge them when he shouldn't. Not a capital crime, just a personal foul. Which isn't to imply that I *regretted* having said it; after you've suffered a certain amount of humiliation, you feel a need to lash out. Fairness and a strict adherence to accuracy become decidedly secondary considerations when you've been treated with contempt for month after month.

I didn't owe the bastard fairness.

But I did wonder, as I strolled up Connecticut in the swampy darkness, with the hundred-year-old cognac sour (and aging fast) in my stomach, how I would feel about everything the next morning. Had I fucked up big time, or had venting all that accumulated poison extended my life by a decade or so? I had a notion that my British grandmother would have been proud of me, which was heartening. Especially since she lived to be ninety-one. Quite an advertisement for venting.

But now I was faced with the vexing question of what to do with the rest of the life I'd arguably just extended, and I certainly didn't have an answer to that one handy. The rest of my life? Hell, the next couple of days would be challenge enough.

Gretchen was asleep when I got home, of course. I undressed in the dark. My tux was damp, was way beyond damp, and my shirt was positively *infused* with mist from one direction and sweat from the other. So I just threw everything into the closet. They were headed for the cleaners anyway, no reason to fold and hang. Gretchen had left the air-conditioning on; after I'd stripped, it gave me a small chill, but the sensation was delicious after the oppressive humidity I'd been enduring for the last couple of hours.

I towel-dried my hair, peed, and brushed my teeth to get the cognac taste out of my mouth, but it was much too late to bother with floss. Fuck it. How much harm could one day's worth of plaque do to a bad motherfucker like me?

When I climbed into bed, Gretchen stirred slightly. I hushed her, but she had been awakened just enough to murmur drowsily, "How'd it go?"

"Great," I said. "It was a triumph."

I SLEPT LATE THE NEXT MORNING. WHEN I WOKE UP, I SMELLED coffee. Still tired, and slightly hung over as well (the steward had poured generously, and I didn't have much experience with cognac), but feeling surprisingly free of morning-after remorse, I staggered out into the kitchen and found that Gretchen had prepared a big breakfast. She was standing beside the little table in our breakfast nook, arranging several platters. Fruit salad, bagels, cream cheese, lox, whitefish spread. A tribute to my people's folkways and the very finest Sutton Place had to offer.

"Morning, honey," she said brightly. After I returned the greeting, she asked, "What time did you come in last night?" I doubt she remembered our brief exchange from the night before. I doubt she knew it had even taken place.

"Very, very late."

"Should I be jealous? Where were you? What were you up to?"

"Let me shower and shave first, then I'll tell you all about it."

"Sounds interesting."

"It is."

"Tease!"

When I returned to the kitchen a half hour or so later, she was sitting at the table, sipping from a cup of coffee. She had *The Washington Post* opened to an account of the MacMillan roast. She looked up and gestured to the paper. "Great write-up," she said. "Sounds like you were a smash."

"Not me. Your buddy was the smash. I just sat there twiddling my thumbs and looking yummy."

She looked up at me sharply, trying to assess my tone and gauge my mood. Unable to do it—she didn't have enough data to work

with yet—she continued, "You're mentioned in the article. Identified as the guy who wrote the speech."

"It isn't even true."

"It's sort of true."

I sat across from her and poured myself a cup of coffee. "Chris
Partridge was there." I took a careful, appraising sip. The temperature was Goldilocks perfection. "We talked a bit, before everybody
went into the big room." I took another sip. "He had big news,
he said."

"Was it about his story?"

"Yes."

A look of anxiety flitted by. "Did he say what it was?"

"Yep. He's found out the name of the president's girlfriend."

She went white. It happened remarkably fast. The color just
drained from her face in an instant. "Oh my God. Oh Ben…Oh
shit." She looked down at her plate, then up at me again. "Did he
say if he was going to publish? What an awful mess! Am I going to
be exposed? Or will he be a pal?"

"I got the impression he probably isn't going to publish. He
seems to have encountered a couple of snags."

"Thank goodness for that."

"Yes, it's a relief all around." I took another sip of coffee, then
casually added, "Her name's Jennifer Sloat."

It just sat there for a moment, an endless moment, while she
processed it. The color rushed back into her face. And kept on deep-
ening.

"Do you know her?" I asked.

"That son of a bitch," she said very quietly—almost musingly—
but quite distinctly.

"Chris seemed absolutely certain of it."

"That lying bastard."

"I take it you don't mean Chris." She didn't respond, so I repeated
my earlier question. *"Do* you know her?"

She looked at me as if she had forgotten I was in the room with her. "What? Oh, yes. Yes, I know her. I mean, I've met her a few times."

"With Steve Rossner?"

"Yeah. And without. Both."

She didn't volunteer anything further. I had a feeling there might be an entire novel of manners contained in those four words, but she gave no indication she was about to reveal its contents. And then her mind was elsewhere again. She had picked up a fork and was now closely examining its tines.

"You're upset," I said.

She looked up at me. "I'm just surprised, is all. Taken aback."

"That's it?"

"Well, I guess maybe my pride's hurt a little." She was making a visible effort to get control of herself.

"You thought you were the only one?"

"I didn't think about it at all. But I guess I kind of assumed it without thinking about it. A stupid assumption."

"Of course, we've only got Chris's word for it," I said.

"Oh, I suspect it's true. I'd be surprised if it isn't, now that you've said it. I just hadn't given it much thought."

"You seem dismayed."

"No, no, not at all. Not dismayed. Just…" She shook her head. "What an asshole. What a complete and utter asshole."

"Chris?"

Her answering look wasn't friendly. "You know I'm not talking about Chris." She got up from the table, walked over to the sink, realized she had nothing to do there once she got there, and swiveled around to face me again. "Listen, Ben, I'm going to tell him it's over. I mean, not at some indefinite date in the indefinite future. The first chance I get. Maybe *I'll* even phone *him* instead of waiting for him to call. Which I've never done, incidentally, even though he told me I could." She shook her head. "And I owe you an apology for dragging this out. It was unconscionable of me, but, you know, I was scared. I was chicken. But I've been kidding myself, waiting for the right moment. There isn't going to be any right moment, so I should just do it and get it over with."

I started slicing a bagel. "Don't do it for my sake."

"No, no, it's overdue. It's ridiculous. He's not Henry the Eighth, he's not going to have me beheaded. I'm sure he won't even have me fired. Too messy. So what am I scared of?"

"No, what I mean is, it's too late. For me, I mean. Too late for it to make any difference." I didn't realize this was true until I said it.

"But I thought this was what you wanted," she said. She was looking at me strangely.

"Yep, it was. Absolutely. But now…I mean, now that you've heard about this Sloat person, and the way it's obviously upset you…it wouldn't be the same gesture anymore. It isn't about *us*."

"But it *is*."

"Except I'll never know that for sure. Neither, I think, will you. Not really. And even Sheffield…if he figures out you know about this other woman, he'll just think it's one of those hell-hath-no-fury deals."

"Does that matter? What he thinks?"

"Yes." I was sick of explaining myself. I was through with analyzing my injuries in order to justify the pain they caused.

"But why?"

Once more unto the breach. No getting around it. Heaving a vast internal sigh, I said, "Because of the position you put me in. Because I asked you to do it a long time ago and you didn't. Because it makes him feel good to sleep with the wives and girlfriends of the men in his ambit, and you were willing to contribute to his well-being in that way at my expense. Because…because of the way he looks at me. Fondly. As if it's okay to like me because he's proved he's something and I'm nothing."

She bit her lower lip. "You really think he's like that?"

"Yes."

"And my doing it now won't help?"

"Not even slightly."

"Then...I mean, in that case, where does that leave us?"

I wasn't ready to answer that question yet. So instead I told her, "I was with him last night. After the banquet, I mean. That's why I got home so late. We spent a little time together, he and I."

The look she gave me was...the only word I can find to describe it is "cross." "You were with him? Where?"

"The White House. Two buds hanging out. It was like the good old days during the campaign, except we didn't play chess."

"This is relevant?"

"You bet."

"You didn't tell him, did you? Ben, you *promised!*"

"No, I didn't tell him. I kept my promise. But *he* told *me.*"

She used a hand to steady herself at the sink. "Oh my God." She shut her eyes.

"It was quite a conversation. Kinda surreal." I started putting whitefish spread on my bagel. Why I was so calm all of a sudden I can't really say, but I was. Calmer than I'd been in almost three months. And hungry. I hadn't been able to force myself to eat much the night before. Probably another reason for my minor hangover this morning.

She came back to join me at the table. "Are you going to tell me about it?" she asked as she sat down.

"Well, what do you want to know?"

"Why are you playing games with me? I want to know *everything,* obviously."

"Yeah, I understand what that's like." This was a cheap shot. But sometimes a cheap shot is good for the soul. "Well...let's see. He offered to give you up. For the sake of our working relationship. His and mine, I mean."

"Christ." Her face was a mask of mortification.

"But he said how much he likes you."

"How gratifying. I guess that makes me a nothing too."

"A different dynamic might apply to women. I think his affection's meant to be *elevating*, somehow."

"Could've fooled me. I sure *feel* like a nothing."

"Still...you'll always have Paris."

I was about to take the first bite of my bagel when she muttered, with patent annoyance, "You know, you ought to consider referencing another movie sometime."

"All right. How about *Grapes of Wrath?* 'Wherever a president fucks an underling...I'll be there.'"

"Jesus, Ben."

But now I was chewing and couldn't make a contribution. So she filled the gap. "Go on. What else?"

I swallowed. "No locker room chat, if that's what you mean. We didn't compare notes or anything."

"This is *ghastly*," she said.

"Relax. According to Oscar Wilde, the only thing worse than being talked about is *not* being talked about."

"Oh yeah, he's a superb argument for being talked about, isn't he? I bet he reconsidered *that* little notion toward the end." She hesitated. "So what did you say when Chuck offered to give me up?"

"Something rude."

"Really?" She almost smiled, but only because she didn't believe me.

"Really. I'm afraid I'm now ex–head of speechwriting. It isn't official, but that'll be taken care of on Monday. There's no way I can stay on. Not after last night."

The smile was gone, replaced by a deep frown. "You're serious." She looked at me with distaste all of a sudden. I was taking another bite of my bagel. "How can you *eat?*"

I stopped in midchomp. "I'm hungry. I didn't have any appetite at the banquet. Now I do."

She shook her head and looked away. "So…what am I supposed to think? That I've ruined your life and destroyed your career?"

"That might be a little melodramatic. I mean, I wouldn't say you've done me any big favors, but…I don't know. Shit happens."

"Now you're quoting T-shirts?"

"Would you prefer me to go back to *Casablanca?*"

"The place, maybe, not the movie."

Our little kitchen was suddenly bristling with hostility. Caught me by surprise. Of course, being caught by surprise wasn't much of a surprise anymore. It had virtually become a habit. "Why are you angry?" I asked.

"Am I angry?"

"Seems like it."

"Hmm…" She considered it. "I thought I was mortified and racked by guilt. But maybe you're right. Maybe I'm also pissed off."

"You're mega–pissed off."

She nodded. Even mega–pissed off, she was determined to be honest about her emotions. "I don't know why. Maybe because things have been happening behind my back."

"Yeah, that must be awful." Today was turning into a veritable Mardi Gras of cheap shots.

"And because…I don't know, Ben, you have this aura…like you're shrouding yourself in some kind of victim's sanctity. I'm not trying to evade responsibility, I swear it, but maybe you're enjoying this a little too much."

"Enjoying it?" Now it was my turn to be mega–pissed off. "This has been the worst period of my life. I've barely managed to hold it together."

"Yeah. Point taken. 'Enjoying it' was a poor choice of words." She pondered for a moment. "This isn't going to survive, is it? You and me, I mean."

"No."

"It's over?"

I met her eye. "Yes."

She looked down at that damned fork again and mumbled, "How long have you known?"

"I probably realized it last night, but I didn't admit it to myself till this morning. Till just now. But it just seems... There's too much *mess*, Gretch. We've let too much mess accumulate. I can't separate *you* from *it* anymore."

"Yeah..." Tears had sprung into her eyes, but she didn't dab at them. Unheeded, they started to roll down her cheeks. "You think we might have pulled through if it had just been some guy?"

"I think so. It would have been a serious setback, but I think we might have gotten past it."

"Except it never would have happened at all. It couldn't. That's the awful, miserable, ironic fact of the matter. You were so important to me, our relationship was so important to me, I would never have jeopardized it for just some guy. The whole idea is unthinkable. It had to be for something like this."

Well, this was ground we'd been over before, and there wasn't much point in debating the fine points one more time. Particularly when we had some really awful, really pressing decisions to make. About the condo, for one thing. Gretchen couldn't afford it on her salary, and I was about to be unemployed. Should either of us stay in it, even for the short term? And where could one or both of us go to live right now if we vacated it?

We spent most of the day talking in circles. Covering a lot of old ground, trying vainly to find some formulation that would give us a sense of mastery over events. We both cried. We both managed to laugh a little. We made love, with more tenderness and more passion than we'd achieved in months. She asked me if I hated her, and I assured her I'd never loved her more. She suggested we try to start afresh, but I told her there was no point. The day was melancholy, claustrophobic, exhausting, and oddly sweet. And it seemed endless, even though we both knew we would someday look back on it and wish it had never ended.

By six, both of us were feeling a little stir-crazy, so we walked over to Pizzaria Paradiso, the way we had often done when we'd first moved into the condo. It was almost a weekend ritual. Even so early, the place was jammed, and we had to wait for a table. Which only added to the valedictory sadness. It was so reminiscent of all those Saturday and Sunday evenings when we were happy, when even waiting endlessly in the crowded foyer for our names to be called was a pleasure and seeing families spending a weekend night together seemed like the promise of future happiness.

When we got home, Gretchen went straight to the bedroom without a word. I went to my desk, took a sheet of paper, and started writing longhand. I finally came up with:

Dear Mr. President,

In light of recent events, it is clear to me that I can no longer serve in your administration. Therefore, I am herewith tendering my resignation, effective immediately.

Sincerely yours,

Benjamin Krause

I was proud of its utter bloodlessness. I had tried several other approaches, and crossed out a lot of extraneous words, before achieving what I flattered myself was a Hemingway-like purity. After sealing the note in an envelope and addressing it, I brought it to Gretchen, who hadn't left the bedroom and was now lying on her back on top of the bed, in the dark, listening to the bluegrass music they anomalously played on the American University NPR affiliate, WAMU.

"Gretch, I'm not going in to work tomorrow. Not much point. But I assume you are."

"I suppose."

"Could you please take this to Sandra first thing, ask her to make sure the president gets it?"

"All right."

She didn't ask what it was, and I didn't volunteer the information. We said nothing else to each other for the rest of the evening. We were completely talked out by then. There was nothing left to say.

The next morning, after a night of uneasy and intermittent sleep, I stayed in bed until Gretchen left for work. Later, over coffee, I was going through *The Washington Post* classifieds, looking at apartment listings for both Gretchen and myself—not a cheerful occupation— when the phone rang. I picked up and heard, "Mr. Benjamin Krause? Please hold for the president."

Oh shit. Certainly a conversation I'd hoped to avoid. And actually believed I might.

As usual, he came out punching. No preliminaries, no good morning. "Ben, I get the feeling I'm not a terrifically popular guy around your place. First Gretchen drops off a note without even sticking her head in to say hello, and then, even worse, there was the note itself. Jesus, if the rest of the country felt the way you two seem to, I'd have to pull an LBJ and not even bother to run again."

"Fortunately for you, Mr. President, that's not the case."

"Yeah. Listen, about the other night…I understand you were angry. And given the circumstances, I can't say I blame you. Plus we'd had all that cognac, neither of us was at his best. So I want you to know…I'm not requesting your resignation. I'm not *accepting* your resignation. I think we can get past this. I need you on my team."

It may be incomprehensible to an outsider, but I immediately felt myself wavering. Was it his position or his personality that did it? The same old unanswerable question that kept posing itself whenever I found myself within his orbit.

So I didn't say anything, which seemed to disconcert him. After the silence dragged out for a while, he said, "And I'm prepared to apologize for any injury you feel has been done you." He spoke so quietly, it was virtually a mumble.

This was, in its way, more than anyone can reasonably expect from the president of the United States. And the choking strain in his voice when he said it was unmistakable. He was going the extra mile, and it obviously was murderously difficult for him. He really wants me back, I thought to myself. The flush of pleasure that followed hard upon that thought was what clinched it for me. I said, "No, I think we'd better leave things the way they are."

"Please, Ben, take some time, give this a little thought."

"There's no point. I've thought about it enough. More than enough. I've thought about little else. I'm not going to change my mind."

"I'm not comfortable leaving things this way."

Was this a tacit expression of remorse, an implicit admission of guilt? Were such feelings even in his repertoire? Did he have any interior life at all to speak of? With people who have organized their existence in so entirely public a way, there are things we can never know.

Although Gretchen might know. Gretchen had been vouchsafed glimpses of the private Chuck Sheffield. When that thought occurred to me, all the old rage and anguish returned. "I really can't help you with that," I told him. "It isn't my responsibility. You'll have to work it out on your own."

THE FAREWELL NOTE FROM THE PRESIDENT WAS MINIMAL AND entirely impersonal. Thanks for my services to the administration and the country, blah blah blah. It was even signed "Charles W. Sheffield," unlike all the previous notes and autographed photographs I'd ever got from him, which were always either from "Chuck Sheffield" or, later, just plain old "Chuck." Well, at least it wasn't inscribed by autopen.

On the other hand, the note from the First Lady was astonishingly warm, full of appreciation and sympathy and good luck wishes, running on for two handwritten pages. I guess I'll never discover how much she knew or suspected, but the tenor of her letter leads me to believe she may have known quite a lot. Her note was signed "Claire."

Maybe I should have asked her to run away with me. Acting in concert, we could have settled a lot of scores, virtually wiped the slate clean.

My quitting so soon after receiving the promotion was awkward, of course. A public embarrassment. The White House, predictably enough, let it be known to a few favored reporters that my work had been disappointing, that I "just wasn't ready for the big job yet." Bastards. But I was a good soldier, I played along (if not quite falling on my sword), answering all press queries with a "No comment." Chris Partridge and a few other journalist friends assured me it was widely assumed something fishy was going on, but I refused to rise to the bait. "A gentleman never tells," is what I said to importuning friends for whom "No comment" wouldn't suffice. The truth is, no one cared very much. It was a two-day page five story, and it would have been a one-day page ten story if anything else of interest had been going on at the time.

At least I was spared having to face Randy. He must have been high-fiving himself all over the West Wing. I was pleased to note he hadn't been reinstated, however. They brought in somebody from outside. A good writer who was known to be homosexual. I mention the latter fact only because I suspect Alice Hahn regarded it as a distinct plus when she chose to hire him. If she could have found a way to arrange it, the entire White House staff would have consisted of gay men and women who looked like her.

What I was going to do with myself next, I had no idea. There were feelers from several senators—the White House spin operation hadn't done irretrievable damage to my reputation, apparently—including Jared MacMillan, but speechwriting at a lower level than the one I was used to had approximately zero appeal. I was approached by a couple of publishers about writing a book. Perhaps they suspected I had a story to tell. Well, I certainly had a story, but the only person to whom I intended to tell it was myself, trying to make some kind of sense of it in these pages. And there were a few...you couldn't quite call them offers, but you might call them *probes,* about writing a column or doing television commentary. Even though I couldn't claim any expertise, the prospect wasn't unattractive. Very few commentators *do* have expertise, after all. But the timing was wrong. I needed some time off.

Gretchen found an apartment within a couple of weeks and moved out soon thereafter. When it finally happened, it was both a relief and a misery. We weren't talking much during that fortnight, we were almost like strangers who happened to share an apartment, even if we did sometimes huddle together for warmth late at night. Waiting for her to leave was awful, like a state of suspended animation with your central nervous system still functioning at peak capacity, but it was clear everything would be even worse once she was gone.

Dying of curiosity as I was, I didn't ask her whether she had finally broken off relations with Sheffield (or indeed, since she no longer owed me anything, had resumed them), and she didn't offer any dispatches on the subject. Nor did I know how she now felt about such matters. Her emotions, which once seemed to be mine almost as much as hers, weren't accessible to me any longer. Not that it was easy to let go. It felt like an amputation. But even though I still experienced intense phantom pain, the limb was gone, and I had to get used to the loss.

And as I say, in those weeks before she moved out, we weren't fighting, we were barely talking. Whatever acrimony existed, whatever arguments, were conducted in silence. I suppose we were each trying to prepare ourselves for the other's absence. And we maintained that stance pretty consistently until the morning she was set to move. She had hired a couple of AU students to help her, and while we waited for them to arrive, she suddenly succumbed to the urge to get a few things off her chest.

"It didn't have to end this way, you know," she said heatedly into the oppressive reigning silence. "This isn't what I wanted. It isn't what I *want*."

"It isn't what I want either. But there are some things that can't be undone, can't simply be reversed by saying 'Whoops.'"

She must have been hoping I'd say something like this, because she rose up and lit into me as if she'd been rehearsing her answer for days, saving it against just such an eventuality. "You are such a *prig*," she said. "I was wrong. I've admitted I was wrong. I made a mistake. But you have to find a way to let it go."

She had used the word "mistake" once before in this connection, and I had allowed it to pass. But this time my feelings were raw, my dander was up, and I pounced on it. "A mistake? I don't think so. A mistake is when you goof once. An affair spread over several months, with God knows how many trysts, an affair that persists even after it's been discovered, that goes way beyond mistake. Mistake doesn't begin to cover it. It's like…listen, someone who crashes a car might be able to say he made a mistake. Even if lives were tragically lost, he might be justified in saying, God, I'm sorry, I made a mistake. A terrible mistake. I stepped on the gas when I meant to apply the brakes. I turned left after I was signaled right. Whatever. But…I mean, if someone like, I don't know, like Ted Kaczynski— you know who he is? The Unabomber, from back in the eighties and nineties—well, Ted Kaczynski can*not* make the same claim. You see the distinction? With Ted Kaczynski, it *wasn't* a mistake. It was a deliberate policy. Even if he regrets it later, he can't claim he just made a mistake."

She stared at me, her eyes flashing. "You son of a bitch," she said. "You keep punishing me, you *insist* on punishing me, and you don't even know why you're doing it, do you? You don't have a clue."

"What do you mean?"

"Never mind."

"Uh-uh. You can't do that, Gretchen. If you have something to say, then go ahead and say it."

She sighed. She was in too deep to back out, but the anger that had provoked the outburst in the first place had drained away with its utterance. So now she was facing not catharsis, just a thankless chore. "Listen," she said, "we've both been swimming in the same pond. We've both responded to the same pressures, the same system of rewards and punishments. And the question you should ask yourself is…is…Oh Ben, honestly, who are you jealous of, really? Is it Chuck Sheffield, or is it *me?*"

It was like being slapped. "What the fuck is that supposed to mean?"

"I think you know what it means."

"Explain it to me anyway."

She sighed again. She was really sorry she had permitted pique to paint her into this corner, but now she was stuck. She began slowly, choosing her words with care: "Getting close to the president, face-time with the president…I mean, that's all anyone cares about around here. It's the fucking Holy Grail. When you were on the campaign plane with him, when you were playing chess with him and everything…it killed me, I admit it. I resented it and I resented *you.* Just the worst, sickest feeling of envy, even though I had no right to it and was ashamed of it and never said anything about it. You had something everyone else wanted. It was better than money in the bank. Well, time passed and then something bizarre happened. Bizarre and totally unexpected, just a weird roll of the dice. An avenue opened up to me, one that was foreclosed to you. I realize it isn't the same thing, I know there's no equivalent for you, I understand what I had was mostly about sex. From *his* point of view, I mean. For me, the sex part per se was no more meaningful than the chess games were to you. But I'm not kidding myself. For him, the whole thing was based, at least initially, on nothing more high-minded than his noticing my boobs. But he did, and the rest followed. And it conferred something on me, some cachet, some glamour, and I didn't have the strength or the character to resist it. I wish I had, but what can I say? I'm human, I've got the ordinary quota of human weakness. But if somehow there *was* something comparable for you, if some equivalent existed, I believe you'd have jumped at it too. Even if it meant betraying me in the process. I'm convinced of that. I think you're at least as jealous of my relationship with him as of his sexual access to me."

Which was when the doorbell rang. The movers had arrived. In the nick of time, I'd have to say. I was on the brink of physical violence. I wouldn't have struck her, of course, but if the movers hadn't shown up at that very moment, I might easily have destroyed all the furniture they had come to carry away.

THE NEXT FEW MONTHS WERE NO PICNIC. I FOUND A BUYER for the condo and moved into a smaller, much less prepossessing apartment. My share of the sale bought me a little time before I had to start looking for a job in earnest, but didn't help me figure out what I was supposed to do with the rest of my life. And no longer having my old job taught me a few lessons about friendship I would have been just as happy not to have learned. Some people remained friends, but lots of others stopped returning my calls. I wouldn't necessarily have been able to predict who would fall into which camp. And all those invitations that Gretchen and I used to receive...they didn't merely slow to a trickle, they dried up altogether, and all at once. As if someone had twisted a spigot. Presumably they were now flowing to my successor.

It wasn't only other people, either. Not having a White House job, especially a fairly visible White House job, proved to be worse for me than I had anticipated. In a one-industry town like Washington, your standing is all tied up with your status in that one industry. I now had none, and it bothered me more than I was comfortable admitting. My relationship to the city became tenuous. I felt peripheral, marginal, a *hick*.

Being without Gretchen was a daily heartache. This isn't merely a lazy choice of words. I woke up every morning with the awful realization she wasn't there beside me, followed by a spinning sinking feeling that made it difficult to get out of bed. And repeatedly throughout the day, thoughts of her would come, unbidden, and would almost double me over with misery. She was the one person with whom I was used to sharing everything that was happening to me—that was the role she had played in my life—and everything that was happening to me now emphatically included the anguish of not being with her anymore. But of course I couldn't share that with her. Which made the heartache even worse. I felt as if I were living through every torch-song lyric ever written.

Of course, I kept reminding myself that during our final weeks, being *with* her had been a daily heartache too. But anyone who's ever endured the end of a messy, turbulent relationship can surely understand how the agony of loss feels immeasurably greater than the pain of being together. Even when separation was necessary for survival.

All my willpower was required merely not to phone her. But I managed it, despite a few near misses where I dialed the first six digits of her White House extension before abruptly hanging up. She never called me either. Other than my sending her the check for her share of the condo sale proceeds, we had absolutely no contact. And I sent the check without a cover letter.

It's probably just as well all those invitations no longer came my way; I wasn't fit company anyhow, and I wasn't going out very much.

Not that I had become a complete recluse. At least once a week

I had dinner with various people I knew, chosen from among the ones who hadn't dropped me cold, and I even started dating a little. But I was aware I wasn't much of a companion, and I often felt a little like an invalid whom charitable friends and family members take on an outing once in a while. I was duly appreciative, but also uncomfortably conscious of being a burden.

Did I ever think about Gretchen's parting words to me? Only constantly. My first reaction was blind rage at what I took to be unfair and malicious self-justification. As was my second, and my third and fourth. But as time went by, I began to let myself wonder about it. She was always so shrewd about people, so sharply intuitive; maybe she perceived something I kept buried, kept hidden from myself. And maybe the very vehemence of my reaction suggested she was on to something. I recognized some dim resonance somewhere within me. I tried not to examine it too closely, but I didn't always succeed. And each time I did, her case seemed more compelling.

I finally got a job just before Thanksgiving. I joined an environmental lobbying firm. My official title was vice president, but that was a meaningless distinction in such a small and resolutely egalitarian organization. The truth is, it was an undeniable come-down in the world, and my starting salary was only about two-thirds of my White House take. But the money was adequate to my needs all the same, and the work wasn't entirely dishonorable, and having any sort of job beat unemployment hands down. Additionally, it gave me the wherewithal to consider my options free of panicky desperation.

Having nothing to do with official Washington took some adjustment. It was a relief in many ways, but in other ways I felt like one of those Russian dissidents from the Soviet era who used to be sentenced to something called "internal exile." I was completely cut off. As if a significant part of my personal history had simply ceased to exist.

There was one odd exception, and it occurred within two weeks of my starting the new job. I attended a reception for some prominent environmentalist or other—my first such function in my new capacity as vice president of the firm—and to my surprise, the First Lady was also making an appearance. Out of courtesy, I deliberately avoided her; it didn't seem right to put her in the awkward position of having to decide how to deal with me. But when I was at the buffet table, placing prawns on a little plate, a young woman I recognized but whose name I didn't know approached me and said, "Mr. Krause?"

I turned to her, startled and a little sheepish at the number of shrimp I had been caught cadging. "Yes?"

"The First Lady would like a word with you."

This was unexpected. I put down my plate and followed the young woman across the room. Claire Sheffield was standing at one end, a small group of people around her. Always a handsome woman, she bore herself with a sophisticated elegance suggestive of her roots in the New York gentry. She should have seemed a trifle out of place here, among all these scruffy eco-nuts. But like most politicians' wives, she was a veteran of implausible assemblages and carried herself with easy grace. "Ben!" she said, extending her hand. "How lovely to see you."

I took her hand. "It's nice to see you too, Mrs. Sheffield." It seemed the wiser course to assume my "Claire" days were over.

She leaned in and kissed my cheek—another surprise—and then pulled me a few paces away from the other people in her entourage. "We miss you, Ben," she said quietly.

I couldn't think of how to respond. Nothing seemed appropriate. So I just said, "Thank you," feeling maladroit and fatuous.

"Chuck too. Chuck and I both." She still held my hand in hers. "He was so sorry to lose you. I realize something personal must have happened between you and him, I understand you felt you had to leave...but you should know, there are no hard feelings at all. Not on Chuck's side, anyway."

What a prince. "I'm glad to hear that."

Her eyes sought mine. Evidently whatever she had to say went beyond mere conventional chitchat. I was afraid, for a brief moment, that she intended to say something about Gretchen, but no, that wasn't on the cards. Thank God. "It's difficult. It's so difficult. Having a personal relationship with someone for whom personal relationships have to take second place. Believe me, our children have had that problem with Chuck too. So have I. But we've made our peace with it. It's part of who he is. We just have to overlook personal lapses. What makes him special is so much more important than any personal lapses."

"Yes, I understand," I said. But I didn't. How much did she know, and what precisely was she trying to tell me? It still wasn't clear to me. It still *isn't* clear to me. What *was* clear to me, though, was how sad and tired and defeated she suddenly seemed. But I don't want to make too much of that. She might just have been having a hard day.

She stared at me expectantly, as if there were something specific she wanted from me, some gesture, some combination of words, that would close the chapter acceptably. But I had nothing to offer. I didn't know what she was looking for and in any case felt no compulsion to supply it. I had always liked her, but this just wasn't my life anymore. It had absolutely nothing to do with me.

AROUND THAT TIME I THOUGHT I WAS FINALLY BEGINNING TO recover a little of my equanimity, but then the Christmas season arrived and it became obvious I'd been kidding myself. When you're alone, you never feel more alone than at Christmas. Additionally, in Washington there are so many White House and other high-level political festivities (all of them covered extensively in the *Post*, of course, and therefore thrust into your ken whether you want them there or not) that the full import of my internal exile was brought home to me all over again. Along with the full impact of my separation from Gretchen; she was doubtless present at all those parties and concerts and things, doing who knows what with who knows whom.

A few days before Christmas the postman delivered a surprise invitation. To a New Year's Eve black-tie soiree in Georgetown that by common consent ranked as the season's single most glamorous fete. Since I didn't know the hosts, I can only assume some computer glitch had retained me on a list from which I should have been excised. Well, I wasn't going to let that stop me. I hadn't attended such a glitzy event since the ill-fated MacMillan roast had changed my life several months before.

Nor had I had another chance to wear my Armani tux.

It was time to let the good times roll. I even invited a date, a woman who worked in the same lobbying firm I did, with whom I had gone out once or twice. No big romance there, but this was the sort of hot ticket you can't keep to yourself. And there's no question she was mighty impressed when I invited her. In fact, although she didn't say so, I'm pretty certain she wriggled out of a prior commitment in order to go.

New Year's Eve was a cold night with fresh crunchy snow on the ground, just the way it's supposed to be. We had to park four blocks away from the party, so jammed was Georgetown, but since the snow had stopped falling that afternoon, the walk from the car to the N St. house was delightful, a "Good King Wenceslas" sort of experience. There were Secret Service agents loitering outside the house, which for one tense moment made me think that the president might be a guest. But then I remembered, no, he and the family were up at Camp David for their own idiosyncratic version of "Auld Lang Syne." Overlooking personal lapses, no doubt.

We went in. The foyer was packed solid, just bodies from wall to wall. The first person I stumbled across was the vice president, who gave me a huge affectionate hug. This was pleasant in itself—we'd always had a good relationship—as well as welcome evidence that my internal exile hadn't made me a nonperson in administration circles. I didn't see her husband anywhere and wondered idly whether she had left him home and whether there was still some possibility he might be indicted. No word of any of that had appeared in the press. Perhaps the Justice Department had given him a clean bill of health, or perhaps they were still building their case. Either way, the absence of any leaks on the subject was noteworthy. Somebody in the press office was clearly doing his job.

When I turned around to introduce my date to the vice president, she had disappeared. Then I saw her across the room, talking animatedly to a prominent CNN personage. She caught my eye and waved me over, but she seemed to be coping nicely, seemed to be having a fine time in fact, and with so many people standing between us, just negotiating my way across the room was a daunting prospect. So instead I went off in search of drinks for her and for myself.

There is an electrifying passage in the second movement of Berlioz's *Symphonie fantastique.* The music portrays a scene at a ball, all gaiety and brilliant swirling motion. But suddenly, with no warning or preparation, there is a lurching downward, and the ball music gives way to music representing the protagonist's romantic obsession. He has apparently caught a heart-stopping glimpse of the woman he loves among the dancers. Thereafter, the ball music keeps attempting to start up again, but for a while it struggles vainly against what Berlioz dubbed *l'idée fixe,* that musical motif of romantic obsession that dominates the entire work.

I felt all that—emphatically including the sudden lurching downward—when I spied Gretchen through a doorway. She was seated on a sofa in a denlike room, a plate of food on her lap. There was a nice-looking man sitting beside her. For a moment the party disappeared and there was only Gretchen. My heart went into over-drive. Then, perhaps feeling my glance upon her, she looked up, and our eyes met.

At which point somebody grabbed me by the shoulders and started pumping my hand. It was a fellow I knew slightly from the corridors and basement cafeteria of the OEOB, someone in the second stratum of the National Security Council. He seemed amazingly glad to see me, considering the superficiality of our former acquaintanceship. It was nice that he felt that way, but my own personal *idée fixe* kept drowning him out, kept, indeed, wishing he'd shut the hell up and get lost. By the time we were done shouting pleasantries at each other over the din, assuring each other how nice it was to run into each other, Gretchen had disappeared.

I wanted to kill him.

And then she materialized at my elbow. I smelled her perfume before I saw her. And I pivoted, and in an instant we were in each other's arms. We fitted together like two jigsaw puzzle pieces. The noise around us was horrendous, the press of people claustrophobic, the heat generated by all those bodies stifling, but we were locked in an embrace and nothing else mattered, nothing else even registered. I was afraid to let go of her; once I did, the *idée fixe* might fade and the ball music might start again, real life would seize hold of us and pull us asunder.

But what choice did I have? We couldn't stand locked together like that forever. Not even for the thirty odd minutes till the old year ended and the new one began. So I reluctantly loosened my grip, and we slipped apart and looked into each other's faces. There were tears running down her cheeks. Without saying a word—the moment was too fragile for shouting, and nothing else would be audible—she took my hand and pulled me through the room we were in, through the den, through the formal dining room where an elaborate buffet had been set up, through the kitchen, and into a smallish pantry area. It was at least a little quieter there, and we were alone.

We embraced again.

"God, I've missed you," she whispered.

It was a delicate juncture, of course. Despite the overwhelming emotion I was feeling—and even with her tears as encouragement—this could still be merely an affectionate reunion between former lovers who hadn't seen each other in a long time and were genuinely delighted, now that all unruly passion was spent, to see each other again. So I was afraid to say anything, although it was definitely my turn to say *something*. I was afraid I might be misconstruing the moment.

"You look beautiful," I finally told her. It seemed a relatively safe observation, and it also happened to be true.

"And you look yummy."

"The Armani."

"That's not the whole story."

I just stared at her for a few seconds. There was so much to say, affectionate banter suddenly didn't seem good enough. Seemed unworthy. "I think of you constantly," I confessed.

She didn't answer, but her eyes were glistening, which I interpreted as a sign of receptivity.

"Listen…do you remember that thing you said to me the morning you left?"

Her face clouded. "No," she said. "Please…don't."

"I need to say this, Gretch."

She put a finger to my lips. "No. No, no, no, no, no. You mustn't. It's the worst thing I ever said. Ever. Not a day goes by when I don't hate myself for saying it. I was just…it was guilt talking, that's all it was. I couldn't stand to shoulder all the blame. I needed to spread it around a little."

"But you were right. Right enough, anyway. It's taken me a long time to admit that to myself. I'd be remiss if I didn't admit it to you too."

She shook her head emphatically. "Uh-uh. I don't agree. 'Cause I haven't been able to stop thinking about it either. And you know what I realize? Even if there *was* a little bit of truth to it—and I'm not saying there was, but even if there was—it still doesn't mean a damned thing. I mean…Jesus, we live in a place…we inhabit a *planet*…where everything conspires to tell us how insignificant we are. You know? If we're even a miserable little cog in a wheel, we're already ahead of the game. The world keeps telling us we're nothing. No matter what we may have achieved, we're still nothing. Someone has always achieved more, and let's face it, *he* feels like nothing too. We don't count, we don't rate, we don't matter. An ant in an anthill has as much prestige. And it's all so common, we don't even notice most of the time. We just accept it as our due. We think it's an accurate assessment of our worth."

When she paused for a moment, I started to say something—something bland and anodyne—but she overrode me. She wasn't finished. "So the thing is, if you love somebody, if that somebody is important to you…Aw Christ, Ben, if you love somebody, the very least you owe that person is to treat him like he counts. Like he's the most important person in the world. Because everybody *else* in the world is sure to be treating him the opposite. We all need that from at least one person. Let the rest of the world place us all in a pecking order. Maybe it even serves some sort of useful social purpose, I don't know. I mean, monkeys do it, maybe we have to too. But that's no excuse for telling the person you love, 'I love you, but let's face it, you're not that great a catch.' For saying, 'I love you unless I get a better offer. I love you until I find someone the world esteems more highly, someone who reflects better on me.'"

I pulled her to me, I held her tight. And I said, "I understand what you're saying, Gretch. And I appreciate it, I really do. But… do you think you could maybe start right now? I mean…it's perfectly lovely, but it's also, just incidentally, reminding me that I'm *incredibly insignificant.*"

She laughed, a wonderfully full belly laugh. And then she murmured in my ear, "All right. Fair enough. Ya ready? Benjamin Krause, you are a great catch, I can't conceive of a better offer, and I don't give a flying fuck where the world ranks you or anybody else. Up to and including the president of the United States. The world doesn't know what it's talking about. And you look yummy in a dinner jacket." She took a deep breath. "How's that?"

"It's a start."

"I'll keep working on it."

"Listen." I stepped back from her, put my hands on her shoulders, and looked her in the eye. "We have so much to talk about. Let's get away from here. Okay? Let's go somewhere."

She frowned. "I came with a date," she said.

"Yeah, so did I."

Her face suddenly became very serious, almost grave. "See, I have this funny feeling...it's almost a superstitious thing...I don't think it's smart for us to kick things off by ditching the people we're with. As if we've learned nothing. The whole idea feels like...like really terrible karma to me." She was staring at me very earnestly while she spoke. "Let's treat them as if they exist independent of our convenience, okay? We came with them, we should leave with them. The way I feel about you right now, right this second...it's not going away. Not anywhere. Not ever. Just call me tomorrow. I'll be home. All day. Hovering pathetically by the phone."

"But I don't have your number."

"It's in the book." She smiled. "You know how it is.... Nobodies like us, we don't need unlisted numbers."

★